REINDEER'S
GOLD

FSC
www.fsc.org
MIX
Papper från
ansvarsfulla källor
Paper from
responsible sources
FSC® C105338

Cover and illustrations by David Covenant

david.h.covenant@gmail.com

1st edition 2025

Publisher: BoD · Books on Demand, Östermalmstorg 1, 114 42 Stockholm, Sweden, bod@bod.se

Printing house: Libri Plureos GmbH, Friedensallee 273, 22763 Hamburg, Germany

ISBN: 978-91-8097-094-5

"Altogether elsewhere, vast/ Herds of reindeer move across/ Miles and miles of golden moss,/ Silently and very fast."
The Fall of Rome by W H Auden

PROLOGUE

Norwegian-Swedish border in western Lapland, April 1, 1945.

The airplane appeared out of nowhere. Like a great bird of prey it soared over the northern ridge with roaring engines. Its black belly was outlined like a dark shadow against the night sky. The plane had almost disappeared from sight before the first villagers emerged from their tents and wooden houses. Those who caught a glimpse of the big bird saw it veer off to the west and over Norway. From the fuselage there were flashes of light.

In the midst of the commotion, a tall figure stood on a large rock, silently watching the plane.

"Sáhkár! We are under attack!"

A half-naked and bearded man came running up to the rock. His eyes were wide open and shining in the moonlight. "Sáhkár!" he repeated. "What was that?"

The tall figure stood calmly watching the airplane as it disappeared behind the western mountain plateau. Some ten seconds later, the sky lit up with a bright flash of light followed by a dull thud. The plane had crashed and exploded. All was quiet and still in the small valley. Those who had come out of their tents said nothing, but just stared in the direction of the flickering light.

"Sáhkár," the bearded man finally said. "What really happened?"

"I don't know," replied the figure on the stone, finally averting its gaze from the spectacle in the distance. "But we have to find out."

He then grabbed a large horn hanging from a rope around his neck, put it to his mouth and blew it with all his might. A dark and powerful roar resounded throughout the valley. The last of the villagers emerged from their tents and houses and gathered around the big rock as they had always done. Soon after, a few hundred dazed souls stood looking at the light and at the man on the rock.

"See that light over there?" He swept his arm and paused briefly while all eyes turned to the west.

"A few minutes ago, an airplane flew over the village. Some of you managed to see it. The plane was on fire and lost altitude. It must have crashed just a few hundred meters into the Norwegian side."

"Where did it come from? What kind of plane was it?" Several voices were heard from the crowd.

"It seems to have come from the north. The aircraft was twin-engined and quite large. That was all I could see."

"They are Germans!" someone shouted.

"I don't know more than you do, but it could well be another

German military transport heading south from Narvik. There have been a few of those before, but never this close."

"What do we do now?" said a woman's voice that seemed to come from somewhere very close to the rock. The answers came immediately and from different directions at the same time. A heated discussion ensued. Some felt that an attempt should be made to reach the crashed plane, others warned of German units that had been spotted at regular intervals some way into the Norwegian side. Sáhkár raised the horn again and silenced the debate.

"We have to get to the plane. There may be survivors and it is not certain that they are Germans. We need to know if it is a coincidence that brought them here or if they came to spy on the village. We leave immediately. I want ten men with rifles and searchlights."

The armed troops moved swiftly across the plateau that cut off the valley on the western side from the outside world. On the other side, a long, narrow valley opened up with an equally long, ice-covered lake in the middle. In the middle of the illuminated lake, they could see the remains of the plane wreckage. The closer they got, the clearer it became what had happened. The right wing was torn from the fuselage during the impact, together with the engine, fuel tank and landing gear on that side. The engine, which had apparently burned even before the plane passed over the village, had caused the fuel tank to explode and it was this powerful fire that still lit up the night sky. The rest of the plane had continued a few hundred meters out onto the ice, where the second landing gear had finally cut through the ice crust, causing the whole craft to rotate half a turn.

On the ice next to what remained of the fuselage were three

people, one of whom was lying motionless on his back. The distance was too great to determine what they were doing, but it was clear that at least one of them was injured. Perhaps someone was also still in the wreckage.

Sáhkár ordered his men to continue along the left bank where they were sheltered by large rocks and mountain birches. When they were less than a hundred meters from the site of the accident, they crouched behind a cairn and looked at the wreck. The swastika was clearly visible on the tail fin.

"A German bomber," Sáhkár concluded briefly. Maybe it was on its way from Narvik to Trondheim or Stavanger. Something caused the engine to catch fire and they took aim at the only flat surface they could find. It is not impossible that they were fired upon by our own people.

He looked out over the ice and saw that only one of the three men was still standing. The fire at the eastern end of the lake had died down and it was harder to make out anything but the silhouettes of the three figures. Sáhkár and his men lay quietly for a few minutes, listening for sounds. Perhaps the Germans had already called for help or there were more planes on their way with the same mission? Just as they had agreed to start moving towards the injured crewmen, they heard voices in the distance.

They lay still and listened, and as the voices came closer, they realized the sounds were coming from the western short end of the lake. Branches snapping, faint flashlights and harsh German consonants. The tramp of boots moving determinedly in the direction of the fading fire. Soon, dozens of dark silhouettes appeared against the light snow in the moonlight. They walked on the ice and approached quickly. Sáhkár estimated that they were between forty and fifty German soldiers. Certainly armed to the teeth.

The soldiers walked up to the only crew member who could still stand. Words were exchanged in German. It sounded like an interrogation. A soldier walked up to the airplane and looked through what was left of the cockpit.

Then the unexpected happened. One of the soldiers started shouting while pointing in the direction of the shore where Sáhkár and his men lay. Loud commands and curses rang out across the frozen lake. Then came the gunfire. Bullets flew over the heads of the ten villagers and they all pressed hard against the ground behind the stone cairn. Soon after, the first explosion followed. It was a mortar shell fired at the beach but far from where they lay. It seemed that most people were shooting blind. Someone had probably registered a movement behind the rocks, fired a shot and the others had followed. Bullets and the occasional grenade whizzed around them until someone called for a ceasefire.

Then the same soldier started pointing in their direction again and Sáhkár realized he had to act quickly. He raised his rifle and took aim through a gap in the rocks. Instead of firing at the soldiers, he fired five quick shots straight at the aircraft's left wing. The last shot pierced the left undamaged fuel tank, causing the entire wreckage to lift straight up into the air in a deafening explosion. The scene lit up for a few seconds as the burning wreckage sailed through the air and landed on ice that had already broken into a thousand pieces around the blast site. The surrounding thin spring ice quickly gave way and the wake spread so quickly that the entire German unit went down into the icy mountain water.

Bouncing arms tried to get onto the ice but only made the hole bigger. The heavy uniforms and the zero-degree water made the fight short. After a few minutes, the small valley was silent again. Only the shining moon could witness that something had happened that night.

CHAPTER 1

The Blizzard

William cruised through the muck and snow-mixed rain that persistently smacked against the windshield and tried to throw the car off the road. The snow on the ground and the poor visibility made it almost impossible to tell where the roadside ended and the field began. Guideposts and road signs blended into the background or had simply been blown away. The only visible reference points were the occasional exit signs that were lit up for a few brief seconds by the headlights. Without them, there would have been no chance to stay on the road. It didn't help much to adjust the position of his round glasses on his nose, it was more of a habit than something that would help the situation.

Although the world outside was in a chaotic state, the mood in the cabin was rather dull. It didn't help to focus on driving, and thoughts inadvertently drifted elsewhere. Perhaps the storm was adding to his already wobbly state of mind, even though he knew it had nothing to do with it. It was just something that contributed to a suitable framing of the prevailing mood. In the light of the headlights, every shadow became an omen, a harbinger that something ominous was imminent.

Every turn of the dark highway seemed like a series of missed opportunities - a relentless reminder of possibilities missed and decisions never made. The normally peaceful willow tree on the crest before the straight suddenly gave a windswept and ominous impression. Unwavering, mighty and timeless, it used to stand there as a reminder that he would soon be home, but now it was just a fleeting shadow against a gray-white background.

Life is as unpredictable as a tree, he mused as his gaze flickered over the snowy landscape. With each lap around the sun, a new annual ring is added to the archive, and the branches become more and more sprawling and irregular. No two trees are alike and each new branch is a path to explore. But isn't every branch also a crossroads where an active choice must be made? Did he ever make an active choice? A life changing decision? Not that he could recall.

After all, each new branch is narrower than the one you left and all paths are one-way. The inexorable passage of time allows you to change direction but hardly to go back and start over again. Somewhere on the way to the crown, sooner or later, everyone is forced to take their first turn, and eventually you find yourself on a dry branch, waiting for the leaves to fall for the last time. William wondered which branch he'd landed on, and whether it was fate or chance that had brought him there. Whatever it was, it was definitely not a result of a brave decision.

But the fact that he (once again) found himself in this godforsaken place on a Friday evening in late March, when the snow was falling and darkness had long since set in, was certainly not just a coincidence. He had traveled here many times before. It was the fastest way home, and since the new highway opened, traffic had slowed down considerably. In addition, there was a roadside restaurant strategically placed along the winding highway that only a few years ago was the only link between his work location and his home. The run-down restaurant, Night Owl, as it was called, was located in a sleepy little town that he could never remember the name of and was the only option at this time of day if you needed something to eat.

Next door to Night Owl was also a disused car repair shop and an old gas station where the service was now replaced by self-service.

Along the frost-damaged stretch of road that ran through the community, there were traces of sanded-down pedestrian crossings, signs that were no longer needed and roadside cameras that were not in use. The homes that could be seen from the car window often had lights out or blinds drawn. Perhaps this was because it was usually late in the evening when he passed, or perhaps it was simply because people had given up and moved away. In any case, the whole place had a desolate feel - like an abandoned western town. William was always amazed when he approached the Night Owl and discovered that somewhere in this ghost town there were lights in the windows. As if, amidst all the scenery, there was actually a real saloon with people in cowboy hats. Perhaps it was an irony of fate that William came to make the most important decision of his life on this particular night and in this particular place.

The working week had begun and dragged on like any other week. The sun had climbed behind the horizon and the orbits of the planets in the sky seemed intact, the evening papers reported no new world wars and the working days had dragged on without inspiration for either body or soul. It was not until this Friday evening that the switch to the railroad track that made up William's predictable life began to shift. It had started as usual with wild protests from the stomach region, just before the sign for the Night Owl became visible, and not long after he was sitting at his usual corner table with a cup of lukewarm coffee and yesterday's egg sandwich in his hands.

❋ ❋ ❋

This evening, the Night Owl was unusually quiet. Apart from the waitress, who seemed to be doing her best to keep out of the way, there were two young men in the restaurant area. They were sitting at a table about ten meters away and diagonally in front of William.

14

There was something about the two men that caught his attention. Maybe it was the fact that there was nothing else to look at, or maybe it was simply the way they looked.

One was slender - bordering on emaciated - with a drawn-out face punished by an unusually pointed nose. His eyebrows ran in a curly V from the root of his nose and outwards. His hair was blond and stood straight up in all directions, as if caught between a construction fan and a glue gun.

His friend gave an almost equally comical impression. His hair was brown, greasy and tied up in a ponytail. The face was deeply scarred, revealing the aftermath of severe teenage acne. The nose was misshapen like a root vegetable, with large air intakes on the sides. His lips formed a constant crooked grin. Like his tablemate, he was scantily clad.

Both men were in their twenties. Their faces, both comical and ravaged, gave a contradictory first impression. He was reminded of the nineties series Beavis and Butthead. The two men seemed deep in conversation, or rather a monologue. It was Beavis who was holding the fort while Butthead tried to fight his way through a mountain of reheated jacket potatoes. The presenting party interspersed his monologue with deep throaty gasps and fumed directly onto the floor. William couldn't hear the conversation because they were sitting too far away. He soon lost interest in the two cartoon characters and returned to the egg sandwich and the old habit of tinkering with his glasses.

Outside, the snow continued to fall with undiminished intensity and the wind was playing with it, sending it dancing in all directions. It had been dark for an hour or so, and the unmanned gas station's lights blinked nervously with each gust. It was unusual for a snowstorm to make its way into central Sweden at this time of year. William assumed it was the last gasp of a rather long and arduous winter - one of those sneaky and unruly winters that came and went as it pleased and always seemed to have one last trick up its sleeve. The snow was also heavy and wet, which made things even more unpleasant for a hard-pressed car commuter. He fleetingly reviewed the past few days, trying to figure out if he'd done anything particularly bad that deserved such an end to the week. Or maybe it was simply the natural law of the devilishness and inherent evil of everything playing tricks on him.

Less than a week had passed since the meteorologists declared in unison and with absolute certainty that spring had finally come to stay. The newspapers reported on the thaw and warned of spring floods and birch pollen. Radio and TV broadcasts tried to outdo each other in the art of interpreting signs of spring. Ornithologists gathered in flocks to await the first crane dance. Motorists queued outside tire shops to change tires, winter clothes were stowed in the closet, and some enthusiastic homeowners even managed to bring out the summer furniture. Then came the blizzard. Like a runaway freight train, it swept in from the Atlantic and shattered all the giddy dreams of spring.

William had been in Stockholm the whole week, spending all his waking hours in the office and thus neglecting the amenities of the big city and anything else that might break the vicious circle. It has become a habit now for several years. Every other week in Stockholm and every other week in his hometown. Every time he went by car, and during almost every trip home, he stopped at Night Owl to get something in his stomach. On a few occasions he'd driven past without stopping and aimed directly at the fridge at home. Then his stomach protested wildly, much like a landmine that explodes when you step on the trigger. His stomach was a blast furnace that had to be constantly fed with charcoal.

At least now he wouldn't be stuck in this dump for a while, he told himself, a faint, unconscious smile tugging at his lips. Earlier in the week, he'd finally decided to take a vacation. Work was in a quiet phase, and he'd accumulated far too many unused vacation and overtime hours. But more than anything, he was simply fed up - tired of the daily commute, the mind-numbing tasks, and the colleagues he could barely tolerate. Truth be told, he was worn out by everything. A vacation wouldn't fix any of it, not really. But it would give him something he desperately needed: space to breathe, and time to think.

Much to his surprise, his boss had been sympathetic to the request and immediately approved two weeks off. Whether it was out of goodwill or for some other reason didn't really matter. Neither did the fact that he had no plans at all for how to spend the time. What mattered was that he was free - free from work in general, and from the Night Owl in particular.

William flinched when he heard the front door slam. He had been lost in thought for a few minutes and did not notice that the two men had left the table. He looked around and could see neither the waitress nor anyone else in the room. Outside the protective shell of the building, a person in a fur hat was struggling to get the tank nozzle into the filling hole. William's eyes fell on the spot where Beavis and Butthead had been sitting only a few minutes before. The small booth looked like a battlefield with bottles, cutlery, half-filled glasses, sticky napkins and messy plates scattered all over the table. Split potatoes and other indecipherable objects had fallen to the floor, mingling with cigarette butts and the occasional recycled portion of coarse snuff. With the exception of some gases and precious metals, the entire periodic table was represented in a few square meters. It was a floor that was seemingly beyond saving.

The gaze wandered among the objects and finally stopped at an object that broke the pattern. Amidst all the clutter under the table was a bag. A strange leather bag, a larger model. He hadn't noticed the odd object before and now he couldn't take his eyes off it. Outside there was the muffled sound of a car engine trying to start. On the third try, it succeeded. Before the thought had time to sink in, William flew up from his chair and went over and grabbed the bag. It was ungainly and heavy. The youngsters may look disheveled and unsympathetic, but he instinctively reacted with the blue-eyed dutifulness that was so deeply rooted in every Swede. He pulled out the bag from under the table, put the thick carrying strap around his neck and stumbled away to return it before the two youngsters had disappeared.

He limped through the side entrance with the heavy bag over his shoulder, kicked open the front door with one foot, stuck his upper body between the door frames and just had time to see a white Volvo 740 skid out of the gas station. The sound of a tired and battered engine quickly died away in the snowstorm. The wind whipped hard in his face and William stood for a few seconds in the doorway. For a moment it occurred to him that perhaps the bag was left behind deliberately. Maybe there's an explosive device in there? The weather and the cold outside brutally killed all thought and William was forced to retreat into the warmth. Once inside the entrance, the machinery started to move again and William decided to hand over the bag to the waitress. She'll have to do the first job of the day, he thought.

The side entrance, which was at the gable end of the building, turned into a toilet corridor that led into the restaurant area. William suddenly felt a strong need to use the restroom and went into the men's room - a place he was familiar with from many visits over the years. He found a booth and put his bag on the floor outside.

As the coffee made its way out the natural way, curiosity struck. What was in the bag? It had an unusual square appearance and was the size of a hockey bag, as if it were stuffed with books. The material was some kind of light brown coarse leather but he couldn't tell if it was real or fake. The bag resembled a large duffel bag deformed by its contents. It had no handle or anything tangible except a large shoulder strap. On the side was a large embroidered figure of a mountain peak. The opening of the bag was covered by a brightly colored leather cover held in place by a shiny buckle with a piece of bone wedged in a rope loop. The object looked well made. A solid piece of craftsmanship that must have taken a long time to complete.

After feeling, squeezing and deciding that it couldn't hold a bomb or anything nasty, he carefully released the piece of bone from the loop, lifted the lid and stared into the bag with wide eyes. Christopher Polhem stared back. The father of Swedish mathematics looked grim. The entire top of the bag was loaded with five hundred crown notes. William gasped as he lifted the top layer. More notes in neat bundles. The whole bag was filled with tightly packed bundles of notes all the way to the bottom.

William didn't have time to get better acquainted with the late mathematician because the sound of a car engine quickly grew louder, a familiar sound that he had heard only a few minutes earlier. A car engine that had not often been in contact with a service workshop. The sound died out and shortly afterwards the door to the side entrance was thrown open. Heavy footsteps moved through the toilet corridor and into the restaurant area. William instinctively pulled the lid of his bag and kept as quiet as he could.

After a few seconds, he heard voices through the gap between the toilet door and the floor. The sound came from one of the men who, with barely concealed irritation, explained to the waitress that a large leather bag had grown feet and left its place under the table. The waitress explained that she had not seen a bag running around the room and wondered why the young man had not brought the item with him the first time. Then he wouldn't have had to look for lost bags. The young man explained that it was none of her business. Or as he put it: "Fuck you bitch!"

William flinched when the front door opened again. This time with a distinct emphasis. New steps in the corridor and a new voice joins the conversation. A voice that firmly but not so kindly wondered why it should take so damn long to pick up a bag. The conversation between the unruly youngsters and the now wide-awake waitress soon developed into a loud argument. William suddenly felt very uncomfortable as he stood there looking at the bag and listening to the commotion outside. It didn't take long for the two companions to figure out that they hadn't been alone in the room when they ate, and that one of the restroom doors was closed and locked. At the moment, it didn't seem like a good idea to walk up to them and hand over the strange object. In any case, it was never going to happen, as everyone had now realized that a dinner guest was missing. William envisioned them all staring at the wretched half-eaten egg sandwich hastily left to die on the table.

The voices were mixed with a new engine noise coming from the front of the building. William guessed that it was the poor fellow who had stopped for gas in the snowstorm a few minutes earlier and was now leaving the unmanned gas station. The two men obviously didn't draw the same conclusion from the situation and quickly dashed out of the premises the same way they came in. The waitress shouted obscenities at them and their mothers who had failed so badly at basic parenting. William stood up on the toilet seat and could see the front through a small, high window. A dark SUV rolled out onto the main road and headed towards Stockholm. Less than half a minute later, the old Volvo passed right outside the toilet window and continued, under great protests from the engine, straight through the lighted station and further out on the road in the same direction as its prey.

William suddenly felt heavy in his body. He sat down on the toilet seat with his face buried in his hands. This had certainly turned out to be a different Friday. Thoughts raced through his head. His first instinct was to leave his bag in the toilet and slip away as if nothing had happened. But then the angry savages would conclude that someone had opened the bag and seen the contents, and perhaps then remember their table neighbor. Or someone else would find the bag before them and perhaps take it with them and the only person they could reasonably remember the face of was himself. Same problem again. He could also walk up to the waitress and hand the bag to her. Say he found it under the table and tried to return it. But then he would be shifting the problem onto her while exposing himself - and what if she found herself opening the bag and standing there with her face in the jam jar when they got back. Given the contents of the bag and the scene that had just unfolded, they could be serious criminals.

He really only had two options: to leave with or without the bag. Under no circumstances could he stay behind. It wouldn't be long before the two geniuses discovered that the dark SUV didn't contain any stolen goods. Perhaps they would even remember William's face from the roadside tavern. Then even Beavis and Butthead would conclude that the bag could be in someone else's hands. He could visualize their face expressions in his head as they realized they had been chasing the wrong person.

William needed to make a quick decision. His car was parked on the gable end where the Volvo had been. He carefully turned the lock to the toilet and peeked out through the crack in the door. The waitress was nowhere to be seen but could be heard far away at the other end. She was talking on the phone, conveying her innermost thoughts about the workplace in general and its guests in particular. At least there was no physical damage to her, he thought.

It was at this moment that William made the most important

decision of his life. He slipped out of the restroom and left the roadside diner with his bag over his shoulder. It wasn't until he was in the car, halfway home, that he changed his mind. But by then it was too late.

Beavis and Butthead made contact with the black SUV after only a few minutes. Instead of flashing and gesturing for the driver to stop, the course of events was somewhat rationalized by simply running the car off the road. The SUV plowed through a snow bank and continued down into the ditch. The Volvo went into an uncontrolled spin in the same maneuver but they managed, with more luck than skill, to stay on the road.

The two men got out of the car and rushed to the SUV, where they quickly realized that it was buried in large amounts of fresh snow. It took several minutes to scrape the snow from around the driver's door so that it could be opened. Once inside, they discovered a grateful but dazed driver who thought some kind soul had stopped to help him out of his predicament. Beavis and Butthead were soon able to establish fact number two: the driver seemed largely unharmed, but because the airbag had deployed, his eardrums had ruptured and he was unable to communicate.

They then dug out the back door so that one of them could get into the car and look for the stolen item. It soon became clear that there was no bag. Faced with this fact, the two young men were forced to retreat and analyze the situation. They left the almost unharmed but extremely confused driver to help himself out of the car.

After a brief consultation, they decided to go back to the roadside bar. They hadn't quite got all their ducks in a row yet, but they were able to cross the man in the SUV off their very short list of suspects. They had also crossed the grumpy waitress off that list. An obstinate bitch - and ugly too - but she was most probably not a thief. They remembered that another person had been in the room while they were eating. A man with a sandwich. A man who was normal in every respect. Otherwise, there was no description. They cursed their lack of observation skills.

When the Volvo rolled into the parking lot behind the roadside bar shortly afterwards, they discovered that the car that had been parked next to theirs had disappeared. After a brief consultation with the waitress, they realized that the car was not hers and that they could go to hell - again. And she knew nothing about the third guest. Butthead had considered whether some alternative method of persuasion could be used to elicit more information but, after an angry look from Beavis, he dismissed the idea. This was not the time to draw attention to themselves and it was doubtful that they would get any more information out of this rabble. Probably she hadn't registered the man very carefully either, given her general absence during the evening.

After a brief and fruitless search of the building, they were forced to accept that the bag had disappeared under their noses. On the way out, Beavis swept the plates and glasses off their still untidy table. They landed with a crash on the floor along with the leftovers. Without turning around to face the speechless waitress, they left the Night Owl empty-handed.

CHAPTER 2

Aftermath

William woke up on Saturday morning with a splitting headache. He thought it was perhaps a little more than he deserved, given that he'd taken both headache pills and fluid replacement before going to bed. Unfortunately, they were taken in combination with half a bottle of Famous Grouse.

It took him a while to remember what had happened the previous evening. At least he thought he remembered sneaking up to the apartment around ten o'clock with a stolen bag. The bag was hidden away in the back of the wardrobe as he was too excited to go through the contents again. Instead, mentally exhausted, he had ended up on the sofa with a previously unopened bottle of whiskey. Now the events of yesterday were creeping up on him again in the guise of a faceless and unwelcome guest tapping his temples with a rhythmically swinging hammer. The half-empty bottle of whiskey stared at him mercilessly from the living room table. He wondered absentmindedly what kind of bird adorned the label. A grouse? A pheasant? A capercaillie? The answer was not forthcoming and he soon realized that he was not really interested in the answer.

He decided to go with the flow and take the day as it unfolded. A cup of strong coffee was the result of the first decision of the day. Then he found the strength to go and get the bag. It was hastily stowed away behind a pile of rubble in the closet. He cursed himself for the unstrategic placement as he impatiently dug through summer jackets and old sleeping bags. The peculiar looking leather bag soon saw the light of day and was placed on the living room floor. William closed the window curtains, checked that the door to the stairwell was locked and turned on the overhead light. The leather cover was removed for the second time and the same astonishment spread across his face as the bespectacled scientist stared at him. It was an unreal feeling to see so much money in concentrated form.

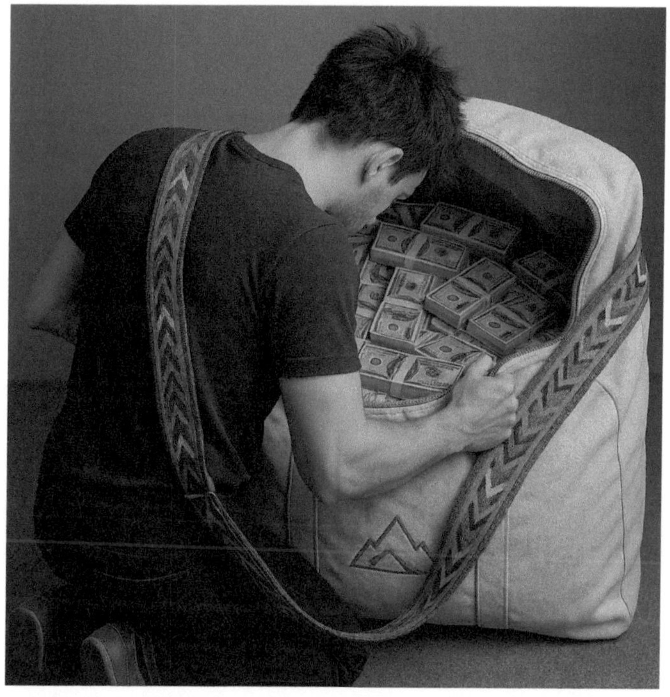

He picked up one of the bundles and flipped through it carefully. Five hundred crown notes all through. Each bundle contained a hundred banknotes. Four bundles crosswise and six lengthwise. Thirty bundles on top of each other. Seven hundred and twenty bundles in total and with one hundred notes in each. He entered 720x100x500 on a calculator and the display showed the number 36 followed by six zeros. Thirty-six million! The thought was staggering. Never before had he seen so much money. He didn't know how to react to the discovery. He couldn't decide whether he was looking at a bag full of gold or a bag of compost that someone had thrown through the window during the night.

His head was throbbing, but William continued his counting game. It was the only thing he could think of to do at the moment. Thirty-six million was the equivalent of about a hundred years' salary after tax. So, after a hundred years of faithful service, he thought, you had earned a bag of money. The honest income suddenly seemed paltry and a small wave of directed anger washed over him as he thought about his work. He sat for a long time on the floor with a few bundles of banknotes in his arms. His eyes were blank and shiny, looking straight ahead. For the moment, he could not assess the situation and what problems he might have gotten himself into.

Then there was a knock on the door. Three distinct knocks that made the letterbox rattle. He jerked where he was sitting and dropped the bundles of notes on the floor. As he unconsciously straightened one leg, which was resting against the leather bag, more bundles went flying across the floor. Who could it be on a Saturday morning? He rarely received announced visitors to the apartment. Yesterday spun in his head and a number of scenarios played out. With his heart in his throat, he stood up and, with uncertain movements, tried to pick up all the notes and put them back in the bag. He fumbled with the piece of bone and the rope loop for a few seconds, then moved the bag into the bedroom and closed the door. The wardrobe would have been a better choice, but it was in the hall by the front door and he couldn't bring himself to move the bag there.

It knocked again, even more firmly than the first time. He made a quick inspection of his own appearance and quickly realized that he'd fallen asleep in his clothes. His hair was tousled and his face unshaven. From his throat rose a scent of a dead animal. He took a deep breath, walked up to the peephole, expecting the worst. Instead, the white-haired nest-like head of his neighbor appeared. Relieved, he turned the lock, removed the hasp and opened the door just as the eighty-year-old Signe, who lived across the stairwell, began hammering on the door a third time. She took half a step backwards when he appeared in the doorway.

"Good... good morning," she said. "I hope I didn't wake you. I saw you come home last night, so I figured you were home."

William opened his mouth to reply but remembered the dead animal wallowing far inside and closed it again.

"Well you see they have been here asking for you. Early this morning they came, both of them. You must have been asleep."

His body stiffened and his face turned white. His mouth opened and closed again as he tried to think of something to say.

"Who? Who was here?"

"Are you not feeling well William? You look sick."

"I ... I have had a hard week," he said, realizing immediately how stupid that must sound. The words popped out of a cloud of whiskey fumes that could probably wake the dead. Signe made a discreet hand movement to cover her own nose, confirming what he already suspected: that nothing he said or did in his current state would be to his advantage.

"I mean the craftsmen. They are ready now. With the whole house. The leak." The words came in a staggered sequence as she discreetly took a small step backwards between each micro-pause.

"The craftsmen ... yes, I remember now. What did they want?"

The pieces were slowly falling into place. The whole block had suffered a water leak in the basement a few weeks ago. A pipe had burst and water had poured out all over the basement. All the tenants living on the first floor were affected because the pipes had to be accessed from above as well. The tenant association had hired two plumbers to fix the problem. As William would be away all week, he had handed over his house key to Signe.

"They just wanted to return the key. But they gave it to me instead. Everything is ready now. They had to break up the floor under the sink in all the kitchens. It smells like sewage and mortar, but maybe you haven't noticed?" she said with a look that suggested it wasn't just sewage under the sink.

Of course he hadn't, he thought, but nodded lazily and said instead that it smelled pretty bad also in his kitchen. He thanked Signe for her help and took his door key. She looked after him for far too long as he closed the door.

It was already afternoon and the hangover should have been in retreat, but his head was throbbing like never before. Over the years he had come to terms with the fact that every now and then he simply got stuck in a dead end of brooding - an eternal search for something that he could not yet put his finger on but which he knew with rock-solid conviction was out there. But this was something different from ordinary brooding - something more animal. He felt as if he were caught between two continental plates; the base of his skull was loose and his thoughts were cloudy, hazy snapshots sailed past the corners of his eyes just before the outlines became visible, and voices echoed somewhere in the back regions. He assumed they were trying to tell him something but could not make out the message.

The phone rang. The caller ID showed that it was Anders, one of his oldest childhood friends. He thought for a few seconds about whether it was a good or bad idea to answer, but finally picked up the phone with unsteady hands:

"Yes.."

"Hello to you too. Almost hung up. How is life?"

"I found a whiskey bottle yesterday. Think half of the contents slipped down."

"So, something to celebrate?"

"No, not really... you know how it is. It seemed like a good idea at the time."

But of course Anders didn't know. Spontaneously pouring himself half a bottle of whiskey was not his cup of tea. Neither was a couple of glasses of wine. Anders was a clean-living person and a fixed point in the lives of his wife and their two children. Both were well-behaved boys in their early teens. Suburban house, dog and a station wagon. A job that he enjoyed just enough, so that he would never change. The wife worked in health care and was medium blond and medium-handsome plus. In winter, the family went skiing in Sälen (they always stayed in the same cottage) and in summer it was off to the Canary Islands, preferably sunny and safe Playa del Ingles. Christmas and Easter were celebrated with the family. William had a standing invitation but had always declined. Anders had never nagged him, decent and caring as he was.

William sometimes found himself wondering what they actually had in common. They were opposites in almost every way and, if you were in that mood, Anders had achieved everything that William had not. A constant reminder that life was running away from him. Then it always hit him in the end - why they were still good friends and why they would continue to be good friends despite their differences. Although neither of them would admit it, and neither would ever bring it up, there was something in the other's life situation that they both admired and secretly looked up to. For William, it was a fixed point in life that appealed. Not necessarily the whole package, but something of what his friend had managed to salvage over the years. A family and a real home would do just fine. For Anders, on the contrary, it was the freedom, and the absence of all these obligations and musts, that he secretly looked up to. Not because either of them would trade their lives for the other's for a moment, but because their interaction gave them a glimpse into a different and more exciting world. A world they wanted to be part of but were not prepared to enter.

"I called because last week you talked about taking a vacation."

Anders' voice broke the temporary silence as he continued,

"Thought I would check if you want to go up to Sälenstugan for cross-country skiing during Easter. They have good tracks up there. But you don't have to stick to the tracks, you can ski on the mountain. Ski touring, you know."

"Yes... yes...I know all of that. But I need to be away for a while."

William didn't know what to say. The situation he was in was so absurd that he could not even think of a white lie. Moreover, he had not recovered from yesterday's private party.

"We leave in a couple weeks. Do you think you'll have time to sober up before then?"

"Very funny."

His brain was working feverishly. He should never have answered the phone. There was no way he could tell Anders about the money without putting his friend and his family in danger. But despite this, he needed help from someone, someone with common sense and whom he could trust. Help to understand how to move forward without revealing too much.

"I need to get away for a few weeks. Get away by myself. I've been thinking about my job and the future."

"Sounds deep. Is everything okay? I mean, has something happened?"

"Everything is fine. I just need something to... something to break the pattern."

He was silent for a while, thinking about how to present the words to his best friend:

"Anders, I'm thinking about a longer leave. Kind of skip work and do something completely different for a while."

"For a while, what do you mean?"

"Well, I do not know. A good while. Try something new. Get off the squirrel wheel."

There was a long silence before Anders spoke:

"William, here's the thing: you really need to get away, try something new or whatever you choose to call it. You can see it a mile away. There is some shit that you are carrying around."

"Ok…go on"

"To those who don't know you, you may appear carefree, but I know there are things weighing you down - a melancholy that can make the most hard-to-please pimples look like nitrous oxide-addled teenagers at an amusement park. I don't know what's weighing you down, but I do know this much: you're not doing anything about it."

Anders allowed the message to sink in before continuing in an equally relentless tone:

"Somewhere deep inside your hungover body dwells an adventurer, an adventurer that needs a firm kick in the ass. Anyway, as far as adventurous thoughts are concerned, they too often stay inside the head instead of being put into action. That's my point."

Anders took a deep breath before continuing:

"I have no idea what you're doing or what you've been through, but maybe it's time to trust your instincts and just take the step. Don't care what I or anyone else says. Don't wait for any approval or directions. Forget about work and other obstacles. Just go."

It took William quite a while to process what had been said. It was so completely unexpected that this came from Anders. He couldn't have any idea about the money, yet he had managed to put his finger on exactly the right point. It was as if he'd always known where to strike but had been waiting for the right moment.

"Well, that was the plan... sort of. To check out for a while."

"Exactly... You need it. I'd love to go with you, but I'm tied up and screwed down. It's easier to say these things to others than to do them myself."

Anders chuckled into the phone and then fell silent. They ended the conversation by making small talk about the missing ski trip and everything that had happened since the last time they met.

By three o'clock in the afternoon, the fresh snow had already disappeared from the ground, but the traces of the storm were still visible. From the kitchen window, William could see broken branches, the occasional blown-over bicycle and scattered garbage bags. The cloud cover had broken up but it was still windy. He decided to stay inside all day. As evening approached, a feeling of unease had taken hold of his body. It went like a shiver through his whole body and his thoughts flew off in all directions. Perhaps he had made a gross misjudgment of the two people in the roadside bar.

They would have appeared as unkempt youths rather than serious criminals. But you never know. What if they had figured out who he was? For the first time it occurred to him that his car had been parked next to the robbers'. His pale yellow Hyundai had been just a few meters from their own car. It had been dark and snowy, but the roadside lights cast a faint glow over the parking lot at the end. If the robbers had paid the slightest attention to his unassuming car, they would have soon tracked him down. The thought was terrifying. What suggested that they had not registered the car was that they had been chasing the wrong person, driving a vehicle that bore no resemblance to William's car.

He suddenly felt the weight of the moment. Someone was probably missing a lot of money. Someone more than the two cronies at the Night Owl. He didn't think it likely that these two philistines had decided to withdraw their honestly earned savings of thirty-six million and then carry the money around in a large leather bag, which was anything but discreet.

* * *

After leaving the roadhouse, Beavis and Butthead had started to argue about whose fault it was that the bag was left under the table. The mood in the car had oscillated between anger and despair. As they approached Westridge, they had still not been able to agree on a verdict of guilt and parted for the evening.

On Saturday afternoon, they met again to decide how to proceed. The who-to-blame issue had to wait for now. Here they had to cooperate. They met at Beavis' home, which was a caravan park outside Westridge. The campsite was always full during the summer but this time of the year it was almost empty. Many campers had left their caravans over the winter months to solve the long-time storage problem. Some of the caravans belonged to seasonal workers who had conveniently arranged accommodation throughout the working season - and almost for free.

Beavis had broken into every caravan on the campsite and stolen -

or 'borrowed', as he put it - forgotten items that could be put to good use. Cable reels, flashlights, canned food, a lined jacket, a pair of shoes and even some money. He had connected the cable reels to an almost hundred-meter-long cord that ran between the caravan and a boarded-up café that ran on maintenance heat during the winter months. The caravan was also on loan - from a German family who spent a few months at the campsite every year. Beavis intended to leave the temporary home in the spring when the first seasonal workers started to arrive.

Beavis' real name was Kenneth, but he had been called "Tube" ever since he tried to get drunk in his early teens by connecting his mouth to the radiator of his car via a rubber hose and sucking in glycol. Kenneth had managed to survive by having his stomach pumped, but was then forever called Tube. The incident with the radiator fluid was the definitive break with everything that had to do with school. For quite some time, he had already been mentally absent from most classes, but after the stomach pump, his body was also absent from the attendance register.

Somehow, he managed to muddle through the last few years of primary school, with final grades that may not have dazzled those around him, but meant he didn't have to repeat a year or be reassigned. This combination of survival instinct and resourcefulness would serve him well in the future. Instead of going to college, he took temporary jobs in warehouses, shops and car repair shops. Wherever he worked, it always followed the same pattern. For a few months he did a decent job but somewhere along the line he always started to lose interest. He would show up late, wreck the truck, argue with the store manager, steal tools, or start selling electronics off the shelves to friends. On one occasion, he was thrown out head first after scratching the entire side of a new car with a screwdriver. This was after the first paycheck had been paid late. The owner of the garage, a bushy man of one hundred and thirty kilos and with a rare bad temper, hadn't even bothered to open the door first but had used Tube's head as a battering ram.

His later teenage years laid the foundations for a career of juvenile delinquency that grew in both frequency and scope over the years. A mixture of luck and cunning had allowed him to escape the long arm of the law until he had passed the age of eighteen. Then he was caught stealing a car and given six months in prison for long and faithful service. This by a united judiciary that had finally tired of his antics and wanted to set an example. During his imprisonment, Tube had made some contacts in the underworld. He felt he was maturing and when he was released after six months, he was ready for bigger crimes.

Butthead - that nickname had followed him since his school days, a chapter of his life he often tried to forget. Behind the desk, he had never quite fit in. Gifted with what could generously be called a nonexistent aptitude for reading, he was generally unfocused, uninterested, and perpetually behind. All in all, a very unfavorable combination for receiving and storing information. Not that it bothered him in the least. After all, it wasn't as a literature professor or nuclear physicist that he wanted to make a career. His talent lay more on the practical side, he thought. He wanted to work with his hands rather than his head. Most of the teachers didn't think there was much to be gained from the practical side either. His potential talents were long absent.

He became known among his classmates as a clown who always wanted to test the limits. During a chemistry lesson, he had the brilliant idea that the school's large swimming pool looked much better in purple. No sooner said than done, he stuffed half his chemistry kit into his baggy pants - including containers of potassium permanganate, glycerol and magnesium. Then he headed for the pool. When no one was looking, he poured half of the potassium permanganate into the deep end of the pool. He would save the rest for later. Perhaps he would visit the aquarium fish in the staff canteen, or maybe he would mix the powder with some other substance in his trouser pockets. In any case, a purple stain had begun to spread in the deep end of the pool, and when a couple of the younger girls shouted in unison that there was a beast swimming around in the pool, it caused a big stir. Some of those in the water quickly tried to get out. One of them was a teacher who had observed the dark spot and in her haste to get to dry land slipped on the tile and broke her jaw. Butthead had quickly removed himself from the scene - unseen but heavily splashed by fleeing and screaming little girls.

Butthead had been pleased with himself. He had committed the perfect crime and escaped detection - almost! If it hadn't been for one small detail he overlooked. An hour later, all the pupils had been summoned to the main hall where the headmaster was waiting to give a lecture on etiquette. The chemistry teacher had discovered the break-in in the chemical cupboard and put two and two together. Because the prank had had such serious consequences, the principal now wanted the perpetrator to come forward. All the students stood in silence, waiting to see what would happen next. After a while, there is a commotion in the middle of the hall and a growing circle of spectators forms around Butthead. At first he doesn't understand what's so damned interesting, but as he follows the stares down to the floor, he sees that his light-colored pants have turned purple and that a dark stain has formed around his shoes. The chemical containers had broken and reacted with the still damp trousers, and the various substances have since come into contact with each other. At the level of the right trouser pocket, the fabric had started to smoke and soon the smoke turned into a bright and intense flame. The magnesium had reacted with the damp trousers. When the surprise had subsided, the pain came. After a wild war dance, Beavis had managed to get his pants off, which continued to burn like a sparkler on the floor. The perpetrator had made himself known.

After the show in the auditorium, Butthead had been forced to listen to the name Funnel. He could never understand the connection between the assigned nickname and the incident at the pool but he had to accept it. As with Tube, it was during this period in his life that things began to go wrong and it was during their first spell in prison many years later that the two of them had become acquainted. Together they had decided to explore the underworld a little more thoroughly.

✳ ✳ ✳

Funnel and Tube were in the borrowed caravan. Outside, the afternoon sun shone through the sparse cloud cover and the thermometer showed 5 degrees plus. The snow had disappeared from the open areas, but there were shadowy patches everywhere, and most of the ground was still white. The ice on the lake was a decimeter thick and the plowed ice channel, which ran around Bear Island and stretched all the way back to the city, was still busy with cross-country skiers.

"Easy come, easy go, Tube said."

Funnel nodded thoughtfully as he looked out the caravan window.

"Maybe we were never meant to own so much cash," he continued, as if seeking some kind of response from across the table.

"Mmmm," muttered Funnel, his eyes fixed on something far away.

Neither of them could quite believe that one moment they had been carrying around millions in cash and the next moment they were empty-handed. It occurred to him that they had never actually counted the money. In the back of the car on the way back from Stockholm, Funnel had roughly estimated the amount at "many millions". Now they would never know how much it was and maybe it was just as well.

"Remember the car parked next to us at the Night Owl?" asked Tube, seeking eye contact with his companion who was still looking out the window.

"Well, I remember there was *a* car there.

He let go of his gazing at the skater far away and turned his focus back to the warm inside.

"Do you remember what it looked like?"

38

Funnel thought for a moment and replied that he probably did not. It had light colored paint, he thought. Maybe it was dirty white. Maybe it was yellow.

"I also remember it being yellow," replied Tube. "A medium-sized yellow car. A sedan, not a station wagon."

"No, not a station wagon. Quite round shapes. Definitely not a Volvo."

"A Jap, I would think. Possibly a Frenchman."

For the moment, it was not possible to get very far in the research. Tube went and got two beers from the fridge. Maybe that would speed up the thinking process.

The sun was setting on the horizon but Funnel and Tube had not appeared outside the caravan for several hours. Empty beer cans started to pile up in the kitchen area. By the fourth beer, the inspiration had begun to recede and eventually disappeared completely. The two companions found no better advice than to simply postpone the detective work until tomorrow and instead focus on emptying the liquid supply. For the moment, there was full consensus.

* * *

Inspector Edward Johnson was summoned to Superintendent Kvarnbring on Saturday morning. It was not unusual to be called in during the holidays, but in this case he had not even received an explanation for the case. Edward could think of a thousand more interesting things to do than spend Saturday in the office, but there was something about the voice on the phone that caught his interest. There was an eagerness and a seriousness in the tone. An excitement in the air and a need to say something more. But as he made his way down the corridor, curiosity gave way to irritation at having his weekend ruined.

"Good morning, Johnson," said Kvarnbring. "How are you doing?" He sank back into the well-padded office chair and gave his colleague a quizzical look as he appeared in the doorway. Both policemen were lanky grey-haired men at the end of their careers. They were in their sixties and secretly looking forward to early retirement if only the opportunity presented itself. They had had a lot to do with each other over the years and had solved some tricky cases together before Kvarnbring was promoted to Superintendent a few years ago. Edward had found it difficult to work with his former partner since he left and became one of those paper turners, and turning papers was not really police work. Both were uncomfortable with the new division of roles and he knew that Kvarnbring was having as much trouble with the changes as he was. Despite the differences, there was still mutual respect between the two colleagues.

"It's Saturday," Edward replied briefly, sitting down in the armchair-like thing in front of the desk. "What can I help you with?"

"Sámi," replied the curator, ignoring the sarcasm of his subordinate.

"Sámi?" Edward repeated without understanding a thing.

"Yes, Sámi. Laplanders…Let me explain from the beginning. Are you aware that there was a traffic accident just outside Arlandastad last night?"

Edward shook his head and delivered a prolonged and poorly concealed yawn.

"What have I got to do with it? I don't work with traffic accidents."

"It was a single accident," Kvarnbring continued. "The driver was seriously injured but will recover according to the doctors."

"Ok, this happens all the time."

"Let me continue," the intendent replied briefly. For the first time there was a slight irritation in his voice. He lit a cigarette and then proceeded with his story:

"It is the man who drove the car who is interesting. He is Sámi and comes from a small village in western Laponia on the border between Norway and Sweden. His name is Niilla Kuoljok and he is the son of a certain Sáhkár Kuoljok. His father, Sáhkár, is the village elder and thus the one in charge in this remote corner of the world. The place is called Luoktajärvi, by the way."

Kvarnbring paused to allow the words to sink in.

"I've never heard of Luoktajärvi," Edward replied wearily. "But then there are thousands of small communities up there in the north and most of them can hardly be pronounced, let alone spelled."

"No wonder you've never heard of Luoktajärvi because it's not even marked on maps. Neither the village nor its inhabitants are known to the public. Despite this, Luoktajärvi, and its original village elder, to say the least, have caused problems that have never reached the ears of the public. He is reported to be as big as a giant, mad as a dog, and cunning as a fox. The inhabitants call him the Mountain King - and the inhabitants are said to be as crazy as their king."

Kvarnbring paused again while looking at his colleague but only got a lazy yawn in response. He narrowed his eyes at Edward and continued in an authoritative voice:

"Luoktajärvi is located in a mountainous and inaccessible area on the edge of Padjelanta National Park - right on the border between Norway and Sweden. This very fact has been the basis of a century-long feud between the two countries. The Norwegians claim that this tiny area, which is no more than a few square kilometers, originally belonged to Troms County and should therefore be part of

Norway. Sweden, on the other hand, claims that the whole of Norway was once part of Sweden. The fact that it was then returned in a moment of weakness does not give the Norwegians the right to seize Swedish territory afterwards. This is more or less how the discussion went on for several years until the First World War gave people something else to think about. Then came the Second World War and well... you probably understand where I'm going with this. Nowadays, people have almost forgotten what they were originally fighting about. On the Swedish maps the area belongs to Sweden and on the Norwegian maps it belongs to Norway. Because the area is so small and remote, you can hardly tell the difference if you put two maps side by side."

Kvarnbring continued, "In Luoktajärvi, on the other hand, the situation has been exploited by playing the parties off against each other. In practice, the small village has had autonomy ever since the dissolution of the Union and has thus been exempt from taxes, registration and other obligations. No one can say where the tax is to be paid anyway, and those who once had views on this have long since fallen by the wayside."

"You were talking about a traffic accident outside Stockholm a few minutes ago and now you are a hundred miles north and a hundred years back in time. Now you'll have to explain to me why I'm here talking Sámi with you on a Saturday morning."

Edward yawned and stared straight ahead. "Do you have any coffee, by the way?"

Kvarnbring ignored the question and continued his lecture:

"The whole ownership dispute over Luoktajärvi had more or less been forgotten until it became clear that something was changing in the small village. All of a sudden, residents started spending money like never before. Snowmobiles, ATVs, construction equipment, and even a helicopter and a couple of seaplanes appeared. The village expanded in width and height. Finally, just a year or so ago, it became clear that the inhabitants had stumbled upon a real gold vein, and since then the village has been under more frequent surveillance. The Norwegians watch from the west and the Swedes from the east. So far, no one has been able to figure out exactly what this gold vein consists of and in order not to revive the old border issue, no one has wanted to push too hard or send people into the village itself."

"And where in this story does the man in the car come into the picture?" interjected Edward, who had now perked up somewhat.

"Niilla is the eldest son of the Mountain King and the likely future heir to the unknown business that is suspected of being built up. It is believed that he is here to make contacts and do business. Incidentally, this is not the first time he has been here."

"So the crazy mountain king has gone and become very rich in later days. Aren't the Sámi a kind of people who live off the land and make a living from reindeer herding?"

"That is certainly the case in most instances. But I am no expert on our indigenous population and I don't even know if the inhabitants of Luoktajärvi can be called genuine Sámi. What is interesting in this case is that old man Kuoljok has now turned to us, that is, the Swedish Security Service. He wants us to patch up his son and send him back in original condition."

"That sounds reasonable, doesn't it?"

"Yes, of course. But it seems that Niilla Kuoljok has been in Stockholm to sell something to the industry. Exactly what the goods are, we don't know at the moment, but one guesses that they are some kind of raw material, such as precious metals. How else would one explain the sudden wealth?"

Kvarnbring put the cigarette in a half-empty coffee cup and continued:

"We believe that this is illegal business. If so, Sáhkár Kuoljok will get his fish warm. If not, it's a great opportunity to smack the Norwegians on the nose in this old border dispute. That is, if we can get our mountain king to push for Luoktajärvi to become part of Sweden."

"Who are *we* and what do I have to do with all this? Why did you call me? From the police's point of view, this is a traffic accident and nothing else, right?"

Kvarnbring leaned forward over the table and narrowed his eyes at the inspector as if to finally get to the point.

"The road accident itself will be conducted like any other low priority investigation. I have already appointed Jörgen Metzner - he was hand-picked by me."

"I don't understand anything," said Edward. You already have a person hand-picked by you - a person who could very well be Sweden's most confused police officer. By the way, *a complete idiot* according to your own personal analysis.

"As I might have said, the elevator doesn't go all the way up, but that's a conscious choice," Kvarnbring added. "Anyway, only a handful of people know what we are talking about now. Metzner is of course not one of them. So, they are investigating an ordinary traffic accident and the unfortunate victim's belongings have been confiscated by me personally."

Kvarnberg hesitated for a few seconds, twirled his bushy mustache between his fingers and continued:

"I want you to get in touch with Niilla and try to win his trust. I want you to find out what is really going on in that remote mountain village and who they are doing business with. It is obvious that there is a connection between the observed activities in the village and the visits down here in Stockholm."

Inspector Edward Johnson almost fell off his chair in surprise. He tried to read the superintendent's eyes to see if he was joking, but was only met by an expressionless stone face that casually twirled its moustache. Just like he always did when he was thinking.

"Why not just treat this as a normal police case and do it the official way? And why the Security Service if it is an ordinary traffic accident?"

"Because it's *not* a normal police case," replied Inspector Kvarnbring emphatically. "The only reason that this case has ended up in my lap is because I can handle it discreetly and professionally and to steer it away from the local police. Remember, Sáhkár turned to Us first, not to the Norwegians and not to any other authority. Nobody wants too much dust to be stirred up or get into a fight with the Norwegians. Sáhkár Kuoljok is probably doing some shady business but we have no proof yet. There is also a suspicion that some companies in the Stockholm region have paid large bribes to take part in business that is illegal, probably without knowing anything about the true origin of the goods. If it later turns out that there are no shady deals, they want to take the opportunity to, so to speak, strengthen ties with a newly rich region."

"They? The handful of people within the Security Service?"

"Yes."

"Do you realize how crazy this sounds to me?"

He stared across the table at Kvarnbring as if trying to get him to retract or at least revise what he had just said.

"Believe me Edward, this sounds as crazy to me as it does to you."

"Have you talked to him yourself?"

"I am the only one who has spoken to Niilla since he woke up last night, apart from hospital staff. It has not really been possible to get any useful information out of him."

"You realize, of course, that it is only a matter of time before this has spread to the wrong ears," said Edward. "Jörgen Metzner may be a police officer with many shortcomings, but he'll soon find out that this is something completely different than a traffic accident."

"That's quite possible," replied the intendent bluntly. "But since Metzner does not work within the Security Service it will push the attention away from us. In any case, I want you to get started immediately. This is what I found in the car."

He placed a cell phone, a wallet, an old map book and a thick green briefcase on the table.

"I have confiscated the cell phone and wallet from our Sámi, or whatever he is. I have dug out the map book from the archive and it is an old fold-out mountain map that is sixty or seventy years old. It is one of very few maps that show where Luoktajärvi is. You will need it. The document folder contains everything written about the area since the dissolution of the Union. Most of it is classified. Maybe you can find something useful there."

"I guess it's not a question but an order," Edward grunted. He could see the whole holiday and the sunny weather disappearing out of the window and it annoyed him enormously. Especially since it was Kvarnbring who had ruined it. At the same time, there was something about this story that tickled his curiosity.

"Exactly right, Johnson! You report directly to me."

CHAPTER 3

The Decision

It was not until Sunday morning that the thought struck him for the first time. The thought that he might not get rid of the money. It started as a slight tingling sensation in his stomach that made its way up to the office. There, like a zealous doorman, common sense was beating the intruder with a baseball bat. At intervals the intruder made fresh attempts to break through the door, and was getting closer and closer to a breakthrough. Until this moment, William had not even considered that he might actually be able to keep the money. Instead, he had been thinking about how best to get rid of the problem. Should he return the bag to the roadside shop? Or would he simply dump it in a trash can?

After long, drawn-out internal debates, he finally concluded that it didn't really matter whether he got rid of the money or not. The only people who could reasonably suspect he had thirty-six million were those two idiots from the roadside inn. And if they somehow managed to track him down, getting rid of the money wouldn't help - if anything, it might make things worse.

The tingling feeling in his stomach wouldn't go away and he knew he was considering the unthinkable. Outside the apartment, the sun was shining again and the snowstorm was a distant memory. Instead of problems, he saw more and more opportunities around the corner. First and foremost, there was the possibility of doing something completely new - a vague and as yet undeveloped idea, a feeling of being able to buy a one-way ticket to a new life. This sense of an easy future was interspersed with more concrete snapshots of exotic travel with sandy beaches and umbrella drinks, beautiful women, luxurious dinners and expensive wines - all flashing before his eyes like a bad ad for the million-dollar lottery.

His window shopping and daydreaming on the sofa were short-lived. The problems and worries started to pile up again like dark storm clouds. How could he spend the money without it being noticed? How would he handle the job? Would he be on the run from now on? And what if the money was fake! This last thought made him quickly get up from the sofa and go and get one of the bundles of notes from his bag. He pulled one of the five hundred notes out of the tightly packed bundle and analyzed it with great care. It was clearly used.

"This is so weird," he said to himself.

He couldn't put his finger on why, but he had expected the notes (if they were genuine) to be smooth and neatly packaged in symmetrical bundles. These thirty-six million had been in circulation. Maybe I've seen too many movies, he thought.

He compared a banknote from his bag to one he fished out of his wallet. The same length, width, thickness, text structure, watermarks and the same feel in his hand. If this is a fake, it's a damn good one, he thought to himself. For a brief moment, he had actually hoped that the money would be bad copies. Monopoly money with no value and placed in the bag to play a nasty trick on someone. In a way, it would have been so much easier. He could have gotten rid of the junk and let the whole thing go.

* * *

William needed to clear his head. There was so much to sort out and Anders' words still echoed in his ears. It was late afternoon, the sun was hanging low over the horizon and he hadn't been out the door for almost two days. He decided to take a drive.

The journey went a few kilometers south towards the city's nearest nature reserve, Bear Island. In summer, hundreds of sunbathing people flocked around the same waterhole like thirsty antelopes. In winter, however, there were not so many people on the island itself. Instead, they gathered along the plowed ice tracks that ran between the small islands in Westridgefjärden and continued all the way to the harbor. He parked his car in the empty summer parking lot in the middle of the island, near the campsite. A few meters from the parking lot, one could directly connect to one of the many walking trails that perforated the entire island. On this particular late winter day, it was more of a slushy ski trail than a cozy walking path, but William was not discouraged.

In the late afternoon sun and in the deserted and scenic surroundings, it was easier to gather his thoughts. In any case, he was stuck with a problem, William reasoned to himself. Whether it was a pleasant problem remained to be seen, but nonetheless, he had gotten himself into trouble. And it wasn't just a bit of sticky fingers, it was a full body bath of bear glue and there was no easy way out. But there were also opportunities. Big opportunities. What did he really have to lose by keeping the money?

Life, perhaps? said reason, hammering a little lightly with his baseball bat on his brow bone. What life? An eight-to-five job with boring chores and car commuting? What exciting things had he done in recent years? Or the last decade for that matter. It was a legitimate question and not the first time it had been asked. Straight to the point and always without an answer. What exactly had he achieved? Or an even simpler question: what did he actually do during the day?

Consultant said the sign on his cubicle. Consultant, plain and simple, written on an A4 with his photo underneath. Not even a name. Just seven letters and a photo where he doesn't even look happy. Possibly a little surprised. He recalled that someone had shoved the camera into his face the very first day he moved into the office in Stockholm. Now he was reminded of that incident every time he entered the booth.

His mother once asked him what a consultant was. It was many years later, but he remembered that he didn't know what to answer. He was not specialized in any field. Bridge designer, mechanical engineer, tax advisor or anything would have been handy to throw out on such an occasion, but he was just a consultant. Sometimes it meant *resource* or *administrator*. A few times, it meant *project manager* or something similar. He was a walking resumé, a drifting resource without a name or home port. A generalist who was shuffled around to fill in gaps. Someone might as well stamp the hourly rate and the word *for hire* on his forehead.

As part of the job it was expected that he occasionally says something wise during the meetings, exchanges information with other nameless resources and periodically produces papers that no one reads. The irony was that there always seemed to be someone willing to pay good money for such things. It was his slim luck for lack of anything else.

William squelched along the snow-slushy forest path. He tried to stay off the ski track itself but soon gave up. In a day or so, it would have thawed into a dirty mass anyway. His thoughts fluttered away as he walked and kicked in the slush. He was in a bubble. He had been for years. When you're inside the bubble, it's hard to understand what's wrong. At best, you understand that something is wrong and needs to be fixed, but it's always easier to just run straight ahead. The law of least resistance prevails everywhere. He was no different in that respect, although he had begun to realize how things are connected.

What was really stopping him from taking the money and disappearing? He had no partner to worry about - long-term relationships had never been part of William's life. Maybe, without even realizing it, he'd internalized his father's old motto after all. Ever since the divorce from William's mother over thirty years ago, his father had maintained that a relationship was like an onion with many layers that had to be built up over time. Time consuming and hard work. Unless each layer was tended, they would start to rot and spread to other parts. Maintaining a relationship is expensive and thankless. "Besides, a damaged onion makes your eyes water," his father used to conclude the lecture.

After all, there had been a few relationships over the years. They lasted from a few weeks to just over a year. The longest relationship had been the most tragic. It was ten years ago that Leena - a short, curvy woman from Luleå - had moved into his small rented flat. At the time, he was living in Stockholm and it was difficult to find decent accommodation. As it always seemed to be in the capital of Sweden. Leena was a very determined woman and she had not only insisted on moving in with him but also insisted that they should get married. Cohabitation is not a marital status but just a term for two people living together, she stubbornly argued. It had ended with William getting married in a moment of weakness in the town hall in Luleå. It all came to a crashing halt six months later and William had kept a safe distance from both stubborn short women and marriages since that experience.

The only real romance had happened five years ago at work. She was an accountant who had been hired for a job that was supposed to last only a couple of months but which, due to external circumstances, ended up taking a long time. The external circumstances were never clarified, but William had spent a great deal of time away from the office to solve these thorny problems.

The woman - Merja - turned out to be a very different kind of colleague, full of unexpected quirks. At first, he couldn't quite figure her out. She would burst into spontaneous laughter or make odd, seemingly unfiltered comments that left him puzzled. But over time, he began to see past the eccentric exterior and discovered a razor-sharp intellect, laced with self-awareness and a disarming sense of humor.

He remembered one meeting in particular: she had suddenly erupted into uncontrollable laughter and had to excuse herself from the room. Later, she explained - still chuckling - that the combination of the shadows on the wall and the PowerPoint slides had triggered some wildly inappropriate associations. He'd asked her, half amused and half incredulous, whether a work meeting was really the best time for that kind of imagination.

She'd just shaken her head and said "William this is a crazy and artificial world and my way of dealing with it is to laugh as much as possible and as often as possible. By the way, did you see what a ridiculous mustache that guy in the front with the pointing stick had?"

After that, they could spend hours talking - about things he'd never spoken of with anyone before. The job faded into the background. And then there was Merja herself - she had a presence he simply couldn't resist. Her brown eyes held a quiet intensity, and her thick, untamed hair reminded him of a lion's mane. She was tall, with long, graceful legs, and yet still favored heels, which let him meet her gaze without having to stoop. There was something about her unpolished, natural demeanor that drew him in - something raw, real, and utterly magnetic.

One thing led to another and soon the first kiss had been delivered. The making out soon turned into more animalistic desires, which were satisfied in Merja's overnight apartment near work. At lunchtime, they would sneak away to satisfy their hunger. Every evening was dedicated to the god of fertility. They were like horny rabbits. Between the fornications, they could lie for hours talking. Time ceased to exist and they lived in a bubble to which no one else had access.

It all came to an abrupt end when Merja had been forced to go up to her parents' home to care for her sick parents. After that, she never came back. They had had phone contact for the first time, which had then turned into postcards, SMS, emails and the occasional short paper letter. After a few months, the contact with Merja had thinned out and eventually stopped completely. It was as if the physical distance had had a negative impact on their communication.

William had never forgotten the time with his long-legged economist. Every woman he'd met since had been measured, consciously or not, against Merja. That brief time with her had become both a cherished memory and a lingering curse. As a result, he had no children, no house, no mortgage - just a rented apartment and a long shadow cast by the past. *I'm the very definition of free and independent,* he thought, giving a half-hearted kick to a low-hanging branch as he passed beneath it.

What about the job? reason insisted but without conviction. William knew this would come sooner or later. He was ready for it.

"I don't give a shit about work," William declared loudly and glared angrily at the squirrel sitting in a pine tree next to the footpath. The squirrel glared back at the moloch as he wondered what he had done wrong.

William thought about the job and the practicalities of just walking into the boss's office and leaving a freshly wrapped and well-seasoned farewell gift on the desk. He shook off his innermost thoughts and soon realized that there were actually no obstacles there either. None at all. Right now he was on a two-week vacation and after those two weeks everything would be very quiet at work; the company he worked for had missed four big orders in a row and he could probably request several more weeks of vacation without objections.

But why would he ask for vacation at all? He didn't even like the job. Maybe this was the big chance. The chance to get out of the swamp and start something new. The chance to do what he'd always dreamed of - to drop everything and just go. Anders' merciless lecture had put his fingers on the right points. Or what the hell, let's be honest, he had put his thumb and forefinger straight into his eyes and twisted around. The pain was strong but the message was clearer: stop floating around like driftwood on the sea and get a grip on your life!

For too long, he'd been drifting along a road he hadn't even realized he was on - a narrow, unchanging path that stretched back farther than he cared to admit. It had been many years since he'd traveled life's broader highway, the one with forks and off-ramps, risks and real choices.

The punishment for not actively choosing your path is harsh and merciless. Without warning, you are diverted onto a one-way road with no option to turn around. The further away from the highway you get, the fewer the choices and the fewer the turn-offs. In desperation and boredom, William had been pushing the gas pedal to the metal to get off the spiky forest road as quickly as possible, with the result that he missed the few turn-offs that were actually available. But now he saw the sign. It glowed with bright colors and pointed with his whole hand.

He stopped abruptly and looked down at the ground with a focused gaze. He remained like that for several minutes, during which he came up with the crazy idea that from now on he would follow his gut feeling - regardless of whether it led him straight into the abyss.

$$* * *$$

It was well into Sunday afternoon and nothing useful had emerged since yesterday's attempt to clarify the situation. Funnel wobbled around the deserted camping area, hoping to shake up the numb joints and sober up so that he could leave the site. They had agreed to make a new attempt to find the bag at the roadside tavern. After all, it was at that place the trail had ended.

On his way back to the caravan, Funnel noticed a car that hadn't been there in the parking lot half an hour earlier when he passed by. It wasn't really anything remarkable, although the parking lot was usually empty this early in the year. Suddenly he saw movement out of the corner of his eye and a person appeared from the dimly lit walkway. A man moving with determined steps towards the car. Out of pure instinct, he crouched behind a conveniently placed recycling station. He didn't want anyone to see that there were people at the campsite this time of year. He watched the man surreptitiously as he approached the car about ten meters away. As he opened the door and turned his face toward the campground to take in the last of the afternoon sun, Funnel saw that there was something familiar about the man. Was it someone he had met in prison? Curiosity made him sit quietly and still among the green and brown bins.

The man got into the car and started driving away from the campsite. Funnel caught a quick glimpse of him through the windshield as he passed close by and then the tired brain cells finally registered a hit in the search database. It was the man from the roadside diner - and a yellow car with a round shape. He memorized the registration number as the car slowly rolled past the low plank that hid the recycling station and onto the road leading to the mainland. Funnel could hardly believe his luck.

The sun was dipping behind the horizon and William started walking back to the car. He felt elated and pleased with himself. Pleased that he had dared to make such a drastic decision. The plan had already begun to form in his head and soon all that remained was to put it into action. He needed to get rid of the car. There was a chance that the two cartoon characters in the pub had noticed a yellow car parked next to their Volvo. That they would then have memorized the license plate number seemed too incredible. They had no reason to notice the anonymous car before the bag disappeared. When this happened, a completely different car had caught their attention - the dark SUV that left the gas pumps when William was in the bathroom. But despite this, it felt very uncomfortable to drive the vehicle away from the crime scene. It went against the normal procedure of every American movie William had seen. The car had to go.

William approached the yellow piece of evidence and opened the driver's door. He stood there for a few seconds looking at the ugly Asian creation, wondering how he could have bought something so insipid. He squinted his eyes across the campsite and on to the water's edge, where the sun was delivering its last light above the horizon.

He thought of Merja and fished the only photo he had of her out of his wallet. It was taken in the kitchen of her apartment. She was standing at the sink with her arms stretched against the door handles of two of the upper cabinets. Her face was looking into the cell phone camera with a surprised smile. As if she'd been caught red-handed. She was dressed in soft pants and a dark t-shirt. He guessed the photo was taken in the morning before breakfast on one of the memorable occasions when they had spent the night together. It was the first and only time he had taken a picture of her and in retrospect it seemed strange.

Emotions unexpectedly welled up in his chest like a bursted dam. He must find her! The conviction was rock solid and it suddenly felt inevitable, like it's always been there, lingering sound in the background. What was he waiting for, why so passive during all these years? To his own defence, he certainly had no idea where she was now. Come to think of it, she probably never told him where she came from. Or maybe he just forgot. It seemed just as strange as the fact that there were no more photos of her, as if it had all been an illusion.

At some point he had searched for her on the internet, but she seemed to have disappeared into thin air. He knew that the surname she gave him when they worked together was not the original one. She had used a more common "son" name when she started working in Stockholm, Merja explained. But if she ever moved back, she would probably take back her real surname again. Her home region was in northern Sweden, that's all he knew, and at some point after they parted he received postcards stamped in Gällivare, Jokkmokk and Porjus, among other places. William soaked up the last of the evening sun before he drove home.

Funnel hurried back to the caravan to announce the good news. His headache was gone and his muscles and joints revitalized. He found his friend leaning forward and sobbing behind the caravan. The thin layer of snow around his feet was stained with a disgusting mustard-yellow sludge that started at the trailer door and ended on the offender's boots at the rear end. This was a crime scene that didn't require much skill to analyze, thought Funnel as he tried to communicate with the perpetrator at a safe distance from the mustard trail. But all attempts to make contact with him were futile.

Funnel took matters into his own hands and ran over to the Volvo to give chase to the yellow car. The key was still in the immobilizer but nothing happened when he turned the key. The car was stone dead! The knob on the light switch showed that the light had been left on. Funnel out his frustration and tried to rip the steering wheel from its mount. He cursed his clumsiness as he thought of the man in the yellow car who had probably reached the bridge leading to the mainland by now. He opened the driver's door and saw Tube staring at him like a question mark. Instinctively he looked down at his companion's boots, which were still smudgy and had left a faintly yellowish trail between the caravan and the car.

"What is happening?" Tube's throat gurgled as he tried to speak. His eyes were dull and watery.

Funnel gathered strength in the fresh late winter air and explained what had happened. Tube's eyes quickly cleared.

"Did you take the registration number?"

"Yes, yes, yes," replied Funnel with confidence in his voice.

But when he searched his memory, the number was gone. Everything that had happened in the last few minutes made him completely forget the most important piece of the puzzle. The cache was not only emptied, but also formatted and overwritten with new information.

✳ ✳ ✳

Chief Inspector Edward Johnson spent the whole Saturday first visiting the scene of the accident and then trying to get to grips with the mysterious little mountain village and its newly rich inhabitants. The injured man had been kept under sedation since a minor operation on Friday evening and was therefore not very useful at the moment. Instead, he was able to focus on what could indirectly be helpful in moving forward.

Edward browsed through the old maps and learned about Sámi

history and culture. He skimmed through the technical details of the accident itself. There was not much to read. The information about the injured person was very scant and largely limited to what he could find in his wallet: a Swedish driver's license, a pair of keys, some cash and - surprisingly - a Norwegian pilot's license. The cell phone contained a few numbers and with some good luck they would lead the investigation further. He could understand why Kvarnbring hadn't sent it for analysis as they usually do, given the sensitive nature of the case. It was now up to him to do the research.

Information about the small mountain village was also scarce. There was no mention of it on the web or in public publications. On new mountain maps of the area, there was not a trace of any colony or village. In the thick file from the police archives, however, there were plenty of classified reports, the oldest of which were over a hundred years old. He decided that he had to sift through all the reports even if it took several days. He quickly skimmed through the top papers but apart from some detailed accounts of the geographical location and terrain of the site, there was nothing useful to progress the case. However, the reports did at least confirm that the place existed and in the old map given to him by Kvarnbring, the mountain village was marked as a Sámi settlement, exactly on the border between Sweden and Norway.

As Saturday night approached, he was not much wiser about the facts, but he knew more about the diverse history of the indigenous people. The history books revealed that the Sámi are not only Sweden's native people, but have inhabited large parts of the entire Northern Calotte, i.e. the northernmost part of Sweden, Finland and Norway, since the early Bronze Age. But it was not until over a thousand years later that any documentation was compiled on the culture and history of the Sámi. They were described as everything from itinerant traders dressed in blue furs and with a love of shiny silver jewelry, to savages and primitive reindeer herders. During the Middle Ages, Sámi culture began to be pushed aside by Norse culture, which meant that more and more areas were colonized. Problems arose particularly around the border areas between Sweden and Norway. The roaming Sámi considered the Lapland area to be their own, which angered both the Swedish and Norwegian crowns. The problem was solved for a time by the Lapland Codicil of 1751, which laid down rules preventing the use of reindeer grazing areas on both sides of the border while paying no taxes anywhere. The second paragraph of the codicil reads: "*No Sámi may henceforth possess tax or urban land in more than one kingdom*". The Sámi were thus forced to choose to be either Swedish or Norwegian.

In the following centuries, border issues spread to Finland and Russia through wars and other disturbances. A variety of treaties, decrees and other agreements forced the Sámi to move back and forth across borders throughout the Northern Calotte. The dissolution of the Union further tightened the rules and reduced opportunities to move across borders. In particular, the new treaties concerned northern Norrland and Troms County. To date, no common solution has been found that all parties have agreed to.

Edward thought of Sáhkár Kuoljok and Luoktajärvi. Nowhere could he find any official information about the small mountain village, even though it seemed to be in the epicenter of the problem area. It was as if it did not exist except in his imagination. He dropped the history book on the table and stared blankly out of the window. He'd become dizzy with all the facts lined up and pondered silently to himself if he ever would be able to use this knowledge again.

He made a cup of coffee and sank down at the kitchen table. The whole kitchen was a mess. The dishwasher was full of clean dishes and the sink was equally full of dirty dishes. There were bills, newspapers and unopened mail on the counter and table. The fridge was more or less empty. It took a lot of imagination to put together a dinner.

Since Beatrice passed away three years ago, the household had fallen into disrepair. He hadn't had the energy to deal with things that were not absolutely necessary for survival. Washing dishes and cleaning were definitely not among them. It was as if all the energy had slowly but surely drained out of him. Like a battery that was never recharged.

Beatrice's exit from the world had not been a quick process. Nor was it a dignified end to a life or a marriage. The cancer and all the drugs had destroyed organ after organ, taking over her body and finally her consciousness and dignity. On two occasions it had been forced to retreat by chemotherapy and other potions, but in the end she had been forced to surrender anyway. They had both surrendered.

He wished he could say that at least he still had a job but that would be lying to himself. They had both looked forward to enjoying their old age together as healthy, happy retirees, but that had not happened. It was never going to happen and in the absence of dreams for the future, the job could certainly be used as a filler, but it wasn't much more than that.

✳ ✳ ✳

On Sunday, he went to Uppsala University Hospital after Niilla Kuoljok was brought out of unconsciousness. At the hospital, he found out that the injuries were a wrist fracture and a severe concussion, as well as a deep cut on his forehead.

"This driver was lucky," proclaimed the doctor on call, cursing the unholy weather that had left hospitals filled with injured patients.

"Tell me, Inspector, who is this man?" The doctor stopped outside one of the doors and looked at Edward curiously.

"I do not know yet. We are still working on it."

"Surely the police must know something. Most of the patients we get here don't lack identity and normally they don't have two guards outside the door," said the doctor, pointing suspiciously at the two uniformed men stationed on either side of the door.

Edward did not recognize the men but assumed that Kvarnbring had a hand in it.

"As I said, we know nothing yet. That's why I want to see your patient."

The doctor glared suspiciously at his guest but finally let him through the door. The guards stared blankly straight ahead and made no attempt to stop him.

The dazed son of the Mountain King was in a pitiful state, with tubes running around his body. His head and left wrist were wrapped in bandages, making him look like a mummy. According to the doctor, he had passed the operation well and was currently contactable. Edward had to promise to proceed calmly and not stress the patient.

When he was left alone with the embalmed Sámi, it occurred to him that he might not be able to communicate in his native Swedish - if it was possible to communicate at all. After all, was he even a Sámi? According to his driver's license, he is fifty years old and has dark brown hair. With all the bandages around his face, it was impossible to tell if it was the same person lying here. As he pondered how to engage the patient in conversation, the patient solved the problem for him by gargling a phrase in a familiar language.

"I'm awake if that's what you're wondering." His voice was thick and strained but his eyes were surprisingly clear and firm. Edward's whole body twitched but he quickly recovered. Edward introduced himself and explained that he was here to ask some questions about the situation. He let the message sink in while he looked at the wrapped bundle.

"Ask away... you'll notice if I pass out."

Under the bandage, Edward could see that the patient was trying to smile. He asked if Niilla could tell him what had happened. The patient harrumphed several times before he slowly started to talk.

* * *

William was sitting behind the wheel of his chicken-yellow car eating a greasy breakfast menu from McDonald's. It consisted of an Egg McMuffin, coffee, orange juice, and some kind of shapeless fried lump in a little paper bag. It was nine o'clock and the trip went a few miles north to his uncle's farm, which was in a sparsely populated area in the northeastern part of the county. Here the snow still lay on the ground and the traces of the snowstorm were still visible in the form of fallen pine trees and the occasional abandoned car in the road ditch.

A few hours earlier, he had finished the conversation with his employer. It went surprisingly quick and painless. His fat and pig-eyed boss did not even try to persuade him. William assumed there were both work-related and personal reasons for this, but at the moment he didn't care which. He was just glad to be out of the misery. The accrued vacation would be replaced with money and the termination agreement would be sent by mail. All phone calls would be diverted through his office. To buy himself some time, he had said he was going abroad on a long vacation and didn't expect to sign any papers for several weeks. He felt both satisfied and relieved after the call. The biggest obstacle was removed.

When the meal was over, he called and deregistered the car. It was a safety precaution, but he knew all traces would not cease to exist even if he scrapped the car or drove it through the ice of a remote lake. The car would still have an ownership history and the digital traces would be easy to follow even if it changed hands several times. So he decided to simply deregister the car and hide it in his uncle's old machine shop up at the county border. If both car and owner went up in smoke, it would at least be difficult to find him physically.

His uncle didn't have any objections or questions and was currently *away on business* as he'd put it. That usually meant delivering a load of gravel around the area with the old truck. Like most other closed or liquidated farms in the northern part of the county, the landowners were multi-taskers and took the jobs that were offered. In most cases, the job usually involved moving a pile of gravel or soil from point a to point b, but it could also involve a broken piece of agricultural machinery that needed immediate attention.

For as long as William could remember, his uncle has had a strained relationship with bureaucrats and government officials. They were, in his view, paper pushers and quacks who were just a few rungs above ragpickers and telemarketers in the social hierarchy. Paperwork had never been his forte and the law could be interpreted differently depending on which side of the table you sat. "The law is guidelines and recommendations" his uncle used to say. Just like speed signs and red lights.

William had not only been offered a place to park the car, but also a replacement car in "mint condition" - an old Range Rover that had been in the machine shop since the mid-nineties. William remembered the car from previous visits. His eccentric relative had a dozen cars scattered around the farm, and most of them were in terrible condition. The Range Rover was different because it was accidentally built into the machine shop between the rear long side and a giant lathe almost twenty years ago. The installation of the lathe was a drunken job carried out by some local talent and took several days. No one noticed the car parked a few meters away. When the car was discovered - or rather, when the lack of an entrance in the wall was discovered - the piping was already laid and the machine foundation cemented to the floor. The car had thus remained in place for almost twenty years before the uncle, in sheer frustration, sawed a hole in the long side of the machine hall in order to free the prisoner. The long-term inmate was given new fresh fuel and some words of encouragement and then started on the first attempt. Despite the happy reunion, the car was never used much. Hence William was offered to buy the old Range Rover when he spoke to his uncle on the phone. If he wanted, he could even borrow the car for a while to see if he liked it. This suited William perfectly as the car was in excellent condition and, more important, registered in a different name.

He made a final phone call to Anders and told him that he had followed the advice and checked out indefinitely. In order not to reveal too much but still give a credible version, he gave the short story behind his and Merjas relationship. He told as little as possible, avoiding any juicy details. He said that he would try to find her and hopefully they would spend some time together, somewhere up in the northern countryside. Probably he would not be easy to reach by phone in the foreseeable future.

Anders avoided the obvious gaps in the story but asked what he would say to anyone wondering if William had gone up in smoke.

"Let's say I've taken a long vacation and I'm in a remote area."

"There's a lot you're not telling me, but sure, I'll pass on the story you just gave me," Anders replied, his voice tinged with irritation.

"I will send you a postcard."

They finished their conversation and shortly afterwards William rolled up to his uncle's farm. It was just before ten in the morning. The Range Rover was parked on the gravel outside the house and the key was in it. He test-started the car and made a brief visual inspection. The vehicle was dirty both inside and out, but the engine ran like clockwork. Satisfied with the inspection, he rolled his yellow Asian into the machine hall and emptied it of its contents. The packing was transferred to the new getaway vehicle. It consisted mainly of the essentials for the next few days: underwear, socks, sweaters, trousers, hygiene items, a laptop, a torch and a passport. Most of his hiking equipment was reluctantly, but deliberately, left behind because it was in such poor condition. He could always supplement along the way if needed.

The bag from the roadside restaurant was replaced by two ordinary sports bags and the money distributed among his other luggage. When he finished packing, he went to the front of the house and left a short handwritten letter. He read it to himself:

I will be traveling and need the car for a few months, maybe longer. I would be grateful if it could be registered in your name for the time being. The key in the envelope goes to the apartment. It would be great if you could pay the bills. The remaining money is for you. Burn the letter. /W

William skimmed the message a couple of times before putting it in an old glass freeze-dried coffee jar along with a wad of banknotes. He hid the jar in the lidded ashtray that stood next to the front door. It looked well used, so it shouldn't take long for the master of the house to discover it. He then got into the black Range Rover, started the engine and began to slowly roll away. As he drove across the gravel driveway, he thought about the letter and the money he had left behind - around two hundred thousand, or as much as could be squeezed into the glass jar. His uncle would understand that there was a smell of a rat but would never talk about it out of sheer principle. Besides, he was constantly in need of money.

William looked out over the sun-drenched snow-covered fields with a broad smile on his face and then headed north.

"Now the new life begins!" he exclaimed to himself.

✳ ✳ ✳

Due to the breakdown of negotiations with the Norwegian Parliament, the Police Bureau has been tasked with strengthening border control around the Luoktajärvi Sámi settlement. As you already know, the Chief of the General Staff has promised resources from your Jaeger unit to carry out the mission. It is of the utmost importance that the soldiers assigned to the task do not enter the Sámi settlement. The postings will be along the recognized land border north and south of Luoktajärvi. These resources shall report directly to the undersigned and no one else.

Detective Inspector Bergeus

✳ ✳ ✳

Edward Johnson sat in his office and recreated yesterday's conversation with Niilla. The conversation had lasted less than five minutes and then the patient had slipped into unconsciousness. The doctor had explained that he might as well go home as it could take hours or days before he woke up again.

Edward left the hospital with many unanswered questions. The story was incoherent and difficult to understand at times. Most of it had to do with the patient's poor condition, of course, but the many layers of facial bandages added to the confusion and Edward had to use a good deal of imagination to put it all together.

Niilla explained that he came from a village in the far north and had traveled to Stockholm by private plane. The reason was business related. On his way back to the landing site and the airplane, he had simply driven off the road in the snowstorm and ended up in a ditch. The story did not reveal any details and Edward did not want to interrupt the flow of words once it had started.

He was probably unconscious from the moment the car landed in the ditch and could only recount fragments of what happened next. When Niilla woke up in the crashed vehicle, he was covered in blood. Edward knew that the blood came from the jacket on his forehead, which in turn was caused by broken glass. Soon after, two people had appeared outside the car - two young men who were shabbily dressed and spoke Swedish. They initially tried to talk to Niilla through the smashed side window but he could not remember what had been said. One of the men had climbed into the back seat because the driver's door would not open and had then found *the bag*. After that, both men had completely lost interest in him and left the scene.

Edward had tried to get more information about *the bag* mentioned in passing, but the patient had begun to disappear into the world of dreams and soon found himself in a deep sleep or unconsciousness.

He scratched his gray hair as he gazed out the third-floor office window, trying to reconcile himself to the idea that this case was much more complicated than he'd first realized. There were many questions but no answers. Edward thought that, after all, he should have gotten much further in this case than Jörgen Metzner, who had not set foot in the office over the weekend.

The phone rang and he picked it up.

"Johnson." Kvarnbring's raspy voice echoed at the other end even before Edward could say a word.

"Yes, of course. Or did you try to call someone else?"

"Come by my office now." The line was cut immediately after.

"You dry old bastard," Edward replied into the emptiness and hung up the phone.

He got up and walked at a leisurely pace towards Kvarnbring's office. He was sitting with his hands clasped behind his head, staring up at the ceiling. He looked crushed and lost in thought. Edward pushed the door shut with one foot and sat down in front of his colleague, who now looked far more worried than a few days ago. Kvarnbring put his hands down, leaned forward over the table and looked at his colleague.

"Have you had a chance to talk to Niilla yet?"

"Yes, in a hurry, before he passed out again. Did not get anything of value really. Thought I'd follow up the conversation as soon as he's awake again."

"Right." Kvarnbring rocked thoughtfully on his chair. 'I've got a bunch of Sámi on my hands myself. Old man Sáhkár sent a whole delegation to meet the boy and to demonstrate his dissatisfaction with the situation in general and the Security Service in particular."

He buried his face in his hands and looked tired.

"To avoid a lot of unwanted attention, I have now been personally appointed to take care of the delegation and sort out this mess."

Edward tried to collect his thoughts.

"They can't have talked to Niilla yet, given his condition, right?"

"No, they have been to the hospital where they were told that the guy will make a full recovery, even though he is currently both unconscious and a little bruised. Instead, they have shifted their focus to the investigation. I have, of course, tried to keep them as far away as possible from both the investigation and the hospital. They are housed in a five-star hotel and I have tried to arrange all sorts of *amenities* - amenities that I will find very difficult to explain later."

Kvarnbring heaved a deep sigh as if to emphasize that this very fact will not make things much easier in the future.

"What have they told you about the reason he is here? What is the man doing down here in Stockholm?"

"Well, they just said it was a normal business visit. I couldn't get any more information out of them. For the moment, let's just say that this is all a bloody mess. I just wanted you to understand the seriousness."

"Do you have any idea where he was going when he skidded into the ditch?"

"No... I just assumed that he was on his way to Arlanda to fly back home." Kvarnbring looked at Edward with a searching gaze.

"I did too at first. But I checked with Arlanda yesterday and they had no guest with his name."

"Maybe he took a private flight?"

"Well, that's about what I managed to pick up from the conversation with Niilla - that he'd arrived by private plane. But there is still no possibility that he and any goods could have passed unannounced. The security service at Arland was very sure about this."

"He must have landed somewhere else. Or perhaps he was not on his way home."

"Niilla claimed he was on his way to the *landing site* or something similar. It was a strange way to refer to an airport but I never got a chance to ask what he meant."

"I will try to get more information from our guests. It should be in their interest that we move forward. Now, if you'll excuse me, I have some work to do."

Edward realized that the conversation had ended. They were already in deep trouble just from all the internal secrecy and politics. What actually caused all of this was now of secondary importance. They sat in silence for a few minutes, contemplating the situation. Outside the window the sun was shining.

❋ ❋ ❋

Funnel and Tube were faced with a fait accompli. The money had slipped through their fingers for the second time in a few days and they had no idea how to tackle the problem. The situation was desperate to say the least. Funnel had tried to soften the blow by suggesting that the money didn't belong to them anyway, but Tube wouldn't listen to that. It was honestly stolen money, he said. For want of anything else, they had searched the internet in the hope of at least identifying the car model. They both agreed that the car was yellow or yellowish and that it had an Asian appearance. That is, round shapes. Funnel got stuck on a picture that showed an emblem of a rounded and slightly slanted "H".

"This is the same emblem I saw yesterday," said Funnel.

"A Hyundai," Tube confirmed. "He drives around in a yellow Hyundai. An ugly one."

After a few minutes, they narrowed down the model by searching car ads. After that, they couldn't get much further without the license plate number.

They left the caravan in the morning to get some fresh air and were drenched by the early spring sun. Tube was too infuriated to notice the spring weather. His gaze was fixed on the ground as he navigated through slush, ice cakes and bare tree roots. The memories of Friday morning came back and he shivered as he thought about it. They had gotten their hands on wealth in a hurry and just as quickly the same wealth was snatched from their hands. As if someone wanted to mess with them, thought Tube. But now the bag was gone and the tracks were covered. As if it never existed.

As far back as he could remember, he had always been short of money. Occasionally he came across some money, but it always slipped out of his hands faster than he could feel rich. Being without money, however, was a normal situation. In fact, when he thought about it, he was a master at getting by without money. Living on what was available was a challenge, and if it got too hard, you could always live on what wasn't available. It worked just as well.

Funnel and Tube slithered across the parking lot towards the eastern end of the island. When they got to the middle, they spotted a dark object that stood out clearly against the light gray gravel parking lot. Tube walked over and examined the object. It was a wallet. His heart skipped a beat as he picked it up and began searching the small pockets. Out of pure instinct, he first examined the large longitudinal compartment in the hope of finding cash. He found a five hundred note and an old receipt from a shop. Nothing exciting. Tube turned and unfolded the wallet and saw the photo of a man on a driver's license. He took a quick glance at it and then passed it onto Funnel.

"It's him!" shouted Funnel almost immediately. "The man in the roadside tavern."

"Are you sure?" asked Tube with doubt in his voice and without recognizing the object.

"Absolutely sure. I remember the face and the round glasses. That's the man at the roadside diner and the man from yesterday."

"William Sleipner is his name according to his driver's license."

Tube bent over and examined the photo carefully.

"Sleipner? Like the pig?"

"As in the horse Sleipner," replied Tube. The pig is called Särimner."

"Horse or pig, it doesn't matter. If this is his driver's license, we have his name and social security number and we should be able to find him easily."

The two companions hurried back towards the caravan. They were suddenly very excited and hopeful and couldn't believe their luck. Once inside the warmth, Tube took out the laptop he had stolen a few weeks earlier from the closed beach-café. They typed in the name from the driver's licence and got a hit almost immediately. The address appeared on the screen and with a little detective work it was possible to find the cellphone number.

"Now we have him!" shouted Funnel with renewed energy.

CHAPTER 4

Papusa the Hitchhiker

William's newly acquired getaway vehicle moved smoothly and steadily like a cruise ship over the bumpy highway. Soon he turned onto highway 70 and continued north towards Avesta. The sun was shining and the spruces along the roadside sparkled with the morning frost. The powerful engine purred like a cat and he was in a great mood.

He looked back on everything he'd accomplished in the past twelve hours and felt a rare surge of pride. He had packed for the journey, quit his job, gotten rid of his old car, and managed to find a new one - all in a single day. But it was the small details that he felt most satisfied with. The bills were pre-paid as far as possible, the rest he could handle via the internet and what fell through the cracks could hopefully be taken care of by his uncle. On Sunday evening, he bought a prepaid sim card for his old cell phone. Not that it would make him invisible if someone really wanted to reach him - his regular phone was in the glove compartment - but it would make him less conspicuous and leave fewer traces.

He also left a red herring by saying he was going on a long vacation. No one would suspect anything for several weeks and during that period he would have time to collect his thoughts and decide on the next step. He was now a professional thief on the run from the law. The thought tickled him and he felt more alive than ever.

But what thrilled him most wasn't the money, nor the fact that he was on the run - it was the sense of direction, the feeling that he finally had a purpose. He had decided to find Merja. And if - when - he found her, maybe they could recapture even a fragment of what they'd shared five years ago.

This time, there was no obstacle in their way. They wouldn't have to sneak away anymore. But finding her after so long and hoping he was still there somewhere in the back of her mind was a long shot. She had probably started a family a long time ago. It was a big gamble and he knew it. The disappointment could be great but it was a risk he was willing to take.

Soon he crossed the border into Dalarna, a roadside sign quietly announcing the new county - as if someone wanted to mark this as the point of no return. Now he had both feet - or at least four tires - planted in the very region where Gustav Vasa once journeyed to lay the foundations of a free Sweden. This, it seemed, was where everything began. By lunchtime, he had already passed Leksand, the road winding gently as Lake Siljan emerged through the car window, calm and glinting in the midday light.

The lake was still covered by a thin ice crust and on the other side was the characteristic Gesunda mountain. It appeared as a majestic mountain range across the crystal lake but William knew that it was only a few hundred meters high.

In Rättvik he stopped at a large gas station to fill up and satisfy his hunger. He selected two fifteen-liter spare cans from the well-stocked shelves and filled them with gasoline, taking the opportunity to fill up the car at the same time. The big beast swallowed almost a hundred litres. In total, the digital numbers on the display went up to two thousand before they stopped spinning. Normally, a four-digit amount would have upset him, but this time he was swimming in money. He paid with his credit card.

He ate a prefabricated salad to compensate for the morning's greasy breakfast. The salad was tasteless and the Rhode Island dressing that came with it didn't improve the overall impression. He washed down the meal with a can of mineral water and finished with a cup of coffee. There was a certain tension in the air when he was about to pay. It was the first time he was about to use the money from his bag and there was, of course, a small risk that they were counterfeit.

This was a situation that he had considered over the past day, the unlikely situation that the money would be fake. The notes certainly looked and felt genuine and they had definitely been in circulation. But he couldn't know for sure until he used them. As a backup story he would claim to have sold an outboard engine to an unknown person who paid in cash. This was essentially a true story but it happened a month earlier, when he sold his four-stroke gasoline engine and replaced it with an electric engine to be used on his old motorboat. A boat that by the way was stored over the winter seasons at his uncle's place. But the fictional buyer would never be possible to trace down and William had no past criminal record. He would probably not even get a penalty even if the money would turn out to be fake. It was anyway a risk that he would be willing to take and the money was not the reason for this trip anyway, it was merely a triggering factor.

But the young woman behind the counter showed no reaction when William, with a stiff smile on his face, fished out three notes from his back pocket, and there was no beep from the compulsory note scan in the cash register.

With a sense of relief he went on to a small grocery store next to the gas station. Outside the glass doors sat a beggar with tattered clothes, holding out a wooden bowl. At the bottom were a few coins. It was a woman of indeterminate age with a shawl wrapped several times around her head. It covered almost everything except her eyes.

Her clothes were baggy and fluttered in the wind. The woman held out the wooden bowl and William stopped in front of her, not knowing what to do. The sensor on the glass wall sensed his presence and opened the door, allowing warm air to seep out of the store entrance. He reached into his back pocket and dug out the bills. He gave her three five-hundreds and put the rest back in his back pocket, then slipped through the door just before it closed and before the woman could say anything.

As he walked among the shelves, he thought about what he needed for the next few days. He had already decided yesterday that the first stop on his trip would be a small log cabin near Fulufjället National Park, not far from Särna and Idre. The cabin was built over fifty years ago by his grandfather, a loner like himself who used to spend much of his free time fishing and hiking in the mountains. Since his grandfather died many years ago, the cabin had remained more or less untouched. As far as William knew, no one but himself has set foot there for years. The cabin has no electricity or running water, so he would have to rely on the gas kitchen, an outhouse and a nearby stream with clean meltwater.

He filled the cart with canned food, powdered soups, bread, sandwich spreads, a few bottles of mineral water, a couple of lighters, a bag of tea lights, some newspapers, and a few other odds and ends that went along on the fly and without thought. As he approached the checkout, he instinctively reached for his wallet in the inside pocket. But there was nothing there. He searched all the pockets but without success. An ominous feeling crept up on him. It was always in his jacket for the simple reason that he often forgets things everywhere. Could he have left it in the car? He paid with the remaining five hundred notes from his back pocket and hurried out to the car. The beggar woman at the entrance had disappeared. No wonder, he thought to himself, she received a decent amount of money and didn't have to sit there in the cold anymore.

He methodically searched the whole car - under the seats, between the seats, in the glove compartment and door pockets, under the folded down back seat, in the clothes and bags. After half an hour, he gave up. He assumed that the wallet had been left in the apartment or in the other car. As long as he didn't drop it somewhere and as long as he wasn't stopped by a police officer for speeding, no major damage was done. He still had his passport, a credit card, a lot of cash and didn't really need the driver's license. The wallet didn't contain anything more than the licence and possibly some cash. He decided to continue without the wallet, but the morning's good mood was gone. The first big mistake had been made. What other details had he missed?

William got behind the wheel and started the engine. He wanted to get away as soon as possible. Then she was suddenly there. The beggar woman who had been sitting outside the grocery store. She stood perfectly still a couple of meters from the car and looked at him through the windshield.

He was so surprised that he completely forgot to be angry by the wallet. He took a closer look at her for the first time and saw that she was small and petite, barely reaching over the large bonnet. William didn't know what to do. Why was she here? Should he roll down the window and say something or should he just honk at her to get her out of the way? He decided that the second method was too uncivilized and started looking for the button for the side window.

When he looked ahead again, she was gone. Disappeared. William sat for half a minute waiting for her to reappear in front of the grill, but when nothing happened, he started the engine. The V8 rumbled to life and he turned left to grab his seatbelt. Then she was standing there outside the driver's door. Her face was only a few inches from the side mirror. He jumped and instinctively leaned away from the window. Now he could see her face a little more clearly, although most of it was still hidden under the shell. There was nothing hostile in her expression; on the contrary, it was disarming. William lowered the window and tried to think of something to say.

"Can I help you?"

She did not answer immediately but looked at him as if considering what to say.

"Are you heading north?" she asked in flawless Swedish.

"Yes... I'm heading north."

"Can I hitchhike a bit?"

He noticed a slight accent this time but could not place it. It was somehow in sharp contrast to her face. Or what could be seen of her face.

"Where are you from?" he asked, regretting the question the second he uttered the words.

"What does it matter? I was wondering if I could hitch a ride with you."

William instinctively glanced at the passenger seat. It was cluttered with clothes, maps, bags and much more. He thought about all the money in the car and the situation he was in. A passenger was the last thing he needed.

"There are buses..." he managed to blurt out.

"There are no more buses running today."

"I am not a bus."

"You have a big car."

"It's full of stuff and I might not be going to the same place as you."

"I can ride along as far as possible. Then I'll find someone else to hitch a ride with."

William was frantically thinking about how to get out of this situation. He had never met a more stubborn person. What was she doing here? A moment ago she was begging outside a shop and now she wants a ride in his car. Where is she going? Is she looking for a new place to beg or is she part of some criminal gang that robs people of money? Does she want to go with him because of the money he gave her?

"So, where are you going?"

"North, just like you."

"To the north?"

"Östersund. I beg you, let me come with you on the road. I've been riding the bus and hitchhiking for days now." Her eyes were pleading, and when the wind momentarily lifted the shell from her face, she looked very young.

"Is it just you?"

"It's just me."

William swore silently to himself. He knew nothing about this woman and what she had told him sounded so strange that it could not be true. Was she a beggar or a hitchhiker or a scammer? Or a begging hitchhiker? Either way, he couldn't let her stand there and pray on her knees.

"Just a moment."

He turned to the passenger side and moved the grocery bag and a jacket to the trunk. She wouldn't discover the money as long as she didn't start digging through the bags.

"I will drive you to Mora. It takes an hour. From there you can hitchhike or hop on a bus that goes straight north."

He reached over to the passenger side and opened the door to show her how to climb in. The beggar woman bent down and picked up a cloth bag, then walked around the car and jumped into the passenger seat. She put the bag on the floor in front of the seat. William released the handbrake and rolled out of the parking lot.

✱ ✱ ✱

Edward had just finished his lunch in the office when Jörgen Metzner appeared in the doorway with a happy smile.

"Hello Edward."

"Hello," Edward replied, caught off guard.

Until now, he had not even thought about how to deal with Metzner given the slightly comical situation his boss had put them in.

"Kvarnbring wanted me to keep you informed about the traffic accident outside Arlandastad."

"So, have you made any progress?"

"Not much to report unfortunately. According to the hospital, the driver is unconscious. All the indications are that it was an ordinary single vehicle accident. The weather was not exactly favorable."

Metzner stood for a moment with his eyes fixed, as if waiting for his colleague to take the next step.

"Ok, then I know. Please come back when you have something new to report."

Edward took a deep breath of relief when his colleague's face had disappeared from the doorway. Metzner was one of those people who was hard *not* to like. An incompetent police officer but a very pleasant person to be around. A person you'd like to go and have a beer with at the pub but who you wouldn't want as a partner when the going gets tough. Not because he would abandon you, but because he would shoot himself in the foot - or his partner.

Edward walked over and closed the door, then pulled out a cigarette and a lighter from his inside pocket. He needed one to relax and collect his thoughts. Smoking was a habit he had learned from Kvarnbring in recent times. The big difference was that his boss smoked two packs a day and had done so for almost thirty years.

Edward usually smoked no more than one cigarette a day. He had calculated that if he were to get cancer from smoking, it would not have time to take hold in his body before he was forced to throw in the towel for completely different reasons. If the old goat, with his systematic mistreatment of his lungs, had survived for thirty years, surely his own lungs would survive for at least another twenty? He knew there was No Smoking in the whole building these days, but as long as the door was closed and the window open, no one would complain. Not as long as Kvarnbring did the same thing and on a much larger scale.

Edward tried to recreate Niilla's disjointed story in his memory. There were clearly gaps in the story that could contain valuable information. He didn't know where Niilla had been going or what the bag contained. What did he really mean by the landing site? Who did he meet in Stockholm and what was his business? Did he get unconscious directly after the crash in the ditch? When woke up, he had blood on his face and heard voices outside. If he had passed out, it could just as easily have been minutes as hours, Edward mused to himself. The car was barely visible from the road. When the police received an anonymous call from a prepaid phone saying that a car was in the ditch just before the Arlanda exit, it was already three o'clock on Friday morning. The roadside traffic camera did not capture the incident because it was mounted too far away and the weather was too bad. He wondered if there could be other cameras that had recorded the incident.

The only way to find out was to go back to the place of the accident again. Edward stubbed out his cigarette, put on his coat and slipped out of the office as quickly and discreetly as he could, hoping that no one would see him. He wasn't in the mood to see anyone right now. As he passed Kvarnbring's room, he peeked through the doorway and saw that the office was empty. He walked the rest of the long corridor and took the elevator down to the basement floor where the car was parked. In the silent underground parking garage, everything was as quiet and peaceful as in a grave. Edward wondered if it wouldn't be better to sit down here rather than up there in the atmospheric corridors. Then the percentage of solved cases would surely rise. A few minutes later he was up in the daylight and reality again.

"What is your name?" he asked.

"Papusa."

She removed the scarf from her head and let her hair down. He saw that she was even younger than he had thought when she stood outside the car. Maybe as young as sixteen or seventeen. Her hair was streaked and dark, reaching well down to her shoulders. The face would have been very pretty if it wasn't so dirty and unkempt. Wisps of hair hung over her forehead and her eyes were bloodshot and ravaged. She looked very tired. Her clothes were baggy and torn.

"Thank you," she said.

"There's nothing to thank me for. I'm going this way anyway."

"I meant the money."

He saw out of the corner of his eye that she was looking his way, as if she were scrutinizing and assessing him.

"You looked like you needed them…"

"It's the first time someone has been so generous."

"It's just money."

"A lot of money. That's very kind of you."

No, that wasn't very nice of me. And not very generous. I just wanted to ease my conscience, he thought.

"You could have walked past without stopping. That's what most people do. And you could have given me a fiver. But you didn't."

William was silent. He did not know why he had given her money. It wasn't something he usually did, although of course he could afford it - it didn't take stolen millions to give a few tens or fifties. Now, for some reason, he'd stopped - just for ten seconds. Ten seconds he had somehow never found in all the years before. The irony of it struck him only now.

"Where do you come from?"

"From no place in particular."

"What do you mean?"

"From nowhere and everywhere. I am a gypsy. My family are gypsies...or Roma."

William couldn't make sense of her story so far. She certainly looked like she just arrived from southeastern Europe somewhere but she spoke flawless Swedish.

"Where is your family then?"

She seemed to ponder the question for a while before answering.

"They are scattered all over the place."

"But where are you from? Where do you live now? Where are you going?"

She looked pained by all the questions and William regretted being so forward.

"It's a long story," she said, yawning longingly.

He left the questions for now. Perhaps she would tell him more if he gave her some time. They passed Vikarbyn and Siljan shone clear and fresh through the car window. Soon they would be in Mora. Where would he drop her off then? Was there a bus stop or train station? He didn't even know where she was going. She had said Östersund, but had she really meant it, or was she just throwing out the only name she could think of to avoid answering questions? He suddenly laughed when he realized that he himself did not know where he was going. The day's route was set, but he hadn't planned much else. They were both gypsies. Tramps.

He looked in the hitchhiker's direction and saw that she'd fallen asleep. Judging by her breathing, she was fast asleep. He swore quietly to himself again and slammed his palm hard against the steering wheel. What the hell was he going to do now? They would be there in less than half an hour. He'd have to wake her when they got to Mora, it couldn't be helped.

❋ ❋ ❋

The Range Rover rolled into the bus station in central Mora just after 2 p.m. Papusa was still fast asleep. William drove up to a large information board and got out of the car. The board was filled to the brim with timetables, information about the city, the bus station and nearby hotels and a lot of flyers for Vasaloppet - the world's biggest ski race - that had already been, but also private ads that seemed to have hung there forever.

A recent timetable showed that there were buses between Mora and Östersund a couple of times a day. The next bus will leave tomorrow morning. If Östersund really was her final destination, she has every chance of getting there from Mora bus station.

He let her sleep in the car for another hour or so before waking her up with a firm hand on her shoulder.

"We are in Mora now. At the bus station. You've been asleep for a couple of hours."

She looked disoriented, like she was trying to find some kind of reference point she knew.

"Here, drink this."

He held out a mug of steaming coffee and then pointed to a sandwich and a bottle of water he had placed on the dashboard in front of her. She ignored the coffee but went for the sandwich and water. She gulped it down in silence.

"I have to continue along road 70 towards the Norwegian border. But from Mora you can go straight north to Östersund by bus. That's where you're going, right?"

She nodded without replying and continued with the sandwich.

"There's a bus leaving tomorrow at eight o'clock. It will leave from this stop where we are standing now. You can buy a ticket on the bus. Is that ok with you?"

She nodded again and took a sip of water.

"I have a suggestion," said William, wondering how to phrase it.

Papusa looked at him as if he was about to come up with a really indecent proposal.

"You look like you've had a rough few days, to say the least. You ate that sandwich like you hadn't seen food in a week, you slept so soundly I didn't know how to wake you up, and your clothes have seen better days…"

"Are you done with the insults soon?"

Papusa glared at him with her big dark eyes and crossed her arms.

"If I give you money, will you try to get something to eat tonight and go to a hotel and get some sleep? You have to wait for the bus tomorrow anyway. There are a couple hotels across the street. Buy some new clothes too. It's still winter in Östersund."

She thought about this for a while before answering:

"And what do you want in return?"

"What do you mean?"

"I mean, what favour do you expect in return? Do you think this is the first time I've been asked if I want money?"

William looked at her and it took a few uncomfortable moments before the token fell.

"Nothing…" William tried to meet her gaze but ended up looking out his side window instead.

"Papusa, you're the one who asked for a ride with a strange man. As far as I'm concerned, you might as well be a mugger or a member of some gang. These are troubled times and no one can be trusted."

"I am not a mugger. I don't even know what it means"

"I didn't think so either, but can you tell me why you are sitting outside a grocery store in Rättvik begging for money? I can't make sense of your story."

"I ran out of money. What could I do? I was hungry."

"Yes, I saw that. But... but what will you do in Östersund?"

"It is my business. I'm looking for someone to come back home with me. Mother sent me. But she didn't have much money to give me."

"And this person is in Östersund?"

"I hope so."

She fell silent and looked away towards the terminal building. William wanted to ask many more questions but he let it go and just nodded. Then he picked up an old, worn glasses case out of the door compartment. It was made of soft black leather and had already been in the glove compartment when he picked it up from his uncle. While Papusa was asleep, he'd put money in it and tied the opening with the loop inside. He handed the case to her and she accepted it with some skepticism in her eyes.

"That's enough money for you to get by for a while."

She felt the glasses case with her fingers, raised her eyebrows slightly, weighed it in her hand and then put it in the cloth bag without saying anything.

"Good. Do what you want with the money but I would be happy if you followed my advice. It's enough money to keep you from begging for a long time to come, but also enough money to get you into trouble if you don't handle it properly. Buy new warm clothes, check into a hotel and try to forget you ever met me."

Papusa sat silently for a minute before wrapping the scarf around her face and picking up the bag from the floor. She then turned to William and said briefly:

"Thank you."

Then she opened the passenger door and got out of the car. She looked at him briefly with an inscrutable look, nodded with a small smile on her lips, and then hurried away along the platform towards the terminal. She did not look back.

William waited until she reached the terminal building before starting the car and drove away from the center.

✳ ✳ ✳

After searching through four caravans, they got lucky. In a storage box under a seating area, they found jumper cables. They didn't even have to break open the doors of the caravans. Tube had already taken care of that several months earlier. It struck him that it was strange that he hadn't found any jumper cables already during the late-autumn inventory round, given all the other finds that had been made.

They went back to their own caravan and connected the dead car battery to the fully charged caravan battery. After a few spasmodic attempts, the engine finally started. Tube and Funnel threw themselves impatiently into the car and slithered out of the campsite. The starter cables were still hanging in the caravan battery and the entrance door was ajar.

They drove across the bridge to the mainland and continued north towards the city center at far too high a speed. It took no more than fifteen minutes to find the address they were looking for. An anonymous brick-red apartment building surrounded by similar unimaginative creations. The facades and architecture suggested that the buildings were erected in the fifties or sixties and then abandoned. They parked a little further down the street to contemplate their next move.

"I think we should just go in and ring the doorbell," said Funnel.

"What do you suggest we do next?"

"Well, we'll just have to talk some sense into him. Like claim our money back."

"What if he is armed?"

"Well, we'll just have to…" Funnel was thinking intensively.

"Here's what we'll do," said Tube to speed up the process. "We have a cell phone number. It's most likely his. We call him and see if he answers. If he doesn't answer, we go inside."

They called the cell phone number but it was seemingly turned off.

"Let's go in," said Tube.

They got out of the car and went to the main entrance. A sign revealed that William Sleipner lived on the first floor. They went through the door and up half a flight of stairs before finding what they were looking for on the right. To the delight of the two companions, the door had a classic letterbox which could be slightly opened.

Across the stairwell was a similar door, and there Funnel put a small piece of tape over the peephole so that they could work undisturbed.

Tube rang the doorbell and Funnel hid behind his back. No one answered, just as they had expected. Tube then fished out a homemade gadget, which he coaxed through the wide gap in the letterbox. It looked like a long fishing hook with a handle at one end and a loop at the other. It took less than a minute for the lock to open. The door was gently pushed open and they entered a quietly darkened apartment.

Right next to the entrance was a long hallway that led to a closed toilet door. On the left, just before the front door, there was a big wardrobe, and on the opposite side a kitchen. At the end of the corridor, on the left, was a bedroom, and on the right, a portal led into a living room. Next to the living room was another room that connected it to the kitchen and a small balcony.

Funnel and Tube searched the whole apartment and it didn't take many minutes to realize that it was empty.

"Should we wait in the apartment until he comes back?" asked Funnel.

His brother-in-arms stood for a while with both hands in his trouser pockets and his forehead in a deep crease.

"Something is not right. The apartment feels somehow... abandoned."

"What do you mean?"

"Well... I don't know," said Tube, throwing his hands out in a frustrated gesture. "I think it looks abandoned. As if the person who lives here left in a hurry. Many drawers and closet doors are open or half closed. There are clothes on the bed. The water to the dishwasher is turned off. The toothbrush and toothpaste are gone from the bathroom cabinet."

"Perhaps he has a very big mouth and uses the toilet brush," suggested Funnel with a grin.

"Or maybe he's at work," Tube added. "There are all possibilities. I suggest we wait a few hours until evening."

He plopped down in the big living room chair while Funnel checked out the huge collection of American corn whiskey that was set out in one of the lower cabinets of the bookshelf. Funnel poured them both a large glass and sat down next to his companion and only friend.

In the years since their school days, they had developed a very strong brotherly bond. It was now not only friendship that bound them together but also a solid criminal record. The results of their exploits were recorded not only in police records but also, and perhaps primarily, in their memories. Like branded cattle, their pasts were linked together for all time. If one falls, both fall. They both knew it.

Tube was the unspoken leader of their little gang. It hadn't been obvious from the start, but as their criminal careers took more advanced turns, Funnel reconciled himself to the idea that his friend actually provided most of the initiative and planning. He was always the one to hatch the best ideas and set the direction. Many times they had stayed out of trouble only because of Tube's quick thinking.

They sat in the living room armchair for a couple of hours before they discovered the map book. An old atlas of Sweden was lying on a black floor speaker next to the coffee table. What first caught Tube's attention was an envelope stuck in the middle of the map book. The envelope was from a telephone operator and contained a PIN and a PIN for a SIM card. On the back of the envelope was a number written in ink. It looked like the sequence of digits in a mobile phone number. Tube put the envelope in his pocket and opened the map book where the envelope had been tucked in. The right side showed the county of Dalarna with Lake Siljan forming a natural center. The finger found its way to a large green spot in the upper left-hand corner of the page. In the northwest, on the border with Norway, was Fulufjället National Park. Tube recognized the name, but he didn't know much else about the area.

In the upper part of the green field, which constituted the national park itself, there was a small mark, a carelessly drawn circle that must have been made with an ink pen. It took a few seconds for Tube to fully realize the significance of the little squiggle. When he did, his heart skipped a beat and he jerked where he sat on the couch. Funnel looked up from his whiskey glass and tried to read his friend's face.

"He's not coming back," said Tube with an inscrutable look.

"What do you mean? What have you found?"

"It is obvious. Everything is so obvious. He left with the money!"

Funnel put down the half-empty whiskey glass on the coffee table, he looked confused.

"He has probably fled here," said Tube and threw the map book on the table. The index finger hammered on the ink circle while Funnel leaned over the table.

"Fulufjällets National Park?"

"I think so."

Tube hastily got up from the sofa and disappeared into the hall. After a minute he came back and continued:

"As soon as we arrived, I noticed that the hall closet was a mess. I then saw that there was a lot of hiking equipment scattered all over the closet floor. An old Fjällräven backpack, a pair of boots, a sleeping mat and some mixed equipment."

"Shouldn't he have taken all that with him if he was going to the mountains?" Funnel looked suspicious.

"We have no idea what he took with him and what he left behind. Perhaps he decided he could afford to buy something new. The equipment in the wardrobe looked to have seen its best days and the guy is a new multi-millionaire. Besides, I think everything in the apartment indicates that he's not coming back anytime soon. I mean, who turns off the water to the dishwasher in an apartment?"

"I guess you're right as usual," muttered Funnel without enthusiasm. "But what do we do now?"

"The ink circle marks an area in the northern part of the national park. It appears to be drawn around one of the lakes but it is difficult to tell with this rough scale."

"I don't understand why he's leaving the map book if he's planning to go to this place."

"No, it's weird. I have to admit that. Maybe he left the map book for the same reason he left the equipment. Look at the pages." Tube held up the worn old map book.

"The map book was printed in 1964. It is fifty years old. Perhaps he didn't make this marking himself at all, just used it to transfer it to a newer map. One that is not sun-bleached, wrinkled and shows something more than fifty-year-old roads."

Funnel admitted that this was a reasonable explanation.

"I don't think he'll be back any time soon," Tube repeated. I think we have to realize that our only clue points 400 km north. I suggest we go there tomorrow."

"Agreed. Let's meet at the caravan tomorrow."

The two young men got up from the sofa to go home and pack. On the way out they took the old map book with them and at the same time stocked up on a couple of bottles of whiskey.

CHAPTER 5

The Refuge

Just after Särna, he turned off onto the long and small road leading up to Fulufjället National Park. Even at this distance, he could see the mountain rising like a great plateau in the landscape, with its characteristic steep sides and flat top. During winter it looked like a big cream cake. The snow was thick until it melted in May, when the temperature hovered around zero. The first fifteen kilometers would be on plowed and relatively well-traveled roads, but after that he didn't know what the local service was like. He had only been up here during summer and even then it wasn't easy to get all the way to the cabin. The four-wheel drive and high ground clearance would hopefully help.

After twenty minutes he reached the turn-off leading up to the cabin. The first part was at least plowed, but after a couple of kilometers the last cabins disappeared and with them any interest in keeping the road clear of snow. He stopped the car where the small road turned into unplowed wilderness. He got out and walked to the sharp snow bank that separated him from the final kilometer that went in a big arc up to the lonely log cabin. Behind the snow bank, which was loose and about half a meter high, the road continued steeply uphill. It was covered with a few inches of fresh snow, but under the powdery white layer the ground was firm and packed. He decided to give it a try.

He walked back to the idling black Range Rover and then reversed a good distance to get going. The heavy car gained speed slowly on the slippery surface but managed to force the snowbank, and a white cloud swirled up over the hood and windshield. Thanks to the four-wheel drive, he managed to maintain the speed on the bumpy road all the way up to the cabin, which was just where the plateau began. He stopped about twenty meters in front of the small red-painted toilet outhouse. Everything looked as he remembered it. Only a little whiter.

He began the arduous task of shoveling his way to the log cabin, which was about fifty meters up on the crest of the plateau. The snow shovel was a surprisingly sturdy old digging tool that he found behind the outhouse. If he'd arrived here just a few weeks earlier, the snow removal would probably have taken several hours, but now it was the end of March and he reached the cabin stairs in half an hour. Under a round stone on the porch, next to the front door was the key - in the same place he'd left it the last time he was here. He tried to remember when it was, and the best guess was summer or fall, two or three years ago.

Inside the log cabin the temperature was the same as outside, but the air was raw and damp and it felt colder inside the walls than outside. The cabin was built of rough-hewn timber with turned joints and the inside consisted mainly of two rooms - the main cabin and a small bedroom. The two rooms were separated by a narrow corridor and a storage room. Everything looked familiar, and no one seemed to have set foot here since last time. It felt good. He would be safe here for the time being.

In the main cabin there was a fireplace and next to the fireplace a large basket of roughly chopped wood. He started a fire and went back out while the cabin was getting warm. He decided to shovel the walkway so he could drive the car up a little closer to the house and so he could get to the outhouse when the need arose. Shoveling snow would raise his body temperature while waiting for the fire to take off.

He tried to follow a system to make things easier. Start at the porch, clear the steps, make neat lines down the walkway, then tackle the driveway in even, satisfying rows. He liked the rhythm of it, the creak of his boots in fresh snow, the puff of his breath in the crisp air. It took over an hour to create a three-meter-wide passage between the car and the cabine and further down to the outhouse which was basically an outdoor toilet and a storage room. By the time he drove the car up onto the cabin and started carrying all the gear into the cabin, the sun had already disappeared behind the mountaintop and the light was dim.

Inside the cabin, the temperature had reached fifteen degrees. William changed into comfortable clothes and started the gas stove he had brought with him. His stomach was in revolt, but he was able to satisfy his hunger with a can of goulash soup, some bread, and fresh, cold mineral water. It tasted delicious.

He looked around the small cabin, trying to familiarize himself. Apart from the fireplace, there was room for a small half-circular kitchen table and a couple of stick chairs. A worn armchair stood in front of the fire. Along one wall was the kitchen area itself, which was not really a kitchen but a long wooden board resting on some concrete blocks in a U-shape. In the middle of the wooden board, his grandfather had lowered an old sink with a drain pipe running down through the floor. The hole was covered with a thick blanket that prevented cold draughts around the pipe. William wondered if his grandfather had given much thought to where the pipe went under the house. He didn't think so.

The walls were decorated with various paintings and hunting trophies. On the floor was a sheepskin that had seen better days. Since there was no electricity, old-fashioned candles and gas lamps were used to light up the cabin. A cast-iron chandelier with a dozen half-burnt candles hung in the middle of the main room. It was almost dark outside and William lit the chandelier and a few other candles in the bedroom and hall. A pleasant glow lit up the small cabin.

In front of the log wall next to the fireplace was a fifties sideboard with carved drawers and doors. Did he ever notice that piece of furniture before? He opened the doors and gave a muffled cry of delight. Inside the sideboard were several bottles of brandy. Some bottles were unopened and over thirty years old. One bottle was a full fifty years old, but it was half full, and the expiry date had probably passed even for brandy. Further into the sideboard there were cut glasses and some cigars. Expectations went high as he opened one of the thirty-year-olds and poured it. The cigars were dry and crumbly and could not be saved but the brandy tasted as fantastic as the goulash soup did earlier. Age had rounded out the flavor and removed most of the crispness. He settled into the deep armchair in front of the fire and sat there until he dozed off.

✳ ✳ ✳

✳ ✳ ✳

Edward was driving along the E4 highway. He pondered over the bag. It was of great importance in order to make progress in the investigation. And what about the traffic accident? Was it a normal single traffic accident or had it really been a premeditated robbery? Or did the man in the hospital just imagine it all? After all, he'd suffered a serious concussion. Right now, there was nothing to go on, but that was first and foremost Kvarnbring's problem and not his own. The worst that could happen was his own removal from the investigation, and at the moment that thought didn't seem very unpleasant at all.

He approached the spot where Niilla's car had gone off the road and carefully rolled along the edge of the road. The snowbank, battered by sunshine, road salt and exhaust fumes, remained as a thin line along the ditch, but the traces of the crash were still visible.

Edward remained inside his car as he lit another cigarette and rolled down the side window. With small puffs of his mouth, he finished the cigarette while his eyes roamed over the surrounding area. A four-lane highway, a large concrete bridge, road signs, ditches, bushes and a lot of traffic. On the other side of the road was a gas station and a hamburger restaurant. For some reason, he had not noticed the gas station the last time he was here. Gas stations were always equipped with surveillance cameras. He decided to pay a visit and get something in his stomach at the same time.

It took a few minutes to get to the exit on the opposite side, but once at the station, he realized it was worth the effort. The buildings and gas pumps were on a plateau with a perfect view of the crime scene and the distance was not even a hundred meters. Edward entered the shop and asked for the station manager. He was shown to a fat, thin-haired man in his fifties who was kneeling by one of the shelves to pick up a package. The man glared irritably at Edward.

"Is it the car wash again? If it's broken, you'll have to go somewhere else. That son of a bitch breaks down every time it's below freezing outside."

"No, I'm from the police," Edward replied, showing his ID.

The manager stared suspiciously at the gray-haired man, who was dressed in ordinary clothes.

"I'm in civilian clothes," Edward continued, as if he could read the other man's mind.

The fat guy stood up with some difficulty, running his hand through his greasy hair as he caught a breath. He still didn't say anything, but his eyes flickered anxiously. Edward thought the man looked unnecessarily nervous but ignored it for the moment. He just wanted to get hold of the surveillance video and decided to move straight to the point.

"On the night of Friday last week, there was a traffic accident on the other side of the highway. I wonder if any surveillance camera here at the gas station may have captured the sequence of events."

"I am not aware of any road accidents."

"The traffic accident took place during the snowstorm and it is very possible that there is not a single witness to the incident. Therefore, the police are looking for possible footage."

"Follow me, the man said, leading Edward behind the counter and into a small office."

He seemed visibly relieved, as if he had just escaped much more uncomfortable questions.

"This is the video surveillance system," he said, pointing to a couple of computer screens, a keyboard and some electronic devices that were spread out over a large table together with pretty much everything else represented in the periodic system.

"They continuously record everything that happens and after a week the oldest recordings are automatically overwritten. Camera four monitors the gas pumps and should be aimed out over the highway."

Edward sat down in the room's only chair, cleared away the traces of a few more or less finished quick lunches. A clear live image of the gas pumps was visible. A woman held a nozzle to the car. A man was moving towards the entrance. Edward looked closer at the screen and tried to place the highway in the background. In just a few seconds, a car passed across the screen at high speed and then it was easier to navigate in the picture.

"Can you go back in time to 2am on Friday night?"

The site manager nodded and made a few keystrokes on the keyboard. A new video sequence became visible. This time the ground was covered in snow. There was a sense of chill in the air but the storm had not yet arrived in full force. The area closest to the gas pumps was clearly lit, but the section of road in the background was also illuminated by a powerful floodlight between the two lanes. The cars passing on the highway in the background were clearly visible although it was difficult to make out any details. The fat man increased the playback speed ten times and after a couple of minutes, Edward saw something strange happening in the video sequence. He asked to have the last few minutes played again at normal speed. Soon the scene became visible again. A car plows through the snow bank at the right edge of the screen, tears up a large white snow cloud, and then disappears from the picture.

"My goodness!" exclaimed the fat man on the chair.

"Do you think I could get all the recorded data from that camera?"

Edward decided that the manager had seen more than enough.

"Of course, anything for the police."

The manager was visibly pleased to be able to help and Edward guessed that he would be even happier when he left the gas station.

Less than five minutes later, Edward was on his way back to the office with a USB stick full of data. He'd finally found a clue.

CHAPTER 6

An Unexpected Visitor

William woke up by a scratching sound and cautiously opened his eyes. At first he couldn't get his bearings. His eyes were dry and the environment was alien. He sat in an armchair in front of a fireplace where the embers had long since burned out. He was in a small room with rough log walls and strange decorations. The legs ached, his back was stiff and his right arm had fallen asleep. The memory of yesterday slowly came back, but he still couldn't understand how he had managed to spend the whole night in this armchair without waking up. He must have been very tired. The wristwatch showed eight in the morning and it was already daylight outside.

The scraping sound came back. It sounded as if it came from outside. He got up heavily from the armchair and walked on shaky legs towards the hall. The sound came from the front door. He peered through the small window beside the door but couldn't see anyone outside. Carefully he lifted the hasp and turned the lock. As he pushed the door open, the scratching stopped. Down by his feet, two small pointed ears peeked out from behind the door frame. On the front porch, a red and yellow striped cat stared at him in surprise. Before William could react, the piece of fur slipped between his legs and into the log cabin.

The cat roamed through the rooms, exploring every square meter of the two rooms, sniffing curiously at the grocery bags and then curling up in the warm armchair in front of the fireplace.

"What a determined sly dog!" William walked up to the cat and gently stroked its fur. Instead of being scared or running away, it purred loudly and rolled over on its back, exposing its belly. When he gently crossed his hand over the belly, he noticed that the cat had many scars hidden by its long hair. Some were quite large and the fur had matted around the healed wounds. The cat was emaciated. Under the long, matted fur, there was not much fat on the small body.

"You must have had a very tough life."

He wondered how the cat had survived the cold winter up here and how it found food. There were hardly any year-round residents on the mountainsides of Fulufjället. It probably hunted voles and mice and slept in a nearby cottage or barn.

William searched the grocery bags for something that might suit such a guest. He fished out a yogurt and a packet of ham sandwiches. When he cut open the ham packet, the cat was there in an instant. It twisted its legs and meowed as loud as it could. There was no way William would miss the message, but just in case, the cat stuck its nose into the half-opened plastic wrapper. William shredded some slices of ham on a plate and scooped up some yogurt on the side. The cat ate as if he had never seen food before.

While the cat satisfied his hunger, William looked out of the window at the back of the cottage. The weather was still good, with a gentle breeze and no clouds in the sky. The temperature had dropped well below zero the previous night but was now rising again. Through the window he had a clear view of the mountain heath and the small lake that lay directly behind the cabin. Technically, it was probably not even a lake. More like a stretched-out pond, barely a hundred meters in diameter. Nevertheless, it was called Black Lake and that's exactly what it was - raven black and mirror-like.

He remembered some of the stories his grandfather told him about Black Lake. More than thirty years had passed and he could no longer remember all the details, but the message was always that the lake was deep, icy, treacherous and held many secrets. It was best to stay away from it. Even then, William had suspected that the stories were made up by his grandfather to keep him away from the lake and thus prevent him from falling in. The edges around the lake were certainly high and sharp and the water was cold all year round. If you slipped in the wrong place, you may never get out. His grandfather's way of conveying this simple message had been to tell intricate ghost stories. Through the frosty window, the shiny black surface, flanked by sharp stone edges, gave an eerie impression. He must admit that.

He thought of Papusa. By now, she should be on the bus to Östersund - at least if she'd taken his advice. He hoped she had checked into a hotel, bought herself some food and clothes. She could certainly afford it - he'd left at least fifty thousand in the glasses case. Maybe even more. But he didn't feel any joy or pride in the move. On the contrary, he felt some anxiety and ambivalence. He could have given her a lot more than that, but then she might get into trouble and risk getting *him* into trouble.

In any case, he would probably never see her again. Yet he could not let her out of his mind. Where was she now and was she okay? She had passed out in the car, completely exhausted. And she basically devoured the sandwich. What had happened to her and who was she looking for?

At the other end of the main room, the cat was no longer feasting on the food. The barrel was emptied and it had crawled back into the warmth and was licking the paws. It was clear that the creature had no intention of leaving the armchair in the foreseeable future, so William went to tackle the morning chores instead. He looked for the outhouse. The mountain air was cold and fresh but dry and at the moment there was no wind. The coldness wasn't as noticeable up here, some 600 meters above sea level, because of the dry air. On the way back, he filled a pan with snow, which he brought inside and melted on the gas stove. Then he made a cup of coffee and ate a hearty breakfast of boiled eggs, ham sandwich, porridge and juice.

With food in his body, it was easier to focus on the practicalities. He made the old bed in the bedroom and then set about unpacking. He placed the clothes on the wooden shelf along one wall at the foot of the bed. The structure was as sturdy and rough as the rest of the cabin. Each sock, underwear, T-shirt, sweater or towel contained a bundle of banknotes. These were distributed in plastic bags, which in turn were packed into two large sports bags. He kept about a million in cash, which he put in the only drawer on the bedside table for the time being. On top of the plastic bags of money, he placed similar plastic bags filled with old clothes before sealing the zippers. He carried the two bags into the small storage room at the end of the hall. The storage room was little more than a spacious closet with pine shelves along the walls. He pushed the two sports bags onto the top shelf and pushed them against the slatted roof so that they could not be seen from below. At the same moment, the cat jumped down from the same shelf and landed at his feet.

The cat twisted around his legs as if it wanted to play. William tried to shoo it out of the storeroom with one foot but it jumped away easily. He stepped over the cat and out into the hall, thinking it would follow him, and then he saw that the creature had got its claws into a carpet. He clawed and tore at it until the mat moved from its position and formed a large crease along one side. When William tried to push the rug back with his foot and lift the cat out, he saw that something had been exposed underneath. He pulled the carpet away completely and found a gap in the floor. The gap was about half a meter square. He'd never seen it before and assumed it led down to the foundation under the cottage. Out of curiosity, he turned the handle and pulled the hatch open. A cold, musty smell hit him in the face as he looked down into the exposed space. The cat meowed and disappeared through the hole without a second thought.

William grabbed a flashlight from his travel pack and pointed it at the darkness below. The crawl space was one and a half meters high and consisted of a number of large stones that ran like a basement around the entire bottom of the cabin. As he bent down and swung around his flashlight, he saw that the space was full of gadgets, boxes and tools. His grandfather had apparently used the crawl space as a storage room and possibly even had a reason to hide the hatch.

William heaved himself down through the hatchway with his torch firmly in hand. The ground was covered with some kind of insulating mat, an older model. In a gap between the large foundation stones, he saw the cat disappear. Instead a sliver of sunlight found its way into the crawl space. He maneuvered around the cramped space on his knees, lifting lids, looking into boxes, digging through piles of tools, and rummaging through bags. Most of what he found were old and rusty tools and personal items of no real interest, with the possible exception of a flea market. Various stuff of no particular interest that had belonged to his grandfather and could be found in any basement or storage room.

A large bundle of cloth, tucked behind a pile of boxes, caught his attention. He unrolled the bundle and to his great surprise he saw that it contained half a dozen old weapons. There were rifles, shotguns, a couple of pistols and even an older revolver. Apart from their age, the weapons looked to be in excellent condition.

In the cloth bundle there were also some paper boxes in different shapes. They turned out to be full of ammunition. A whole arsenal of weapons. Had his grandfather been on the level? Was it for hunting, poaching or perhaps something even worse? Or was he just a collector of old stuff? How much did he really know about his blasphemous relative, given how rarely they had met? Perhaps the answer lay in all the junk that was yet to search through.

Next to the cloth bundle with weapons was a large army-green backpack. It was full of hunting equipment of various kinds. A heavy camouflage jacket with matching pants and boots, a tent, sleeping pad and sleeping bag, a hunting knife, can opener, alcohol stove, a telescopic fishing rod, gloves and a fur hat, a couple of maps and a lot of other things stuffed into small bags. He turned back to the small arsenal of weapons. Maybe it was just as well to have a weapon under his pillow now that he was on the run and living alone in the middle of nowhere.

He picked the gun that looked the most modern (or least ancient) - the only one he recognized - and put it in his pocket with a box of ammunition. He knew little about guns but recognized the thirty-year-old Pistol 88, or Glock17 as it was officially called, and the usual 9mm cartridges. Hardly something for poaching, he thought for himself, as he maneuvered his way to the hatch opening and pulled himself up into the storage area. The backpack, gun and ammunition went with him.

William closed the hatch to the crawl space and placed the floor mat on top. The cat would have to scratch at the door if he wanted back in. He put the gun and ammunition in the bedside table along with the money. He was now an armed thief on the run.

Once up in the warmth of the cabin, his thoughts drifted to his visit to Bear Island a few days earlier and the lost wallet. It suddenly occurred to him that the last time he could remember holding it with certainty was in the parking lot of the caravan park. That was when he had looked at the photo of Merja. Where did he put his wallet after that? Was it on the roof of the car? Or did he put it back in his jacket pocket? A shiver went through his body. What if it was in plain sight in the parking lot? Or if it had been on the roof of the car and fallen off on the way home. Then it could be lying anywhere. If he dropped it in the parking lot, someone should have contacted him. His number could be found on the web. But then he recalled that his phone had been intentionally turned off. He decided to turn it on and answer the next time it rang.

✳ ✳ ✳

The white Volvo rolled slowly along highway 70. Funnel was careful not to exceed the speed limit as he sat behind the wheel munching on a giant bag of candy. His criminal record was strained enough as it was. Besides, they wanted at all costs to find the man who had so contemptuously slipped through their fingers several times over.

Funnel had picked up his companion early in the morning at the caravan on Bear Island. He had been in the process of unloading a boarded-up caravan of useful things. Exactly what he meant by "useful" was not clear from the brief explanation, but in any case the items were in two equally stolen bags. Tube had then outlined his plan. The first part of the plan was easy to understand: go to Fulufjället National Park. The second part was a little fuzzier; it would be formed on the way, Tube had said. Now they were halfway there and still didn't know what to do when they got to the national park.

In any case, they needed to get a better map of the area, a hiking map, a terrain map or, at worst, just an overview picture. On the old map from the 1960s - which was surprisingly detailed - they could make out a group of small blue dots that were probably small mountain lakes without names. One of these dots was encircled by the carelessly hand-drawn circle. But the marking was large in relation to the blue dot they hoped to identify. It could just as well be a rough positioning to show roughly where the cottage was for someone who was interested. Furthermore, the blue dot was not necessarily a lake. The dots could be anything from well-known mountain lakes to misprints and spilled blueberry soup.

Apart from the uncertainty of where to look, there was an imminent risk that the scribble on the map had nothing to do with the money. Perhaps the man was even back in the apartment and had already discovered that someone had paid an unexpected visit. But it was their best and only chance right now. Sooner or later they would find him. His identity was revealed and he could not disappear.

✳ ✳ ✳

Edward spent Monday night rewinding the sequence around the accident back and forth in the hope of finding some interesting details. There wasn't much he could make from the video. The cars passing by after the crash had nothing to do with the accident itself and, in the gathering storm, no road user had even noticed the crash. Perhaps it was a ghost that Niilla had seen outside the car window after all. He hoped that the police specialists could get more information and therefore sent a copy of the full footage.

Dan Anderson from the documentation analysis group called as early as six o'clock on Tuesday morning to ask questions about the material. Edward sat up straight in bed and grabbed the phone.

"Yes?" he replied in a gruff, freshly awakened voice.

"Good morning, have you woken up yet? It's Dan from the analysis department."

Edward ignored the rhetorical question and got straight to the point:

"Have you found anything?"

"Well, I've had at least ten minutes to study the material so I understand the question."

"Funny guy. Then why are you calling in the middle of the night?"

"I have a question for you. Is it the sequence with the white car you are interested in?"

There was silence on the phone for a few seconds.

"What white car?"

"Have you not seen it? The car that stops after the crash."

"I don't have time for riddles. I have only seen the accident itself. I haven't seen anything interesting before or after."

"I see," replied the voice on the phone. "If you jump forward in time almost an hour, a white car stops in the same place. Two people are visible. They don't seem to have anything to do with the crash itself but I think you will find it very interesting."

Edward stood up in bed in a few seconds and replied in a slightly less gruff voice.

"I want you to focus on the sequence with the white car! Need to know everything you can get through image analysis and common sense. Car model, license plate, faces, weapons, sequence of events and so on. Preferably a name and an address. Call me as soon as you have something!"

Edward hung up the phone and went into his study to start up his laptop. How could he have missed this! It must have had to do with tiredness. He clearly remembered Niilla's incoherent story about how he had seen two young men outside the car.

Edward played the video until just before three o'clock on Friday morning. Almost immediately a white Volvo appeared in the picture. The clock in the upper right corner of the picture showed 02:55. He had simply never looked that far. He ran the sequence without pausing and zoomed in as much as he could.

A white car pulled over to the side of the road in almost the same place where the dark car went off the road less than an hour earlier. The driver's side door opened and a man hurried out and around the back of the car, standing wide-legged by the snow bank with his back to the camera. The man tilted his head back and held his hands in front of his body. It looked like he was peeing, Edward noted.

The man stood like that for a minute or so, rocking his knees and looking generally content with the situation. At least from behind and from a great distance. When he finished the procedure and buttoned his trousers, he stood for a few seconds looking out over the ditch. He then turned his head to the right and probably noticed the traces of the previous accident. He then ran to the passenger side of the Volvo and forced a second person out of the car.

Together, they climbed the snow wall and disappeared down and away from the camera's view. After just two or maybe three minutes they become visible again. This time one of them was carrying a bag in one hand. They rushed into the white Volvo and seemingly tried to drive away as fast as they could. In the rush to get away, the rear-wheel drive car skidded and ended up with its rear across the double lane roadway before the driver finally gained control of the vehicle. Within seconds they were out of sight.

Edward's heart pounded with excitement as he tried to process what he had just seen. He played back the sequence and watched it again. Then once more. It was still not possible to see any details but suddenly Niilla's story made sense. He must have been unconscious for almost an hour. The people in the second sequence probably had nothing to do with the accident itself. However, they were an important piece of the puzzle. Nor did the bag necessarily have anything to do with it. It seemed more like a series of random events.

He called Dan in the data analysis department and asked if it was possible to get a better picture of the rear registration plate from the short sequence when the car crosses the road. He promised to get back as soon as he had found something. Edward went out into the hall and fished a cigarette out of his coat pocket. This was worth a cancer stick and his mouth tasted like sewage at this time of day.

* * *

He sat in the armchair with his feet resting on a small stool, enjoying the warm afterglow of the fire. In his lap was a knocked-out cat. It had suddenly appeared in the main room while William was reading in front of the fire. After a bit of detective work, he finally found the four-legged creature's own entrance by the blanket covering the hole around the drainpipe under the sink. The cat's local knowledge was a little too good to be a coincidence. He'd obviously been here many times before and the crawl space was his private entrance.

William thought of the two guys at the dirty table in the roadside tavern. How did they come across the money? Where are they now? Did they, like himself, simply stumbled across the bag? They didn't look like serious criminals, but more like unbrushed mischiefs. Either way, they would never find the cabin. He felt calm and relaxed up here in the mountains. He always had.

By the fireplace there was a basket of old newspapers and magazines that served as fire starters. At the top of the pile of newspapers was a black and white tourist booklet about northern Dalarna. He picked it up and leafed through it sporadically until he found a short section on Fulufjället.

He could read that Fulufjället is not really an ordinary mountain of gneiss or granite, but more like a large pillow of sandstone. The sandstone was formed almost a billion years ago in a shallow sea at the equator and because sand is nutrient-poor, most mosses and lichens grow there. Not so long ago, there were still mountain huts on the mountainside. They were used during the summer when the animals were released into the forest and the mountains to graze. However, as no reindeer have wandered onto the mountain heath, the lichen cover has been able to grow thick. Today there are shelters, resting huts and hiking trails on the mountain. People rent boats and buy fishing licenses. Yet there are many quiet, isolated areas for those who want to stay away.

On the small side table next to the sofa was the coat bag with the leg locks and the colorful scrolls. What did the embroidery on the outside mean? It looked like a mountain peak, but with a little imagination you could make it symbolize anything. He lifted the leather flap and examined the inside of the bag. It was certainly handmade, but it was also very well made. He had examined the whole inside, outside and underside before he saw it. There was a small engraved text on the inside of the lid: "Luoktajärvi". But what did it mean? Was it the name of the maker of the bag, or was it the name of a place, or something entirely different? Was Luoktajärvi the name of the mountain peak?

In the atlas of Sweden that he'd brought from home, there was no mention of Luoktajärvi. Perhaps the community, if it was a community, was too small and insignificant to be included in an atlas of Sweden, or maybe it was simply not a geographical place. He thought of the maps he had found down in the basement. Maybe they were more detailed. He got up to fetch them and the cat whined in displeasure as it was relegated to the floor.

There were two plastic folders with maps rather than two individual maps. The folders contained yellowed broken paper maps that had been folded in the wrong place more than once. Most showed high-resolution areas around Fulufjället and had probably been used for hunting in some form. Or possibly poaching. Some were old mountain maps covering areas further up in Sweden such as Kebnekaise, Sarek, Padjelanta and Stora Sjöfallet. They contained lots of strange names representing everything from mountain stations and lakes to Sámi villages. Quite a few contained names that reminded him of Luoktajärvi. He began systematically searching the mountain maps. He had plenty of time.

✳ ✳ ✳

Tube wrestled with the unwieldy twenty-liter tanks that were crammed with diesel. It was one of five diesel tanks they had brought all the way from Westridge. Both containers and contents were found at the campsite during the winter. Some of the seasonal guests usually left fuel behind to be used for heaters or as reserve for their cars. Some diesel had been hosed down from visitors in the parking lot, just a few liters from each car - little enough to go unnoticed.

Now he was struggling to get the diesel into the car's tank. When the last drops had been transferred, he threw the can away and sat down panting in a snowdrift with a cigarette in his hand. He looked across the visitor's parking lot to the small grocery store where Funnel went to make some minor purchases. They hadn't eaten anything since they left the campsite in the morning hours and he fantasized about what would be in the grocery bag.

Funnel came out of the entrance a few minutes later with a couple of well-filled plastic bags.

"I think we'll go to that rest area we saw next to the lake just before we turned off," he said cheerfully.

"I am starving. I must have food now!" replied Tube.

"Eeeeh, I don't think that's a good idea... let's get going first so we can eat in peace."

Tube looked suspiciously at his companion and then jumped into the car. They pulled out of the parking lot and drove back towards the rest area they passed half an hour before. The rest area had an old wooden table with flattened logs to sit on. It was hidden from the road by some spruce trees and was idyllically located right next to a mirror-shiny lake.

"Now tell me why it was so damn important to come here," snapped Tube after his friend turned off the engine.

"Well... I'd rather not actually. Weren't you hungry? Aren't we going to eat now?" Funnel took out one of the bags and started rummaging through it.

"Because it can't be that you forgot to pay for the party, can it?"

"Look at these sausages. He fished a bag of thick bratwurst out of the box. Everything is here! Candy, sandwiches, cigarettes, beer…"

"So you didn't bother to pay for all this?"

"I... I didn't have enough money."

"Then you should have shopped less! Or come back and get more money from me. What if you get caught on a surveillance camera? Or if someone saw you sneaking out of the store."

"Sorry... it was out of habit I guess. It's in my DNA. Funnel stared shamefully into the grocery bag."

"You're such a fathead! Now we may have the police after us for shoplifting... when we're looking for millions!"

Tube snatched the bags and got out of the car. He walked over to the log table and emptied the contents with demonstratively exaggerated body movements. He continued to scold his friend until he eventually cooled down and grabbed a sandwich.

* * *

It was ten in the morning when the analysis department called again. Edward was already in the office and jumped on the phone after the first signal.

"Yes?"

The voice was impatient and irritated, but there was no time for subtlety right now.

"This is Dan. I'm sorry it took so long but the image quality was not the best. We had to use a number of tools and…"

"I don't give a damn what tools you use. Have you found anything useful?"

There was silence for a few seconds while Dan swallowed his pride and then continued with an unchanged voice:

"We got the license plate number and I have taken the liberty of looking up who it belongs to. The car is a white Volvo 740 from the late eighties. It's registered to a Jari Kolmerinta. He has a criminal record. He's even done time."

Edward felt a large stone fall from his chest. Finally, a breakthrough.

"Great work."

"That's not all I've found out," continued Dan. The passenger is probably Kenneth Olsson - Jari's buddy and childhood friend. They are in their twenties and have both served time together for various petty crimes. Their faces and criminal records also match what you can see on the video sequence. However, I could not find a registered residential address. Not for any of them. And it's been months since they did anything stupid. At least according to our rolls.

"Absolutely brilliant Dan. See if you can get anything more during the day. For example, if the car passed any tolls during the night of the accident."

He smiled to himself as he hung up the phone. The analysis department had saved him a lot of work by searching the criminal records themselves. It was becoming increasingly clear that the people in the white vehicle stumbled into this story by chance and at the same time came across a bag with unknown contents.

The phone rang again. His momentary enthusiasm clouded as soon as he heard Kvarnbring's troubled voice on the other end.

"Edward, we have more problems."

"Is that even possible?" Edward sank back into his chair with the phone pressed against his right ear.

"Yes, you can count on it. I will come over."

Within minutes, Kvarnbring's drawn face was visible in the doorway. He stepped in and closed the door behind him, standing in the middle of the floor with a blank stare. Edward watched his colleague without saying anything. He looked as if he had aged at least ten years in just a few days. His hair was spiky and silver gray. His shirt was carelessly tucked in under his belt and his face seemed even more weather-beaten than usual.

"Niilla has disappeared. He is not in the hospital."

Kvarnbring walked over to the visitor's chair and sank down with his face buried in his hands. After a long pause that seemed like an eternity, he started digging in his pockets for the cigarette packet. With shaking hands, he picked up a cigarette and then held out the pack to Edward. Without a word, he also took a cigarette and put it in his mouth. There was no point in not smoking when Kvarnbring was in the room.

"But how is that possible! Didn't you have guards posted?"

"Just some poor guy on the night shift. The guard claims to have seen nothing strange all night. Just the occasional doctor. We think he fell asleep at the post."

"But... you mean a seriously wounded patient just got up and left the hospital? He looked like a mummy the last time I saw him and was fast asleep when I left the room. There's no way he could have slipped away by himself."

Edward's office was filled with smoke before Kvarnbring continued:

"You haven't heard everything yet. The Sámi who came down from Luoktajärvi the other day have also disappeared. The hotel manager called me and told me that everything was left in a big mess. However, they paid for themselves. Substantially, it might be added, and in ready cash."

"Do you think they went to the hospital to pick up Niilla?"

"I have no proof but it looks like it."

"So, what does this all mean?" Edward looked at his boss.

"In theory, we could just ignore that anything has happened and go back to sleep."

"In theory?"

"Yes, in theory. In practice we have a more complicated situation and we are not the only ones that know about this undercover operation. We have a traffic accident and a victim that has suddenly disappeared, so both the hospital and the ordinary police are missing an injured and anonymous person. To the security service this person happens to come from a region that does not exist and he was suspected of illegal business and likely he has also been illegally removed. And all this happened on our watch."

"What about you? You look sick. Are you okay?"

"I'm fine. Do I look that bad?" He looked at Edward almost pleadingly, as if hoping for some kind of pity.

"Seriously, yes. You look like a corpse."

The words faded and remained unanswered. They smoked their cigarettes in silence. Edward was troubled by the news. It had come completely unexpectedly and overturned the entire investigation.

✳ ✳ ✳

Funnel and Tube found a chart of Fulufjället National Park in a hotel reception in Särna. It showed more detail than the fifty-year-old map book, instead of one lake there were twenty small ones. At least five or six of these lakes could be the right one. Tube suggested that they make an effort to find the yellow Hyundai before it got dark.

"If we search the area systematically, we should have no problem finding our thief."

Funnel nodded in agreement.

"In any case, we have nothing to lose, except time."

A few minutes later they turned off road 70 towards Fulufjället. After another half hour or so, they had circled the entire national park so that they were between the Norwegian border and the lakes at the northwest end of the park. The snow was thick on the ground, but had been since they crossed the county border into the valleys. The weather had changed from sunny and calm to overcast and windy. Almost no traffic was visible.

A few small roads, not even marked on the new map, led up the slopes in an easterly direction. They selected a few small roads that looked good enough to drive on and started systematically cutting them. They assumed that if they couldn't get around in their own car, neither could the man they were hunting. At least not in the car he was supposedly driving.

"If we don't find a Jap in a couple of hours, we'll have to find somewhere to stay and continue tomorrow," said Funnel. Hopefully the weather will be better then.

"Agree, we will not find anything in the dark."

But darkness came faster than they had hoped. With no street lights or other sources of light, it was difficult to continue the search. They decided to go back to Särna and try to find some accommodation for the night.

"It will be easier to find him in daylight and with a steady breakfast in the stomach," said Funnel. He was struggling to keep the rear-wheel drive car on the road. The high beam was broken on the left side, but so far Tube hadn't said anything. The combination of darkness, rear-wheel drive, worn winter tires, poor lights and lousy road markings made it hard to stay on the road and Funnel was relieved when they agreed to give up for the day.

Tube sat silently for several minutes before saying anything.

"I'm afraid we might lose him."

"But... he's still up there in his cabin, right?"

"He most certainly is. That is, if he is in Fulufjällen at all. But there is a risk that he has hidden the car and cleared the tracks. If he hides in a cabin in the mountains, it will be almost impossible to find him."

"But tomorrow it will be daylight again," Funnel tried.

"I think even in daylight it will be a difficult task. Like looking for a needle in a haystack. We have a map, but it only tells us which end of the haystack to start searching."

"What do you suggest? Should we put an ad in the gas station?" Funnel gave his friend an ironic look.

"Let us call and surprise him. Scare the shit out of him. So he shits his pants and hands over the money voluntarily."

"We already tried that. The phone was shut off. And we would lose the element of surprise. Now he doesn't know we're looking for him."

Tube nodded thoughtfully.

"Yes, but we don't really know anything about this guy except that he's stolen a lot of money and fled north. We can safely assume he's not going to show his face in public."

"He also dropped his wallet right in front of us and left a clear trail in his apartment. It doesn't look like we're dealing with a cunning criminal," Funnel tried.

"No, I agree. This is an average Joe who stumbled in through the wrong door. If we call him and scare him, I think he'll throw in the towel. After all, we know his name, what car he drives and roughly where he is. Plus, we know he's stolen a lot of money. We have his wallet and we've been to his apartment."

"Ok, go for it. Let's hope that he answers."

Tube took out his phone and dialed. This time the signals went through.

✳ ✳ ✳

William woke up to the sound of a phone ringing. He had dozed off on the sofa for the second time in 24 hours, and through the windows he saw that darkness had settled over Fulufjällen. The wind was persistently tugging at the house. The fire was out and it had become cold and raw in the house. The cat was nowhere to be seen and the mountain maps lay scattered on the floor.

It was a familiar signal but very weak. Suddenly he realized that it might be about his missing wallet and swung himself off the sofa as fast as he could. The sound came from the bedside table in the bedroom. He ran into the room, grabbed his cell phone and answered it in an eager voice:

"Hello?"

It was quiet at the other end, but there was a faint background noise, which meant that he was at least in contact with someone. He waited a few seconds before asking if there was anyone at the other end. A male voice answered:

"Is it William Sleipner?"

"Yes, it is me. Who am I talking to?"

There were a few more seconds of silence, which felt very uncomfortable.

"I have found your wallet and would like to return it. Where can we meet?"

William was about to say something ill-considered in sheer joy before he realized how stupid it was. It was the first time he thought about what to say when someone asked where he was. And there was something that didn't feel right about this person.

"I am on vacation and will not be home for a while. Would you mind handing it in to the police?"

"You are on vacation?"

"Yes."

William hesitated whether to say anything more.

"How timely."

"I beg your pardon?"

"That you are on vacation," replied the man at the other end with clear irony in his voice.

William didn't know what to say. It was starting to feel uncomfortable.

"You have something that belongs to us."

"Who am I talking to?"

Again silence on the phone before the voice was heard again.

"It doesn't matter who I am. We've met before. You have stolen something from us and we know your name, what you look like and where you are now."

William was silent. He realized that it must have something to do with the bag.

"We saw you in a dirty roadside restaurant along the old Stockholm Road. You sat opposite us and you stole our bag. Just so you don't doubt what I'm saying, we know you drive a yellow Jap, we've been inside your apartment and we've drunk your whiskey."

William broke out in a cold sweat. It was Beavis and Butthead from the Night Owl. He tried to buy time by playing ignorant.

"I have no idea what you are talking about."

"You're William Sleipner, right? Then you know what I'm talking about. You were at the Night Owl on Friday night and now you're going to return what belongs to us."

"Which bag and what is in it?"

"Stop playing dumb. You know very well that it is stuffed with money."

He kept quiet. Now there was no doubt about it. A great sense of unease had set in. They had been inside his apartment, rummaging around.

"We know that you are in Fulufjällen. Tomorrow at ten o'clock you will meet us at the gas station in Särna and hand over the bag."

William flinched involuntarily when he heard Fulufjället mentioned. How could it know where he was now? Had he left his map book out? Yes, that must be it. They had been sitting on his sofa, drinking his whiskey and seeing the markings in the map book.

"What's it gonna be? Either we come up and get you by force or we make a nice handover tomorrow and forget about this incident."

Was it a tremor in the voice he heard? His mind raced. How could they know which cabin he was in? There was no way from the markings in the fifty-year-old map book. And why didn't they just go up unannounced and surprise him? It occurred to him that the youngsters from the Night Owl hadn't looked like serious criminals and they probably had no idea where he was. They wouldn't go to the police either, because the contents of the bag were hardly theirs. And the yellow car they had seen had now been replaced by a Range Rover. Slowly, confidence returned.

"I find it hard to believe that I have something that really belongs to you but if you want we can meet tomorrow at the place you suggest and clear up the misunderstanding."

"Good... and make sure you have your bag with you."

"How do I recognize you?"

"We recognize you."

The call was cut off. William hurried to the window and peered out from behind the curtain. He stood like that for several minutes, looking out into the pitch darkness, but he could see nothing.

With his adrenaline pumping, he walked around the cottage, feeling the window hooks and drawing the curtains. He turned off some of the lights and bolted the front door from the inside. He took the gun and the ammunition bag out of the bedside drawer, then sat down on the sofa and tried to collect his thoughts and familiarize himself with the weapon.

The situation had drastically changed from a cozy vacation to an escape for life. Or at least an escape from two unpleasant people who knew far too much about him. He had the money but they had the psychological advantage. Who knew what they were capable of doing?

He had tried to buy time by saying he would attend the meeting the next day. Of course, he would never show up but hopefully he would have time to make the right decision and, if necessary, leave the cabin. He suddenly realized that he couldn't contact Merja as long as the situation looked like it did. Not without risking her life too. He was a prisoner with thirty-six million in an old wooden cabin in the wilderness. The adrenaline in his body had been replaced by anger as he reflected on the situation.

For an office rat who never served in the army, loading a pistol was easier said than done. The magazine held 17 cartridges and he didn't even know how to open the magazine. There were also some accessories that he later identified as a barrel cleaner, speed loader, holster and extra magazine.

After some initial struggle he managed to insert the rounds in the magazine and push it back into the grip. He then made a mantle movement with the slide and took aim at the logs along one wall. The gun went off on the first try and the recoil made his arm jerk upwards. With horror-mixed delight, he dropped the gun and walked over to the hole where the bullet was expected to have entered. With the help of a candle, he managed to identify a deep mark in the dried-out log and on the floor lay a flat lead bullet. He didn't know what to expect - a hole straight through the wall or a bullet stuck in the wood - but the flat little lump of lead on the floor looked pretty harmless.

** * **

Security Service archives, internal correspondence
Date: June 22, 1920
From: Chief of the General Staff
To: Superintendent Hallgren

I apologize for the delay but I hereby get back to you regarding the meeting we had last week. My contact confirms your concerns. It seems no better than them playing us off against each other. To us they say that the Norwegians slavishly follow the new Reindeer Grazing Convention which severely restricts the right to winter grazing in eastern Troms County. They have apparently told the Norwegians the same thing - that as soon as they graze on the Swedish side, they will be driven away. The Sámi Parliament does not want to deal with the villagers. They claim that the Luoktajärvi people are not real Sámi... Yes, you read that right.

The problem is that no one can tell which side of the border they are on even if they stay in their houses and do not move an inch.

In any case, the Minister of Foreign Affairs suggests that we leave the matter alone. His Norwegian counterpart is apparently of the same opinion. I will hereby contact the head of the regiment upstairs and call off the search.

KG

❋ ❋ ❋

Since he could not use the ordinary police resources, he had searched Niilla's phone himself. Only three calls were recorded and the address book was empty. The number was linked to a new prepaid card and had probably been used only for this trip. It had been purchased on the morning of Thursday, March 26 from a kiosk in Märsta. The phone was an unlocked smartphone of a cheaper model.

Edward guessed that Niilla had landed his private plane on Thursday morning and then, for some reason, left again in the middle of the night. But he surely wasn't flying himself this time, regardless of his pilot license. Wherever he went after the hospital he did not travel alone, most likely he was transported in a wheelchair.

He looked at the cell phone display again. Two of the calls were to unknown numbers that could not be traced in the usual way, i.e. by searching the internet. He had to wait and see if the police needed to be involved in any way. They would have no problem tracing the calls and linking them to the person, time and place. The third number went to a trading company in Stockholm: *Swedish Wrapping AB.* The company was registered at an address near the goods terminal in the harbour area.

He scrolled through the phone to see if he could find anything else of interest but it seemed pretty much unused - even the protective plastic remained on the display. By chance, he opened the map application and saw that it had been used. A marker was placed between Märsta and Sigtuna. Edward zoomed in and saw that the position was indicated right where land and water separated, not far from a Nature Reserve. His heart leapt in his chest when he realized that it corresponded well with the area where Niilla had stayed. The phone card was purchased in Märsta and the car had driven into the ditch just before road 263, which runs between Märsta and Sigtuna and branches off the E4 highway not far from the accident site.

Edward took out the keys he'd received from Kvarnbring. One of the keys was probably from the car that Niilla had driven. The other was more difficult to determine. Perhaps the answer could be found at the map position? The next morning he would pay unannounced visits to two different places.

CHAPTER 7

A Bold Plan

It was seven o'clock in the morning on April 1st and everything was ready to go. He'd been awake well past midnight, wrestling with the details until they clicked into order and the decision became clear. The plan was bold but once his mind was made up, a rare sense of calm settled over him. For the first time in days, sleep came easily.

The well thought-out plan in the back of his mind and the old gun under his pillow made him feel at ease with the situation, even though he'd asked himself several times whether he could really use the gun against another human being. Would he, when really needed, have the courage to point the barrel at someone and pull the trigger. There was no obvious answer, but for the moment the presence of the cold steel felt good and it was good.

William looked out of the window at the small lake behind the cottage. It was barely visible in the morning mist. He wished he would have had the opportunity to spend a few quiet days in the mountains, but now he could forget all such thoughts. Even if the plan worked out, he knew he would not find peace in the cabin for the foreseeable future. He just had to accept the new situation.

The bags and other packing were moved to the car. The cabin was almost empty except for some food he had left for the cat. All the footprints would melt away in a day or so. The April heat had already taken its toll on the fading snowscape. Soon there would be no sign of visitors around the little log cabin.

He cleared away about ten million of the stolen goods. He packed six million into two plastic garbage bags, and a generous four million in travel cash was spread out in the rest of his luggage and in a floor compartment of his car. It was all part of the plan that he would soon put into action. The rest of the thirty-six million remained hidden in a tin box in the crawl space under the log cabin. It was unlikely that anyone would find the money, but if they did, the tin box was well hidden under a lot of tarps and the top layer of the box was filled with newspapers and magazines.

In the Range Rover's spacious cargo area, he placed the large backpack from the crawl space. All the equipment seemed to be in good condition, even if it might not be the latest model. The camouflage jacket and shoes fit perfectly, although he wanted to remember that his grandfather had been slightly smaller. Perhaps his back had shrunk slightly during the last years of his life.

Included in the travel pack were also the pistol, a number of cartridges, the old mountain maps, some clothes and the leather bag with the mysterious name Luoktajärvi engraved on it. He didn't have the time or peace to search through all the mountain maps, but the many similar names suggested that it could be a community in the western part of Laponia, or possibly a lake, a mountain or a Sámi settlement.

It was half past seven when the Range Rover slowly rolled down the small road that led to the cabin. He was no longer relaxed and his heart rate had risen noticeably. What seemed like such a watertight and brilliant plan just a few hours ago now seemed to have fundamental flaws in its entire construction. Instead of being bold, it suddenly seemed foolhardy and ill-conceived. But he told himself that there was no turning back now, that the only option was to do what he was about to do. The train had already left the station. His antagonists already knew who he was and if they didn't get their way, they would certainly make his life miserable in one way or another.

✳ ✳ ✳

Just after eight o'clock, he slowly rolled past the gas station in Särna. A light powder of snow covered the ground. There was no doubt that this was the place they would meet. It was the only gas station within a reasonable distance. His heart skipped a beat as he passed the meeting point even though it was almost two hours away. On the other side of the road was a hostel with a gravel parking lot partly hidden by some trees. Further away was a small grove of trees and from there he would have a good view of the meeting point when the time came.

He turned off towards the hostel parking lot, which was located along a small cross street. The whole parking area was empty of both cars and people. He guessed that it was off-season for both skiers and hikers. At the far end of the large gravel parking lot were some green waste bins that most likely belonged to the hostel. William took a deep breath and thought one last time if this was really such a good idea. He quickly shook off his doubts and took out the two plastic garbage bags containing bank notes. He opened them and checked the contents. He had put a layer of clothes on top of each bag, but if someone just looked beneath a couple of T-shirts, socks or a pair of underwear, that person would soon get the surprise of his life.

He tied the bags tightly together and then went to the waste bins. One brown bin contained compost and a green bin contained residual waste, packed in various plastic pouches. He put the money bags in the green bin and rearranged some of the existing garbage pouches and put them on top. Then he went back to the car and drove off a couple of hundred meters along the cross street to park out of sight.

It was only half past eight but William wasted no time. He took a

133

pair of binoculars from his rucksack that he'd found in his grandfather's hiding place under the cottage. Then he walked back along the cross street and up to the grove of trees that lay between the hostel, the gravel parking lot and the highway. Through the grove was a small path that ran to the next cross street. It was a shortcut if you did not want to use the bike path. He walked along the path, trying to look like any other pedestrian. Halfway down the path, he saw that he could keep an eye on both the gas station and the gravel parking lot from here. He felt that he had been incredibly lucky so far. He had coldly expected to sit in the car somewhere but this was much better.

Not wanting to arouse suspicion before it was time, he continued along the path to the next cross street. Then he walked the parallel street back to the car where he would wait for his two blackmailers and hearten himself for the unwanted meeting.

Edward was stuck in the morning traffic on Lindroad. Most people were going in the opposite direction, but the road seemed to have jammed just before he could turn off towards the harbour. The atmosphere in the long queue of cars was charged to the limit, as it usually was at this time in Stockholm traffic. Motorists honked their horns, pedestrians waved their fists angrily and cyclists zigzagged between people, vehicles and lamp-posts. Even the dogs were barking at each other.

After half an hour, the queue had moved enough for him to see what had caused the traffic jam. It was a road repair just before the bridge that had halved the number of lanes. The poor motorists who had to get from Lind Island to the mainland were the worst affected.

Soon after, he located the address in the harbour. It was a large factory premises located in an industrial area that seemed to be buzzing with activity. He stopped in front of what appeared to be the main entrance. Above the door was a large sign that was not ashamed of itself: *Swedish Wrapping* it said in stately white letters.

Inside the doors was a small, unmanned reception area, and behind the counter were some offices and a corridor leading to a door. He suspected that the factory itself was behind that door. Swedish Wrapping produced packaging of various kinds according to its website, a website that would not win any design awards for clarity or innovation.

Since both the reception and the office were empty, Edward took the liberty of walking up and checking the door down the corridor. It was unlocked so he opened it and just as he had guessed, the factory premises were inside. Even the factory was seemingly silent and empty. Somewhere in the background was the muffled sound of laughter and voices.

Edward took the opportunity to look around. Everything looked like a typical factory workshop: production lines with special machines, cartons, pallets and crates, the occasional forklift truck and lots of shelves with tools and debris. Along one wall was a large opening that led to a space adjacent to the loading bay. Apparently, this was where the goods were shipped out by truck. The room was filled with pre-packed cartons. He looked into an open box and found stacks of snuff boxes stacked close together. Thousands of small round cans ready for delivery.

"How can I help?"

The voice just behind his back made him flinch and turn around. A middle-aged man with a moustache had entered the room without him noticing.

"Are you looking for someone?" the man continued.

There was nothing hostile in the tone or choice of words. Just a reasonable assumption that Edward was lost.

"There was no one at reception to ask and nowhere else either for that matter."

"I understand that. This company believes in regular and shared coffee breaks. Everyone sits in the break room across the production hall. "

Edward nodded briefly.

"I come unannounced and would like to exchange a few words with the foreman or manager of this company."

"Then you have come to the right place. I am the factory manager. Sven Kempe. Everyone calls me Svempa."

Svempa held out his hand.

"Edward Johnson from the Security Service," replied Edward and returned the greeting.

"Oh dear, have we committed a crime?"

"No, not that I know of, anyway. I'm actually investigating a traffic accident and... well, it's quite complicated. You could say that the victim was quite seriously injured and now he's on the run from the hospital."

"Do you think he escaped here? Here in the factory?"

The foreman looked surprised.

"No, I don't think so. The man we're looking for made a call the day before he drove off the road. The call went to a number registered to Swedish Wrapping. It is possible that the person who answered may have some information that leads us further in the search."

Edward held out a post-it note with the number. The foreman looked at the note and thought for a while.

"Yes, that is one of our numbers. We have a number of wall

phones scattered around the building. I think this number comes from the factory hall but it is something I can check. Then there are quite a lot of people running around here so it's not certain that I can find out who received the call even when I know which phone was used. But the police should be able to do that themselves."

"Yes, possibly. I thought it would be easy to just go here and see the person in question but I was wrong. Anyway, I would be grateful if you could ask your staff. The call was made at lunchtime on Thursday, March 26."

"I'll ask the guys if they know anything. But it might take a couple of days. A lot of people are sick right now. By the way, what's the name of the person you're looking for?"

Edward thought for a few moments but decided to give him Niilla's full name. The foreman promised to get back to him. Edward thanked him and asked about the snuff boxes.

Foreman Svempa was happy to talk about something else. He gave a vivid description of the company's history, production process and products.

"We're a pretty small company, you know. Around fifty employees. Plus some part-timers. The big production volume is about metal boxes as you may have noticed. And some of the orders are for snuff boxes, usually sold to tourists in gift shops. There are a lot of smaller specialty jobs like these boxes."

He walked over to one shelf where there were a number of snuff boxes of various sizes that were not yet put into transport boxes. Edward saw something shiny in a crate standing alone along the wall. He picked up one of the shiny things and moved it around in his hand. It looked like one of those silver-plated gift boxes that the company provides instead of a gold watch after thirty years of service. It was roughly the same size and shape as a snuff box, but gave an exclusive impression and that was probably the whole point. On the lid was an elegant engraving that said "Reindeer's Gold". He wondered if the object might be coated with white gold.

"Who orders a snuff box like this?" Edward asked.

The foreman took the object in his hand and looked at it for a while.

"I really don't know. We have about a hundred customers and they all have a lot of strange requirements for their products. These ones also come in different sizes, different engravings and sometimes gold plated. It's not sure that this is meant to be used as a snuff box. You can't imagine what people use the stuff for sometimes."

Svempa held up the box in the light, pointed with professional pride to an almost invisible splice in the manor, and began to talk about their metal manufacturing process. Somewhere along the line,

Edward started to lose interest and excused himself, saying he needed to get back to his other business. He thanked the foreman, who promised to come back once he'd questioned the staff about the conversation, and then left the premises.

When Edward turned onto Lind Road again, the traffic jam had eased somewhat. If he didn't have any new mishaps, it would take less than half an hour to get him to the coordinates in Niilla's phone.

Just before 10am, William got out of the car and walked towards the hostel. His heart was pounding and he was more nervous than he'd ever been before. He arrived at the grove and turned onto the small path. Halfway into the grove he stopped and looked around. No one seemed to be around. The gravel parking lot was as empty as it had been an hour ago, and across Highway 70, at the gas station, a lone person was filling up his car.

Suddenly there was a rustle in the foliage and William almost fell backwards in fright. He just had time to look in the direction of the gravel parking lot and the hostel before a bicyclist passed at breakneck speed right behind him. William saw the back of the caped teenager flying past on a mountain bike painted red with shiny shock absorbers on the front forks. The teenager threw out a short apology with a squeaky voice. William regained his composure and quickly realized that this improvised path was probably the cyclist's own shortcut. He probably wasn't used to meeting shady characters on his morning walk.

At the gas station, things suddenly happened. Just before ten o'clock, a white Volvo 740 turned off the road and parked in the guest parking lot at the water and air station. A thin person got out of the car and started to walk towards the building that hosted the gas station's shop. William took out his binoculars and quickly realized that it was one of the men from the Night Owl. The one who talked the most - the skinny man with the pointed nose and the curly v-shaped eyebrows. That's Beavis, he thought excitedly! Soon after, Butthead also emerged from the car and walked over to his companion.

Through the binoculars, William managed to note the license plate number of their car. By sending a text message to a 4-digit number at the Swedish Transport Agency, he immediately got an answer to who owned the vehicle. It was registered to Jari Kolmerinta. There was no time to do any further research. He hoped that one of the men in the car was this Jari.

A few minutes passed without any action, but suddenly the phone vibrated in William's hands. The rehearsed phrases played in his head before he answered:

"William here."

"We are at the gas station. Where are you?"

"I am in the neighborhood."

"We are in the parking lot. A white Volvo. Meet us there."

William takes a deep breath and answers:

"First, I would like you to hand my wallet to someone in the shop."

"Don't try to fool us! The voice was grumpy."

"I can't fool you. You already know who I am and where I live. Leave the wallet at the gas station and you'll have your money. Tell them you found it at one of the pumps and that you've contacted the owner, who will come and collect it as soon as he can."

There was silence on the phone for a few seconds.

"Ok, we'll call you in a few minutes."

The call was disconnected.

Soon after, Beavis entered the store with something in his hands. As far as William could see through his binoculars, it was a wallet or at least something similar. After a few minutes he came out empty-handed. William was on edge, so far the plan had worked.

The phone rang again.

"Your wallet is with the bitch at the gas station. All you have to do is show her your ugly face and you'll get it back. But first we want to see the cash."

William tried to pull himself together as best he could. This was the moment. The million-dollar question was at stake, and he couldn't mince his words.

"You will get your money. Here is my proposal, and please consider this carefully before answering: we all have as much to lose. If you hang me out to dry, I will do my best to fight back as much as I can. I will claim that the money came to me by accident and that I intended to return it all along. This was my original intention, by the way. It will be word against word and you can guess who will sound the most credible and who has the most to lose."

He let the words sink in.

"Anyway, here's the deal: you get half the money and I keep half. I can hardly believe this is your honestly acquired fortune. You've stolen or found the money, then lost it and now you get a second chance."

"You... you're not in a position to set the terms here. How do we know you're not screwing us? How do we know we're getting half the money?"

"You know as well as I do that there was 12 million in that leather bag. And if you haven't counted the money, you'll just have to trust me. I offer six million in two plastic bags. Do you want to know where it is or not?"

This was the big bluff in Williams' plan. The big gamble that risked bringing down the whole company. During the first conversation he got the impression that these guys had no idea how much money they had come across. Now he offered them a smaller share instead of half. When he previously distributed the bundles of banknotes in the two plastic bags, the corresponding amount looked considerably more than when they had been stacked like bricks in the large square leather bag.

"You are fooling us! Where is the money? We can go to the police. We know who you are."

"Listen to me very carefully, you thugs. Either we split the money or I keep it all and then all three of us will be in trouble, especially you two. I know who you are too and what your names are. Is it you or your friend called Jari Kolmerinta? Anyway, I think you both know that there is a waitress at a certain place who will be happy to point you two out and tell the police that you have been running around like hooligans during her shift looking for a bag."

William paused for a moment before continuing in the same relentless voice:

"Let's call this a balance of terror. We're sitting on each other's laps and if the balance is upset, all three of us will go down. I'll tell you where the money is, but I want an answer to a simple question first: where and when did you find the bag? Don't even try to tell me it's your own money, or I'll hang up right now."

It was quiet at the other end, but there was rustling and talking in the background. Eventually the same voice was heard again:

"We found them. Some guy had driven into a ditch outside Stockholm. It was during the snowstorm. We don't know who it was. We just stopped at the roadside to pee."

"Was it the same night you left your bag at the roadside cafe? Was he injured?"

"It was the same day but in the middle of the night. Or early as hell if you like. The guy was injured but not seriously I think. Seemed mostly shocked and confused. We saw the bag in the back seat and took it."

"So you left an injured man in a ditch and ran off with his money?"

"We called 112 and reported the accident! Isn't that enough? How honest are *you* really? Enough with the bullshit questions. Give us the money!"

William thought about what had been said. It all sounded plausible, and if it was true, it was just as he'd suspected and hoped; the crooks had stumbled across the money. They hadn't robbed or hurt anyone - they had even called to report the accident. In all likelihood, they probably did not even know that the bag contained money when they stole it. It might have looked tempting where it lay in the back seat, and when they opened it later, they were in for the shock of their lives. They had stumbled upon Pandora's box and had no idea how to handle the situation. Amidst all the excitement, the box was forgotten and another equally clueless person made the same discovery. He was simply dealing with clumsy petty thieves who were now desperately trying to get their jackpot back. William knew he now had the upper hand.

"I think you're telling the truth and I'll keep my promise. The bags are in a green bin across the road, at one end of the hostel parking lot. You're going to have to do some digging to find something. Call me when you've made your decision."

William hung up the phone and picked up the binoculars again. For a few moments there was obvious confusion in the other camp and then an impromptu consultation followed. Shortly after, the two companions jumped into the Volvo and turned out of the gas station in the direction of the hostel. William hurried along the path towards the far cross street and then crossed the road towards the gas station. This part was not in the original plan but was completely improvised. It was a new opportunity that had presented itself: to get his driver's license back without having to rely on the goodwill of the two cartoon characters.

The woodland partially obscured the view between the gravel parking lot and the gas station, but if any of the men were looking towards the pump station at that time, they would have seen him enter the shop doors. Behind the counter was a stout woman dressed in the gas station's formal clothing. It took a couple of minutes to convince him that he was the person on the license. Only when he recited his full name and social security number and showed a striking resemblance to the person in the photo was she satisfied.

Less than five minutes passed before the phone rang again and in that time William was able to leave the store and hide behind a free-standing storage room with gas cylinders.

"We found the bags with your dirty clothes on top. How do we know it's six million? "

"You have to count the notes in each bundle. There are 120 bundles in the bags. "

"We will notice if something is missing."

You haven't noticed anything, William thought.

"Does that mean we have an agreement?"

"We have an agreement. But if you cheat us with the money or if you contact the police, we will find you. We know where you are."

"I don't think so. And should you surprise me with a visit, you will get acquainted with an old Glock17. I'm not a good shot, but as the name suggests, I can afford to miss sixteen times."

"Just remember what I said."

The phone was disconnected.

From his hiding place behind the LPG bottles, William could see the white Volvo rolling out of the hostel cross street. It turned right and continued south along Route 70. He sank to his knees in relief. It had cost him a lot to play the role of an ice-cold gangster. The facade had cracked, but now it no longer mattered. Everything had worked flawlessly and the two crooks were on their way home again. He was six million poorer, but what did that matter? The money wasn't his anyway. The only side effect was that now there was absolutely no turning back. He was as involved and complicit as one could be. In the past, he might have been able to get rid of the money and report the two cartoon characters, but that was no longer an option.

William walked back towards the Range Rover on shaky legs. The thin blanket of snow crunched against his shoes. The morning fog had lifted and the sun was coming out. It was time to implement the last part of the plan.

CHAPTER 8

The Boat House

Security Service Archive, classified letter

Date: March 16, 1945

From: Chief of Staff General Staff Corps

To: Head of the Security Service

The fighting around the village of Luoktajärvi has now been confirmed by a squad unit from the Norrbotten Regiment. According to the information available to me, the fighting was between German soldiers and armed villagers. When soldiers from the Jaeger unit tried to make contact with the villagers, they themselves were fired upon. I have read the reports written in connection with the border surveillance missions carried out between 1910 and 1920. I understand that this has been a hot potato for a long time, but it is now of the utmost importance to put an end to the fighting as soon as possible in order to avoid being drawn into the ongoing world war. I have therefore ordered the Fourth Battalion, which has hunter units in Abisko and Sjangeli, to disarm the villagers and stop the fighting with the Germans. Hopefully they will not fire on Swedish soldiers.

Chief of staff

* * *

The second location was harder to find than he had first thought. It had taken him several hours because of a simple mistake. The position was marked between two overgrown dirt roads and as far out to a lake as it was possible to get. The gravel roads, or grassy paths were not marked on the map, which made the search difficult. He also wrongly assumed that the coordinate must have a significant positional error because it was given in water and not on land. He had therefore searched along the road. In reality, the coordinate showed exactly the right position.

Right by the water, Edward finally found a large dilapidated wooden house on an overgrown forest plot. Its windows were shattered, its porch slumped like a tired beast resting on broken legs. At the entrance there was a sign informing you that you had arrived at "Grangårdens Scout Camp". The site was so neglected that there could not have been any activity here for many years. The house must once have been a beautiful turn-of-the-century house with imaginative ornaments in the eaves and windows. It had at least three floors and an attic but the façade had long since lost its luster.

The forest had nearly swallowed the old camp whole. Tall pines crowded together, their branches knitting a dim canopy overhead, while brambles clawed at the remnants of a once-clear trail. Edward's trained police eye picked up fresh tire tracks in the muddy, spring-damp road that led to one side of the house. He knew it could mean anything: that some curious person had been driving around looking for a potential summer house to buy, that a burglar had been here, or that whoever owned or managed the property was out checking that everything was in order.

In one corner of the overgrown camp, he discovered a well-prepared path that led diagonally down to the water. The path was a few meters wide and leveled with sand or stone dust. In the sand there were clear traces of a small vehicle or possibly a tractor of some kind. The path was perhaps a hundred meters long and ended at a wooden jetty surrounded by tall reeds. The jetty was wide, sturdy and about thirty meters long and pointed straight out into the water. At the end of the jetty, hidden among the reeds, was a large boathouse with its long side facing the jetty end. It was an old, classic, red-painted boathouse that had certainly once been used for its intended purpose. The position of the building matched exactly the coordinates he had found in Niilla's phone. It couldn't be a coincidence.

Edward walked towards the boathouse with unsteady steps. The dock ran seemingly straight through one long side of the building via a wide wooden door painted black and smelling of tar. In the middle of the door was a fixed handle, and under the handle hung a metal hook with an open padlock. What if someone was here right now? How would he explain himself? The fact that there was no car or any kind of transportation vehicle in the driveway suggested the opposite, but it was impossible to know without looking inside the building. Edward drew his service weapon for the first time in years. The last occasion was ironically in his own home when he thought he was being burglarized in the middle of the night.

Beatrice had woken him up in a deep sleep and just after midnight. She was sure that someone had broken into the apartment. Sleep-deprived, he'd dug out his service weapon and sneaked out into the hall. On the sofa in the living room, he had found a drunk neighbor who, in his drunken stupor, had taken left instead of right while looking for his apartment door. Since the main entrance was equipped with a door code, they were habitually careless about locking their own door and that was probably why the neighbor had managed to get the door open in the first place. The deadbolt was not only wrong on the right and left but also on the floor. Edward let him sleep it off on the sofa and went back to reassure Beatrice. In the morning, the stairwell neighbor had woken up late in the morning with a severe headache and badly disoriented. They treated him to breakfast and then pointed him in the right direction.

Edward gently pulled the door handle and felt it open. Not so strange really, given the isolated location, he thought. You can't find this place unless you're really looking for it - and that's not likely either. He took a deep breath and inhaled the oxygen from the late afternoon air. It was thick and fresh. When he opened the door and stepped into the building, he was in for a big surprise.

The jetty on the inside turned right along the front side. The far side had huge sliding doors that were almost completely open to the water. Between the sidewalls floated a large amphibious aircraft. Edward estimated that the wingspan was at least twelve meters and the length at least ten. A simple wooden bridge had been built along the side of the aircraft.

Edward did not announce his presence, but walked with cautious steps along the jetty on the side leading to the bridge. Not a sound could be heard under the rough planks, only a faint rustle of wind from the opening in the wall. The smell of fish and tar still lingered in the wood, and high up around the rafters hung nets and hemp rope. The whole building was lit by small windows and the big opening.

The bridge on the short side was perhaps two meters wide. A sturdy long bench had been built along the front wall, and on the bench were a couple of metal boxes and a plastic barrel that looked like an ordinary thirty-liter yeast barrel for wine. Under the bench were a bunch of wooden boxes, the size of picnic baskets. All the boxes had folded lids and were empty. In front of the long bench was a four-wheeled transport cart. It looked like one of those hand-pulled carts that could be borrowed from larger greenhouses or even amusement parks. All over the room were gadgets and other signs that someone had been here recently, including a coffee thermos with the lid unscrewed and a fleece sweater hanging over a bridge post.

Edward looked down into one of the metal boxes and saw a lot of small silver-colored cylindrical containers stacked on top of each other. He picked up a container and got his second surprise of the day. On the front was an engraving he had seen just a few hours earlier that day: *Reindeer's Gold*. It was the snuffbox-like thing from the factory in the harbour, but possibly slightly heavier. He fiddled with the small container for a few seconds before he managed to open the lid. At first glance, the contents looked like dried grass and Edward therefore first suspected that it was cannabis. But the contents of the jar lacked the distinctive sweet smell and the consistency was more like moss than grass. He took some moss between his thumb and forefinger and smelled it. Like moss, it smelled forest and grass. But there was also something more. Something hard to place. A faint touch of manure perhaps? He sniffed into the yeast barrel and smelled the same scent but slightly stronger. Edward looked at the engraved metal boxes and realized that he was on to something strange.

He was on the run again. Not literally, but almost. Despite that, it felt good. It was crazy how quickly a person can adapt to a new environment or situation. A few days ago, he was an office rat, just another name in the labor statistics. A gray shadow that left no trace behind. Now he was a hardened criminal, zigzagging between the raindrops, hoping to avoid the legal system and save his own skin.

He had become several million poorer in an instant. But it didn't matter. If you could afford to lose a few million, you probably didn't need it in the first place. He reminded himself that it wasn't about the money. It was never about the money, which by the way wasn't even his money, it was about the excitement and about breaking patterns. It was about breaking free from the shackles of everyday life. And he had succeeded. He felt more alive than ever and regardless of what happened next, nothing would ever be the same again. He thought of Anders' words: *trust your instincts and don't care what others think.* That's exactly what he'd done - and so far, he hadn't regretted it for a single second.

After leaving Särna, he turned the bumper east towards Sveg. Then he drove the E45 north towards Östersund. He considered crossing the border into Norway and heading north via Trondheim and the E6, but he felt uneasy about the luggage. Although border checks were rare, at least for people traveling in ordinary cars and this far north, he didn't want to take any risks with several millions and a gun hidden in his car.

At Östersund, he turned off towards the city center, which was only a few kilometers from the E45. He sat by the window at Frasses, eating a hamburger with a clear view of the car - and the millions stashed inside it. After lunch, on a sudden whim, he turned off the main road and headed toward Östersund Central Station, just a few hundred meters away. He edged along past the bus stops, along the platform and outside the terminal building. Just as he started to feel stupid enough to roll past the terminal entrance for the third time and look through the car window, he saw her. She was sitting on a bench at the end of the building, facing the sun. He barely recognized her. The baggy clothes and the scarf covering her face were gone and she looked like any other train or bus passenger.

He briefly wondered if he should leave, but before that thought could take hold, Papusa had spotted him. Maybe she recognized the big Range Rover or maybe she saw him through the side window. He rolled down the window and waved at her, and she waved back before getting up and coming over.

"I thought you were heading for the Norwegian border," she said, slinging the cloth bag over one shoulder.

"There was a change of plans. I thought you were going to Östersund."

"Yes, this is Östersund, right?"

"Are you on your way again?"

"There was a change of plans," she replied with an attempt at a smile.

He looked her over from head to toe and saw that all her clothes had been replaced by functional clothing and on her head was a plain cap. She was still a somewhat frail apparition, but the abysmal fatigue seemed washed away. Her eyes were bright and clear and her hair no longer hung like vines in front of her face. Only the cloth bag was left.

"I see you followed my advice," said William.

She shrugged and looked past him into the car.

"I have to go to Malmberget. Is your bus going there?"

"This is still not a bus."

"Well, what are you doing here then?"

A very valid question, he thought, and consulted the asphalt below the window before answering.

"I stopped for lunch while passing through and had a whim. My bus is not exactly going to Malmberget but to a couple of places nearby."

"Can I go with you?"

"Does it matter what I answer?"

She ran around the car and climbed into the passenger seat. She put her bag on the floor at her feet just like last time.

"You are not that careful Papusa. Would you jump into any car?"

"This is not just any car. I've ridden in it before."

"Yes, and you fell asleep after only a few minutes."

"I have traveled thousands of kilometers and have done well so far. I've taken the beggar bus from Bucharest and hitched a ride with all kinds of trash. If I get into trouble, I'll just bring this out."

She put her right hand into the cloth bag and took out a small kitchen knife. William flinched instinctively, but before he could open his mouth to say anything, she had put the knife back in the bag.

"Safety precautions," she said apologetically when she saw William's reaction. "The toughest part was the journey between my home village in Romania and Bucharest. I hitchhiked with truck drivers and even rode behind a tractor. You have to be on your guard all the time."

William didn't know what to say, but just nodded and turned out of the parking lot. He continued towards the E45, which after a few kilometers turned off to the northeast. They drove for a while in silence. Papusa looked out of the window and saw the snow cover getting thicker and the landscape changing. Up here, winter ruled, and it held everything in an iron grip. Spring was still far away. He guessed that winter must feel as distant down in Mälardalen as the coming spring did up here.

"Did you find the person you were looking for?" he asked, breaking the long silence.

"No, he had moved on."

"Who are you looking for?"

"A relative. Mother says he must come home."

She paused and looked out of the window. Perhaps she was

looking for the words, or perhaps she was hoping William would steer the conversation in a different direction. Eventually she continued:

"My father died a few months ago and since then we have had neither food nor money. We are struggling and can't get much help from anyone else. Everyone is in the same situation. People borrow money from usurers and buy tickets to Sweden or somewhere else in Europe. Anywhere is better. Some people go to Sweden to find an illegal job."

"What happened to your father?"

"My father worked in a coal mine. It was the only job there was. He earned just enough money to get by. Then the roof of the mine collapsed one day and ten men never came home. The mine closed again. We've been struggling ever since, and my mother became desperate."

"I'm sorry about your father. They sat in silence for a while and Papusa looked absent-minded."

"I've been thinking about your Swedish," William tried tentatively.

"What's wrong with my Swedish?"

"It's absolutely flawless, but there's a subtle accent that I don't recognize."

"We lived in Turku for a while with a cousin of my father. He thought we should try our luck in Finland, but we didn't get a residence permit and they wanted to send us home after just a few months. Just before we were to be deported, my little sister was born. Then we were allowed to stay for a couple of years and I went to a Swedish-Finnish preschool. But we were sent home in the end anyway. I learned Swedish and a little Finnish, but my parents only learned a few words and my sister was too small. Since then we have been floating around Europe: Romania, Hungary, Bulgaria, Germany and back to Romania again. I can't remember all the places. We've stayed in caravans and with friends. The only thing I know is that we have been driven away every time and I didn't have much use from the language either... no one speaks Swedish.

"Until now."

"Yes, until now."

They passed Strömsund, Dorotea and Vilhelmina in silence. When they arrived in Storuman, the sun was low in the sky. Although there had been a few stops during the day, he felt like he had run a full marathon. He explained to Papusa that he too had a hard day and that they would most likely end up in a ditch if they kept going. They checked into a simple hotel and were each given a room in the same corridor. The receptionist had said something in passing about *when kids get into their teens, they don't want to sleep in the same room as their parents anymore*. Papusa found this hilarious and managed with great effort to keep a straight face.

William, too tired to appreciate the humor of the situation, went to his room and took a long hot shower. When he came out of the shower, he was so exhausted that he fell asleep almost immediately.

The word "Reindeer's Gold" must have something to do with the contents, that much was clear. But it was impossible to determine exactly what was in the small boxes and equally impossible to guess who the recipient was. He opened a few boxes at random and noticed that they all had the same contents. Edward took a couple of pinches from one of the boxes and put it in his pocket. The idea was to send the moss-like substance for technical analysis to shed light on the mystery.

Not a sound had been heard in the room since he entered. Edward gained new courage and decided to board the airplane. Before doing so, he used his cell phone to take pictures of what he'd seen. The metal boxes, the storage boxes, the boathouse and the airplane. He was careful to get the registration number on the fuselage.

He then went out onto the narrow gangway, which ran parallel to the wing, and saw that the cabin door was wide open. Was someone hiding inside the airplane? He looked into an empty passenger cabin, dimly lit by the boathouse overhead lights. In the dim light, he saw a number of chairs lined up on either side of the aisle leading to the cockpit. He boarded at the rear end of the cabin where the ceiling height was less than one and a half meters. At the back of the cabin was a partition with a small door. Edward guessed that it led to a toilet or kitchenette that had been installed afterwards. The cabin had six simple passenger seats and on almost every seat and on the floor below there were various packages and bags. Most of it seemed to be related to food: rice, pasta, spices, olive oil, canned food, soft drinks, beer, yeast packages and the like. There were also some boxes of phones and various electronic devices.

On the inside of the cabin door was a plastic information map showing the type of aircraft, the cabin layout and the location of emergency equipment. According to the map, the aircraft was a Cessna 208 Caravan Amphibian. Strangely, the layout showed eight seats. To the left of the cabin door, six seats were plotted and so far everything matched reality. But directly to the right there should be two more seats and there was instead a partition with a small inner door.

Edward became curious and opened the inner door. Behind it was a small storage room that was no more than a meter long. The space was dark and if it weren't for the smell, it would have passed unnoticed. He smelled the faint but persistent aroma of manure that he experienced just a few minutes earlier. Edward turned on a small LED light that was on his key ring. In the light from the lamp he saw a number of small wooden boxes. The same boxes that stood on the bridge but with the lid on. On the walls there was a cabin window on each side. The sunshade was pulled down. It was clear that the whole space was some kind of retrofit. The back row of seats had simply been removed and separated by a wall.

He counted 15 wooden boxes and they more than filled half the space. Edward crouched down and stepped through the door to access one of the wooden boxes. The lid was secured with a simple locking device and it was just a matter of pushing the hook to the side and folding up the lid. He was not surprised to see that the box contained a number of neatly packed and well-filled aluminum cans. He did not need to open the other boxes to realize that they had the same contents. They were pre-packed and stacked for delivery. Someone had been here just recently, preparing them for departure.

Suddenly there were voices and the sound of muffled footsteps moving on the wooden jetty outside the boathouse. Edward almost dropped the LED light in fright. He turned it off and looked out one of the rear windows of the cabin. Soon two people became visible. They stopped in front of the long table on the jetty and were talking intensely about something. They were too far away for him to make out any words and the distance and the angle was too poor to see their faces. All he could register was that they were two male voices. He considered for a moment whether to confront the two men but decided against it. The risk was that he would get into trouble before he had a chance to understand how everything was connected.

He moved further into the small space and carefully pulled up a few centimeters on the sunshade covering one window. The light that seeped in was just enough for him to orient himself in the space, but it was still not possible to see the faces of the people because they were partially obscured by the wing. Suddenly one of the men started walking towards the airplane.

Edward got cold feet and looked around the makeshift cargo compartment. It was dark and both sides of the compartment were loaded with wooden boxes. He felt like being in a coffin. Behind the crates, he noticed an opening to another compartment, which was screened off by a shutter. He guessed that this was the actual cargo space behind the fourth row of seats. It was probably intended for luggage and other items that were not wanted in the passenger compartment.

As the man stepped onto the pontone, the plane lurched. Edward then took the opportunity to crawl into the rear compartment and found that there was plenty of room there, even though the ceiling height was very limited. The fuselage was equipped with some soft absorbent material that was probably intended to protect travel bags from external damage. At the same time, he was worried that his movements would cause the plane to heel over in the water. After all, he was in the stern of an airplane floating on water.

However, the man did not seem to notice the stowaway. After entering the cabin, he continued forward towards the cockpit. Edward felt the man's mass moving forward in the airplane. For a few minutes everything was quiet and still. Then he felt an external force pushing the airplane backwards and shortly afterwards the powerful turboprop engine started working. Slowly the speed of the propeller increased and soon everything was a rumbling chaos.

Edward felt the adrenaline surge through him. Where was this heading? He hadn't anticipated things escalating so quickly. It had been years since his job stirred this kind of excitement - and he'd been through more than a few tense situations. But despite everything, he felt calm where he lay behind the wooden crates in the soft and secluded luggage section and if something should go wrong, he always had his service weapon.

He couldn't help wondering what Kvarnbring was up to. The old goat was probably still sitting in his office, chain-smoking and twirling his mustache.

The craft made a few turns and then shot through the water. After a minute it lifted off from the calm bay and Edward noticed that it was already past 19. Through the window he saw that dusk was not far away. He was amazed that it was so late. The search along the two forest roads with all the small paths and other detours must have taken several hours. He followed the terrain with his eyes and assessed that the pilot was flying north along the coast and the Åland Sea.

After half an hour, the aircraft started to lose altitude. The sun was about to disappear behind the horizon and it was difficult to judge where they were. All he could see was a shimmering red sea and a jumble of small islands and islets. The pilot set the amphibious craft down in a passage between two islands. The surface was calm so it could hardly be very far off the coastal strip. The pontoons sank into the water as the craft lost speed. Shortly afterwards, the engine was switched off and they lay bobbing in the water.

A few minutes passed without anything happening. Then he saw the shadow of a large boat through the cabin window. It was the broadside of a small freighter of some kind and it was moving very slowly past the airplane. Then he heard the sound of a motorboat approaching. When it was almost level with the airplane, the pilot went back and opened the cabin door. Edward was on edge. He took out his service weapon and put the safety on with sweaty fingers. This was the moment it would happen. Some kind of handover would take place. Voices were heard and a few phrases exchanged in broken English, but this time it was not possible to make out more than a few words.

The airplane lurched and the door to the smuggling compartment opened. The wooden boxes were moved to the motorboat, one by one.

He saw that someone in the boat was receiving the boxes but it was too dark to see his face. Instead, he focused on the louver that separated the luggage compartment from the added space with the crates. Through a gap he could see straight into the dimly lit cabin. No food or anything else seemed to be moved from there, only the boxes from the smuggling room. Edward lay motionless and barely dared to breathe. At any moment the pilot could pull up the shutter and then he would not fail to discover him.

Soon the boxes were delivered and the motorboat quickly departed. Everything went in just a few minutes. The pilot closed the cabin door, went back to the cockpit and started the engine. The plane hit the gas and soon they were airborne again.

Edward exhaled and wiped the sweat from his hands and face. He took the safety off the gun and put it back in its holster. Through the window he saw the islands again as faint dark silhouettes and tried to find a reference point that he recognized. Using the horizon, he realized that the pilot was continuing in a northerly direction. He was surprised that the aircraft did not turn back south now that the handover was completed.

But there were more questions than that. What did he actually witness? Clearly, it was some form of smuggling. The contraband consisted of small metal cans filled with a moss-like substance. The cans were filled in the boathouse, which appeared to be some kind of distribution center. The metal cans were then packed into small wooden boxes that were flown to a pre-designated meeting point somewhere in the outer archipelago of the Åland Sea. There, a ship was waiting to transport the cans to an unknown destination. Presumably to some eastern state on the other side of the Baltic Sea. One thing was certain: the contents of the cans must be extremely valuable. Otherwise they wouldn't have gone to so much trouble. The airplane alone must cost tens of millions and operating it would be expensive too. The whole operation was probably illegal as hell, but apart from that he had to admit that he was might impressed with the arrangement. This was managed by professionals, not ordinary gangsters.

He needed to call Kvarnbring as soon as possible and tell him what he'd found out, but of course that was not something to think about while he was huddled in the luggage compartment of an amphibious aircraft, with unknown final destination.

Edward paused in his thoughts and lay down in the narrow storage space to straighten his back. There was nothing else to do and it was actually quite comfortable and plenty of space once laying down on the back. The sound of the engine was soporific and the thin air soon put him asleep. He dreamt that he was flying.

CHAPTER 9

To My Schatzi

William was alone in the breakfast room, occupying the most secluded spot with a view through a large window. Papusa had not yet appeared and for the moment he was content to be alone. Physically and mentally exhausted as he was, he'd slept deeply and was now taking in the grandeur of nature. Through the window glass he looked out over Lake Storsjön. The air was damp and slightly misty, but the hotel was close to the water and guests could enjoy the view in all directions. A large terrace surrounded the entire building and encouraged people to go out, but William and Papusa seemed to be the only guests at this time of year and the terrace was probably only used during summer.

Breakfast was simple but tasty. After finishing his third cup of coffee, he spread out the mountain maps on the sturdy wooden table. The oldest was wrinkled and yellowed and printed in 1956. The newer ones were from the seventies. The map from the fifties was the largest and most detailed (over a square meter when fully unfolded) so he started searching it, inch by inch. If such a place as Luoktajärvi existed, it would soon make itself known.

As he systematically worked his way through the map from corner to corner, his thoughts turned to Merja. He had already started to process the recent events and felt comfortable letting her back into the game. But where should he start looking? The only clue he had to go on was a short handwritten letter. A paper with *Gällivare Townhouse* printed in the footer along with a switchboard number and an address.

It wasn't much to work with and the few postcards he'd received were all postmarked in different places in northern Sweden. But at least it was a starting point and he was getting closer to the right part of the country anyway. In addition, he had a traveling companion to consider and Malmberget was just outside Gällivare. It was only 400 km away and would take around five hours by car if the traffic was calm, he estimated. It wouldn't be a problem to get there before the town hall closed for the day if he decided to do so. His gaze floated out over the white waters of Storuman and he did not notice that his index finger had long since stopped moving over the mountain map.

He was jolted back to reality when an elderly woman came in and asked if he wanted more coffee. It was the same woman who had been at the front desk yesterday. He guessed that she was the only staff in the hotel: the governess, the receptionist, the maid and the waitress. He said yes, shifted his focus back to the map, and soon realized that he had to start all over again with the finger search.

He didn't know how long he'd been sitting there with the map in front of him when he finally found what he was looking for. At first he just skimmed past the letters without reacting, and it took a few moments before the processing was complete and he could go back. In worn letters it said *Luoktajärvi*. The text was printed just over the border line between Norway and Sweden. To make it clear that Norway was not part of the map, the colors had been toned down, making the text extra difficult to find. Luoktajärvi was marked as a Sámi settlement located between three mountains. The symbol of the Sámi settlement was almost completely hidden by the border line.

What struck him was how remote the place was. It was in the western part of Padjelanta National Park, and there were no roads or even snowmobile trails that were marked and connected the settlement to the rest of civilization. Everything around was wilderness. The closest hint of civilization was the Padjelanta trail and the Staloluokta mountain station.

He drew a circle around the symbol of the coexistence and unfolded the newer maps on the table to see if he could get more information about the place now that he knew where it was. To his surprise, he discovered that it was not marked on any of the other maps he'd found in his grandfather's hiding place. Either the location had been removed from newer maps for one reason or another, or the level of detail was lower. Instead of a settlement or community, there was a small lake on the newer maps.

He thought about what to do next now that he had identified the location, or rather, now that he knew it was a geographical location and not something else. As far as Luoktajärvi was concerned, he didn't really have any reason to visit the place, but curiosity tickled him. In addition, there were a couple of other reasons, the last of which had been creeping up on him more and more over the last few days. Firstly, he would be in the area anyway because he was going to look for Merja. "In the area" meant at least 100 km from civilization, but this was, after all, Lapland where distances were often great. Secondly, a small pang of guilt had begun to gnaw at the back of his mind. He liked to think that the guilty conscience was a growing desire to satisfy his curiosity by unraveling the mystery of the strange leather bag. But there was something more - the growing realization that someone was looking for that money, and it wasn't the goofballs in the Volvo. He needed to understand what happened to the man who drove into the ditch in order to sleep well at night. At the same time, he realized that he couldn't expose himself. It was likely, maybe even very likely, that the owner of the bag was a criminal. Who carries that much cash around without being in trouble with the law in one way or another?

"Good morning, Captain. Are you planning an invasion?"

William was jolted out of his reverie and looked up at Papusa standing in front of the table. She was wearing a black T-shirt and sneakers and had both hands casually tucked into a pair of dark blue stretch jeans. Her hair was damp and tied up in a bun. For some reason, all of this made her look even younger and even more petite.

"Invasion?" he said, tasting the coffee that had long since gone cold.

"All the maps," she said, gesturing to the table cluttered with elaborate maps and booklets strewn across plates and cutlery.

"The maps...well I'm thinking of blowing up the dam in Akkajaure and was looking for the best escape route from there.

He tried to smile ingratiatingly and began folding the mountain maps. Papusa went to get a croissant and a glass of juice, and then sat down opposite him at the table.

"Maybe you're keeping secrets, she tried. Come to think of it, you never told me where you are going and why."

"I am looking for a person, just like you. An old friend I lost touch with many years ago."

"Is that all? Your friend must be very difficult to find given all the maps."

"That's not all... but that's all I can tell you right now. I don't want to drag you into something that's none of your business."

She looked at him with a face that looked as if she'd just listened to a child caught with his fingers in the candy jar and then tried to explain that things were not as they seemed.

"You are not as innocent as you look, behind those round glasses and with your disarming face. At least that's what I think."

"I'm not sure if it's a compliment or an insult."

"Take it as you like. I think you are involved in something illegal."

She leaned back and took a big bite of the croissant without taking her eyes off him. William thought he could see a faint smile in her dark eyes.

"And what makes you think so?"

"Are you kidding me? A few days ago, you gave me a fortune in cash. Were they just lying around in the car? And today you're sitting with a table full of maps and saying that you don't want to involve me in something that I have nothing to do with. Need I say more?"

William opened his mouth to say something but closed it again and leaned back on the sofa with his arms crossed. He looked out over the lake, forgetting for a few seconds that there was someone sitting opposite, watching him with amusement. His thoughts drifted back in time and he remembered the events of the past week. It suddenly felt unreal and at the same time a little uncomfortable. Without thinking, he took another sip of the cold coffee and coughed when it reached his throat.

"I didn't mean to push," said Papusa. "I've been in trouble with the law too. All my life, in fact. It's not something I think about anymore. It's just the way it is."

"So we are in the same situation? Is that what you want to say?"

"I don't know what you have done but I don't care. It can't be that serious. You seem like a decent guy after all. Papusa smiled broadly and poured herself the last of the juice."

"I can't tell you anything," said William. "The less you know, the better for both of us."

"Ok then, as you wish."

She shrugged and looked out of the window. It was now ten in the morning.

"We are not really Roma," she said suddenly and without taking her eyes off the window.

"What do you mean by that?" William put the coffee cup down on the table.

"We, my family, are not real Roma."

He looked at her across the table. It struck him for the first time that she didn't actually look like a gypsy. Sure, her hair was dark but she looked more like a central European. Perhaps Austrian, South

German or possibly Slavic in origin.

"What are you then?" he asked.

"We are Jews. Among many other things. My great-grandmother grew up in the Sudetenland on the border between what was then Czechoslovakia and Germany. Her name was Kristyna. When Hitler took over the Sudetenland in 1938, she fled east to Hungary. She could not have been more than a teenager then. She lived there for 5-6 years before she met a man in Budapest and got pregnant, he was my great-grandfather. Soon after, she was forced to flee again. Kristyna, who was still pregnant, went east to Romania with many other Jews and my great-grandfather remained in Budapest where he was captured a few months later by the Russians who thought he was working as a spy."

"So your great-grandfather was Hungarian?"

"No, he was Swedish."

"Swedish?"

"Well, at least according to my mother. According to her, his name was Raoul and he came from Sweden. Raoul Wallenberg."

William gave a sudden laugh and then picked up the cup of coffee again before he remembered the cold tar-like sludge at the bottom. He leered at Papusa and expected her to be laughing or giggling as well, but she just calmly gazed back at him across the table.

"Raoul Wallenberg?" William gave Papusa a suspicious look and unconsciously reached for the coffee cup again with one hand. "Do you mean the famous Raoul Wallenberg? The one who saved jews? Give me a break."

"Yes, I know it sounds strange. And according to the stories, Raoul managed to escape from Hungary."

"Are you inventing a story just to cheer me up?"

"I only tell you what my mother told me and what her mother and father told her. But I am not making anything up. I swear that I am telling the truth."

"Wallenberg was captured by the Russians in 1945 and transferred to Moscow where he was executed as a spy two years later."

"That is the official version. One of many. According to my mother, he got into a fight with a German soldier and managed to overpower him. He stole the soldier's clothes and identity papers and left his own with the soldier. In the chaos of the final battles for Budapest, the German soldier was arrested by Russian security services shortly afterwards and Wallenberg managed to escape on a German transport plane when soldiers were being evacuated from the war zone. There were witnesses to the events, including a Jewish woman who later fled to Romania and met Kristyna in a refugee camp."

"But what became of him if he was not captured and executed?"

"There is no definite information, but according to the story, Wallenberg ended up in Norway on the same transport plane that was also used to fly German soldiers home from Norway at the end of the war."

"This sounds too incredible to be true," said William.

"I know. But my great-grandfather spoke fluent German, he looked like any other Aryan or German soldier, and had already spent several months deceiving the Germans in Budapest. He knew exactly what to do. Besides…"

Papusa fell silent, bent a little to one side and dug in her jeans pocket with one hand. Then she put some folded papers on the table and with a barely perceptible smile on her lips.

"What am I looking at?"

"These are three copies of postcards. The first one is postmarked January 29, 1945 in Berlin and was sent to my great-grandmother's sister in Gyula, Eastern Hungary. Do you see the words written in the middle of the postcard?" Papusa pointed to the center of the copy of the postcard. It read *To my Schatzi*.

"*Schatzi* roughly translates to *darling* or *sweetie*. It was apparently the word my great-grandfather used when addressing Kristyna."

"Now, I don't want to spoil the party, but isn't that something that could be on thousands of postcards?"

"Remember that the postcard was dated about a couple of weeks after the traces of Raoul disappeared and it was sent to the sister whose husband was already dead. He was killed in the war in 1944. And who would mix Swedish and German on a postcard?"

"But still…" William didn't really know what to say. It was all so unreal, yet it made sense in some strange way. The fact that Papusa would make all this up just to make fun of him was even more unlikely.

"And then this…" Papusa put the second copy on the table and pointed with her finger. It clearly said *To my Schatzi* and in the same handwriting: *To my darling*.

"It was stamped on Tromsø on February 27, 1945," Papusa continued. "This postcard was also sent to my great grandmother's sister."

"And the last copy"? William asked in a whispering tone.

"The last postcard is the strangest. It's dated March 1945 and contains the same text, *To my Schatzi*, but it doesn't say where it was sent from. But do you see the picture here?"

She pointed to a black and white image copied next to the text.

"Is it the front of the postcard?" William asked.

"Yes, exactly, and I think I know what the picture is. It's Tranoy Lighthouse in northwestern Norway. The lighthouse tower itself was built in the 30s, but the buildings around it are older. So the lighthouse and the buildings around it looked exactly like this in 1945 and still look like this today."

"Is that where you are heading?"

"Yes, that's where I'm going. And look here, she pointed again at the lighthouse."

"What are you pointing at?"

"See the cross? Someone has deliberately put a cross on one of the windows of the lighthouse."

"I see now," said William. "But what do you hope to find?"

"I do not know. But I have nothing to lose. My mother asked me to go because I speak both Swedish and English."

"Is Kristyna alive today?"

"No, she died already in the sixties. At the end of the war, she went to a temporary refugee camp in the Romanian countryside with many other Jews. Hungary was officially fighting on the side of the Russians and almost all the men took part in the war. My grandfather was born in a tent city with almost only women. A little later they came into contact with Roma and my grandfather grew up and became part of them."

"So your grandmother is Roma?"

"No, not even my grandmother is Roma. She is Russian, from the Black Sea region. The whole of Europe was falling apart at that time and whole towns and villages were leveled. People were fleeing everywhere. My grandmother is still alive."

"Why has it taken 80 years for someone to start digging into this?"

"My great-grandmother never saw these cards. They were found in a family drawer that came from my great-grandmother's sister in Gyula, in Hungary. The postcards were actually discovered by my mother. She knew that her grandfather and grandmother had met in Budapest during the war and that her grandfather was Swedish and called Raoul. It was she who realized that it must be about the famous Swede who was supposedly captured and executed after the war. But since the trail ended in 1945 anyway, the only difference being that it ended in Norway and not in Budapest or Moscow, she did nothing with the information. Until a few months ago, when she sent me here."

Papusa suddenly looked tired. As if the last few days and weeks had started to take their toll. They sat for a long time while both looked out the window in silence.

CHAPTER 10

In Gällivare

Security Service Archive, Internal Correspondence

Date: April 5th, 1945

From: Chief of Staff, General Staff Corps

To: Head of the Public Security Service

Once again, I have to agree with your assessment of the lunatics in Luoktajärvi. Not only did they manage to deceive a whole German company, men and all, straight into a frozen mountain lake with bad ice. They also succeeded in overpowering and disarming the Swedish fighter platoon of thirty men. The platoon was sent back on foot and without weapons, but at least they got to keep their clothes. The headman of the villagers is reportedly called Sáhkár Kuoljok. The platoon commander remembers in particular how he pulled down his trousers and showed his ass as the men marched away.

I have informed the commander-in-chief about the embarrassment and he wants to keep a lid on it. The lunatics in the village seem to be doing best on their own and if more German soldiers come, he does not think we are helped by our own soldiers anyway.

He insists, however, that the reconnaissance at the border must be resumed again, but at a safe distance from the madmen and with a focus on the remaining German occupation force. He believes that they may try to cross the border to Sweden somewhere in the Laponian Wilderness.

Chief of staff

❋ ❋ ❋

When Edward woke, everything was dark and eerily silent. He lay on his back, motionless, in the exact position he'd fallen asleep. For a moment, disoriented and groggy, he couldn't remember where he was. Then, like a slow-moving tide, reality crept back in. He held his breath and listened. Somewhere in the distance, barely audible, came the low, steady hum of an engine - not the sputter of a propeller, but the smooth, deep roar of a jet. It sounded like a jet airplane taking off. But there were no voices, no footsteps, no signs of movement inside the cabin. The stillness was unsettling. Had the pilot left the plane? The thought lodged itself in Edward's mind, bringing with it a ripple of unease.

He raised himself up on one elbow and pulled the sunshade apart a few centimeters to orient himself. Sunlight seeped straight into his face and he had to pull the shade back a little to avoid being blinded. After a while, his eyes adjusted and he could look out. At first he saw nothing. Just a large, white, flat surface. Then he realized he was in a snow-covered airport. Further away in his right field of vision was an airplane. Probably a standard Boeing 737 or Airbus 320. Further to the left he saw the terminal building and a couple of service cars. Outside the terminal building he saw a boarding staircase on wheels. It was definitely a small airport but impossible to tell where.

He looked at his watch and saw that it was just after six in the morning. The weather was slightly hazy, just enough to dim the sunlight slightly. The phone vibrated in his inside pocket. He thought for a moment that it was lucky that he at least had the presence of mind to turn it off. The display showed an internal police number. He didn't answer. Now was not the time. When the ringing finally stopped, he noticed several missed calls - all from the day before. Including one from Kvarnbring and one from Dan in the analysis department. He decided that they had to wait until he got off the plane.

He pulled up the shutter of the extra cargo hold and saw that it was empty. This was to be expected, given yesterday's activities. He shuffled into the empty space and into the cabin. His back felt stiff and his shoulders ached. Edward got back on his feet and saw that both the cabin and cockpit were empty. Through the windows he got a better overview of the situation. The airplane stood at one end of a large snow-covered terminal slab. Behind the plane was a hangar with an open door.

Edward pulled the handle of the cabin door and it opened outwards. Then he jumped down on the ground and looked around. It felt strange with an amphibious aircraft on the ground, but the landing wheels stuck out from the pontoons and then it worked like any other airplane. He walked over to the opening in the hangar and looked in. The building was lit up and inside were a couple of small propeller planes. At the nose wheel of one of the planes, a man in overalls was kneeling and struggling with something. Edward guessed that the guy was a mechanic.

No one else seemed to be in the hangar, so he decided to approach the guy with determined steps. He only reacted when he heard Edward's authoritative voice behind his back.

"Are you the person responsible for this hangar?"

The overall man stood up as if at attention, his back straight and fumbling with his greasy hands as if he was unsure where to hide them.

"Yes, I am the mechanic here."

He saw that the man was young, in his twenties and perhaps a few years older. On his chest was written in large letters: *Gällivare Airport*. That solved that question, Edward thought. But if the pilot had flown straight to Gällivare, it wouldn't have taken much more than 5-6 hours to get here. That meant that they could have landed several hours ago.

"I have some questions about the Cessna outside the hangar. Do you know how long it's been there?"

"It was already here when I got here. My shift started at four this morning. But... but who are you? You're not supposed to be here."

Edward decided to take advantage of the opportunity and took out his badge. He held it out in front of the pale mechanic's face.

"I'm from the Security Service, investigating a crime. The amphibious airplane out there is part of the investigation. I would need to ask you a few brief questions."

The mechanic just nodded and wiped his hands on his overalls.

"Do you know why the plane is outside the hangar?"

"It is in for a short repair and overhaul. One landing gear needs to be checked. After that we have scheduled maintenance, a refuel and then we roll her out again."

"How long will it be here? When will the aircraft be used again?"

"I just know it's going in after these two." He made a sweeping gesture towards the two propeller carts in the hangar. "I guess it will come in tomorrow and be ready the day after. No one has given me a deadline and it usually takes as long as it takes. "

"Have you met the pilot or anyone else who came on the plane?"

"No, I have never met or even seen anyone flying this plane. But it comes in occasionally for repair or service. Once a month or so. It's always outside the hangar when I go on my shift. Should I ask the hangar manager if he knows anything?"

Edward thought about the possibility of getting more information but decided it was best not to. He didn't want to reveal his presence too much. He narrowed his eyes at the young mechanic who unconsciously took a half step back.

"Now I would like you to do three things. The first is not to say a word about me being here. Otherwise you could ruin the whole stakeout. Second, I want you to call me if you see anyone boarding the plane. Third, I want you to show me out of here again."

The man nodded gravely as he took the hastily scribbled down phone number and gestured with his hands for Edward to follow him. They went through a side door that led back out to the snow-powdered parking area again. They continued along a metal fence that connected the hangar to the terminal building. Halfway between the buildings was a revolving gate with a code lock. The man pulled his card and let Edward out. They nodded briefly at each other in agreement before the overall man turned on his heel and walked back to the hangar.

Edward looked around and then followed the fence towards the small terminal but from the outside. He passed a long-term parking lot and then a very short taxi queue consisting of a lonely taxi driver half-sitting on the hood smoking a cigarette. He went into the terminal building and read the departure board. There were two Stockholm flights during the day that he could catch. One in the morning and one in the afternoon. If he jumped on a flight during the day, he had to rely on the mechanic calling soon. Otherwise, he risked losing his way. If he stayed, at least he would be in place when, or if, the phone rang. Besides, he wondered if it wasn't time to pay a visit to that mountain village. After all, he was looking for an escaped patient who was reportedly from this very village. And possibly also a criminal who lacked a telephone, a driver's license and a pilot's license.

Edward decided to stay for a few days, at least to begin with. His back was stiff, his stomach empty, and he badly needed a shower. There were also calls to make - conversations he couldn't put off much longer. After a quick stop at the restroom, he returned to the taxi queue, trying to pull himself together for whatever came next.

The taxi driver, cigarette dangling from his lips, looked up and asked if he needed a ride into town. Edward, who'd had a moment to gather his thoughts about this unfamiliar place, nodded and got into the car. He assumed *town* meant Gällivare, but he didn't ask. This wasn't the time to reveal how little he knew about where he was.

Ten minutes later, the taxi rolled into a hotel in central Gällivare. Edward checked into a room and then went down to the small shop at the reception and bought the essentials: toothbrush and toothpaste, underwear, socks and a triangle sandwich. He then went up to his room to make his calls and maybe get a few hours of sleep in a soft bed.

Tube peeked out through the curtain gap in the caravan for probably the hundredth time. Just like before, the car was standing there in the same place, about fifty meters from the caravan. It effectively blocked the only exit from the campsite while the location allowed a good view of virtually the entire area.

On only one occasion did they catch a glimpse of the person and that was when, under cover of darkness, he'd left the vehicle to pee. In the dim moonlight they had seen that it was a uniformed man. More precisely, a police officer. The first time they suspected that they were being followed was on their way back from Särna when a police car appeared in the rearview mirror. They had both been on edge because of the valuable cargo, but it wasn't until half an hour later that they realized they were probably being followed.

By the time they had passed Avesta, there was no longer any doubt and the atmosphere of tension turned to one of great frustration. They were convinced that William Slepner had tricked them and set the police on them.

"That damn pig screwed us over," whined Funnel as they started to approach the campsite.

The police car had stayed all night and now it was still there, waiting like a hyena watching over a wounded wildebeest. They never had a chance to hide the bags of money. The boxes remained in the recess where the spare tire should have been, hidden only by the thin trunk carpet. If the policeman decided to search the car, he could not fail to find the money. The mood was desperate, but there was nothing they could do.

✳ ✳ ✳

It was late afternoon when they reached the town hall Gällivare. William had been driving for over four hours and his travel companion was asleep ever since they rolled past the monumental landmarks of Porjus, the gigantic water dam and the large-scale hydroelectric power station, two symbols of industrial ambition in the remote north. The landmarks passed unnoticed as Williams' mind was spinning at full speed. Everything Papusa had told him was so incredible that he could barely process it. He simply needed to disconnect his thoughts in order to focus on his own errands.

Once in Gällivare he parked the car outside the town hall and let Papusa sleep. William hoped that he would be able to find the right person, whoever that might be, and that the officials would be more accessible than they were in his own town hall. There, you were lucky if you saw anyone at all inside the reception or the rest of the building. If it wasn't sickness, childcare or vacation, it was meetings, workshops, education or business trips. It was like a black hole where people disappeared without a trace and those few who had not yet been swallowed by the black hole were quick to refer to other people or other days of the week and then disappear into thin air themselves.

He doubted Merja still worked there. After all, it had been five years since he received the letter - neatly written on official town hall stationery. She seemed to have moved around a lot already at that time. Still, he was tense and perhaps a little worried. He was not quite ready to meet her after all the action in the last few days. In addition, he was rather disheveled and tired after the long car ride.

At the reception desk sat an old gray-haired man with glasses. William introduced himself as a friend of a person who had worked at the town hall several years ago. Her name is Merja, he explained, and he thought she may have been a temp for a while, working on

181

financial matters. He described her appearance and age. The man at reception was helpful and suggested that Berit could help. He assured her that if anyone knew who Merja was, it was Berit. Berit had worked here for a hundred years. Maybe two hundred, the man joked.

The receptionist called Berit who answered almost immediately. He explained the case and passed the phone to William.

"I think I know who you mean," said Berit. "She was hired and probably worked here four or five years ago. Who are you, then?"

William clasped his hands and suppressed a roar of excitement.

"I am just an old friend. We lost touch many years ago. Do you happen to know where she's gone?"

"Oh, I see. In that sense. No, I don't know where she's gone. People come and go these days. There's so much rotation of people in this house. But I remember most of them, you see. She was easy to remember. Colorful girl. Good with numbers and quick-witted."

"Do you think there is anyone else here who knows where she might have gone? Someone she was hanging out with?"

William's disappointment must have shone through to the other end of the line. At least the receptionist looked at him sympathetically.

"No, I don't think so. She was only here a couple of days a week and for a single summer, you see. But I would ask Gunvor. Yes, Gunvor knows for sure."

"Gunvor? Who... who is that?"

"Yes Gunvor Lindstrom, the landlord. That's where she lived when she worked in the area. But I do not know if Gunvor is still alive. She was a very sick, poor woman. Had all sorts of issues."

"Do you know where Gunvor lives... or lived for that matter? Is it someone you know?"

"Everyone knows Gunvor. She has lived here all her life. Now she's old, probably ninety. If she's still alive. When her old man died, she started renting out rooms. Mostly to get in touch with people, they say."

"Does she live in town?" William repeated.

"She lives in Malmberget. Along the main street. The big yellow house beyond the grocery store. Located on the same street, you see. A huge house. As old as her. But your girl probably doesn't live there anymore. Gunvor stopped renting out rooms when she got too sick."

William thanked her for her help and went back to the car. Papusa woke up when he got into the driver's seat. He told her they'd both been lucky - the tracks led to Malmberget, giving them both a reason to head there. Since she had no plans for the day, they agreed that Papusa would come with him to visit the older woman.

He drove straight to Malmberget to try to find the yellow house. It didn't take many minutes before he located both the grocery store and the big house. It was from the turn of the century and built in two hefty floors. The carpentry joy was visible in every corner and the size of the house was unusual in his part of Sweden where most buildings are small and relatively new. Most of what changed and evolved in the village followed the same frequency as the mining cycle, albeit slightly out of phase in time.

He stopped in front of the turn-of-the-century building and made his way up the cobbled path. It struck him how freshly painted the house looked, and how meticulously the grounds were maintained. Not something a ninety-year-old lady could manage. The doorbell was modern and the signal echoed through the house. Soon the door opened and a woman in her thirties greeted him kindly. She was tanned and blonde with a short modern haircut and dressed in light-colored clothes. When she spoke, it was without a trace of the broad northern dialect that the woman and man at the town hall had spoken.

William was pretty sure he'd come to the right house but it was obviously the wrong woman.

"I'm sorry to drop by unannounced, but my name is William Sleipner, and I'm looking for an older woman named Gunvor. I'm guessing that's not you," he said, offering a tentative, hopeful smile.

"You've come to the right place," said the woman, returning the smile. "Gunvor is my grandmother. She's been unwell lately and now lives in a nursing home not far from here. What's the matter?"

William wished he'd spent a few minutes changing his fleece sweater for something more presentable and maybe even used some deodorant. He suddenly felt like a very sloppy salesman in front of the attractive woman in the doorway.

"It's a long story but I'm actually looking for one of Gunvor's former lodgers. She lived here for a period several years ago and worked at the town hall in Gällivare. I was advised to come here."

The woman looked at him suspiciously at first, searching him with her eyes from head to toe. But once she'd decided that he was neither a missionary, nor a salesman, nor a burglar, she thawed out.

"I understand that. Unfortunately, I can't help you myself. I have no connection to either Gällivare or Malmberget, apart from my grandmother. My husband and I took over the house when my grandmother became ill. She's been in and out of the hospital ever since and last year we arranged for a place at a nursing home nearby. What I can do is to show you where the nursing home is and introduce you to my grandmother. It will be easier for you to visit her when you are with me."

"That would be extremely kind of you. I have traveled days to get here."

She held out her hand and introduced herself. She then asked William to follow her as she drove ahead of him. The place was only a kilometer away. She led him through a couple of corridors before they came to a dimly lit ward. In a large lounge, some elderly people sat in front of a TV. In one corner, two older men sat in armchairs playing chess. The blonde woman exchanged a few words with a nurse and then moved on through the lounge to a corridor with a number of numbered rooms. William followed.

She stopped at one of the rooms halfway down the corridor. The door was ajar as in most rooms. She signaled William to stay outside and then disappeared into the room. After a few minutes she came out again.

"You are lucky. She's awake and it's one of her better days. God knows how many good days she has left. She'll see you now. I'll wait outside and you two can talk in peace."

William thanked her and entered through the doorway. The room was small but well laid out. A small hallway served as both entrance and kitchenette. Adjacent to the hallway was a private toilet and straight ahead was a combined bedroom and living room in miniature. The living room basically consisted of a sofa, a couple of chairs, a floor lamp and a small round table. The woman was lying in a half-folded steel bed in the bedroom area. She was awake and looking at him curiously.

"Come in, said Gunvor in a weak voice. You've traveled a long way to find an old friend, I see".

William walked up to the steel bed and stopped at one side. In the dim light, the woman looked ancient. Her face was gaunt and her skin dry and wrinkled, but the eyes were alert and searching.

"I'm very grateful that you can receive me, even though... well even though... it's late."

"Even though I look more dead than alive, you mean?" The woman smiled at William when he didn't know what to say. She blushed a few times before continuing:

"Who are you looking for? I've had a few lodgers over the years."

"Her name is Merja and she worked for a while at the municipal building in Gällivare. That was about five years ago. But it's quite possible that she worked in other places in the area too."

William started to describe her but the old woman interrupted him:

"I know Merja. She lived with me from time to time. She worked in different places around here and then she rented one of my rooms. A sweet girl. She helped me with so many things when I started to get worse. She was my arms and legs at the end. Do you two know each other?"

"Yes, we are... it's complicated. We know each other well."

Gunvor looked at him with a hint of a smile. William waited for her to continue, but the old woman started to cough and rattle, and then she lay there catching her breath. He waited a while until she had calmed down before asking the crucial question.

"Do you know where she went?"

"I think she used to go back to her home village. At least that's what she told me. Every week she went back. But it's been years since I saw her. Maybe she's somewhere else now."

"Did she ever tell you the name of her hometown?"

The old woman cringed and then looked up at William.

"She was very sparing about her private life. But at one point she told me about a little village in the mountains."

"A village? Is it a place you know?"

"Yes, and that's probably why she told me. We got close, you know. Such a sweet girl."

She fell silent and went through another rinse program. This time it sounded worse. William asked if he could do anything but she just waved her hand dismissively. Soon she looked up at him again. He got the impression that she *wanted* to tell him this.

"I was born in a Sámi village not far from Ritsem. I lived there until I was seventeen, when the whole family moved away. Those were troubled times. We heard rumors that German soldiers and Norwegian resistance fighters had clashed just a few miles away across the border. We were afraid of what the war would bring, so we moved to Gällivare and then Malmberget. I have remained here ever since."

She fell silent again, her face grimaced and her body tensed. As if it was preparing for the coming coughing attack but it didn't come and the woman exhaled and continued.

"When I was a child, I heard about a mountain village on the border between Norway and Sweden, just a few miles from our own community. The inhabitants were said to be outlaws and homeless. They were neither Sámi nor Swedish or Norwegian. There were nasty rumors about them. Rumors that they stole reindeer and lived around. That they were violent and dirty."

"Was she from that village?"

"Yes, she was from there. I think she told me because I had grown up in the area myself and had heard all the rumors. She said it was all a lie."

"Do you know the name of the village? Does it have a name?"

"It is called Luoktajärvi. In Sámi we call it something else. You could never pronounce it."

William stopped breathing for a few seconds. Luoktajärvi, that's where the bag came from! Luoktajärvi was the ghost town that had disappeared from the maps. He could hardly believe that it was a coincidence that a more or less unknown village made itself known twice in the same day.

"You know about Luoktajärvi? Almost no one does these days."

"Merja... Merja might have told me at some point," he lied.

He didn't want to bring up the case even though he was pretty sure that no information would leave this room. He hesitated whether to ask anything more about Merja, given that the two seemed to have been in close contact. It was increasingly clear that their contact, their romance, had been one big cloud of fog. An undemanding happiness in a bubble without beginning or end. Suddenly the bubble was there and just as suddenly it was gone. He wanted to ask what Merja's surname was, but the question seemed so stupid that he couldn't ask it and claim to know her at the same time.

William looked at the old woman in the bed. Gunvor was her name. She was around ninety now, living in a care home in Malmberget. She'd grown up in a Sámi village during the war and had spent most of her life in a yellow house not far from here. After her husband passed away, she began renting out rooms for companionship, but her health had since declined. She talked about sons and daughters and granddaughters and their husbands and pretty much everyone else in the town until she started to look tired. Frustrated, he realized he knew more about Gunvor and her family - people he'd only just met - than he did about the woman he'd once shared a relationship with, the very person he'd traveled across Sweden to find.

The old woman in the bed was suddenly asleep, rustling peacefully with each exhalation. He stood for a while in the dim light and then went out to the waiting blonde. She asked if his questions had been answered and he nodded thoughtfully. They parted at the parking lot and he watched her as she headed back the way they came. The sun was low in the sky and he was beginning to feel both hungry and tired.

When he got back into the car, Papusa was gone. In her place there was a handwritten note on the dashboard.

I have to continue my journey by myself. Thank you for everything. Good luck with Luoktajärvi. /Papusa

On the passenger seat, the old map lay carelessly folded. He didn't even have to unfold it to find the ring he had drawn around the symbol of the Luoktajärvi community. He chuckled and sank into the seat. The map had been in the bag behind the driver's seat and she must have been curious. There are no limits for that girl, he thought. It wasn't surprising, considering her background. He folded the map and put it in the glove compartment.

He went back to Gällivare and checked into the first good hotel he could find. He left his luggage in the car but took most of the money with him, everything that lay loose in the luggage and not hidden in the car's chassis. He collected the notes and put them in a backpack together with a change of clothes and a toiletry bag. Once in the hotel room, he took a shower and put on new clothes. Then he went out again to find somewhere to eat and make plans for tomorrow. He already missed his travel companion.

✳ ✳ ✳

Security Service Archive, Internal Correspondence

Date: February 19, 1964

From: Commander of I19/IV, Skier Battalion

To: Head of the Third Squad of the State Police

Hello Bertil,

I hope you had the opportunity to read the report that I sent last week. In addition to the observations set out in the report and clearly explained by Lt Anders Thulin, I would also like to highlight some remarkable things that Anders explained orally.

The reason why this is not included in the report is that it only focuses on the reconnaissance for the clearing work after the crashed helicopter. The instructions have always been not to move near any Sámi settlements. I would like to point out that Lt Thulin has in no way violated these instructions, but during the week he spent in the area he has come into contact with a small mountain community that is not marked on the map. I cannot judge whether the information is of value but I will leave that to you to decide.

According to Lt Thulin, the village and its immediate surroundings are located in a large valley surrounded by three mountais. In winter, such a valley should reasonably be a cold spot, especially this far north. But most of the valley-sink was snow-free far up the mountain sides. In the center of the valley-sink, a light mist rose from what Thulin thought was a lake. He thought that perhaps no one had noticed this before because the village is very inaccessible.

The inhabitants rarely seem to leave the valley floor but Thulin observed some activity on two occasions. The first occasion was when the reindeer left the village for winter grazing via a pass in the western part, i.e. towards the Norwegian side. But there also seem to be alternative routes. On the second occasion, two young men were observed "emerging from the mountain", as Lt Thulin put it. It was in the middle of the night on the eastern side. The men were moving

* * *

Edward lay half-asleep in his hotel bed while he listened to the recorded voice messages. The most interesting call came from Dan in the analysis department - he had called five times. Yesterday, while Edward was sneaking around like a burglar, Dan had a breakthrough in the search for the white Volvo and its owner. During the same afternoon, it was caught on camera by a traffic surveillance camera north of Borlänge.

The camera's task was to collect statistics on which vehicles were using selected roadways. Together with a number of air-filled "tubes" placed over the roadway, a fairly complete picture could be obtained of all vehicles using a particular stretch of road. Two parallel air tubes could, among other things, measure a vehicle's speed by recording the time between the first and second pass of the front wheels. It could also give a fairly clear indication of which vehicle it was by using the speed to calculate the wheelbase between the front and rear axles and then comparing the information with a database; thousands of wheelbases were stored in a database where most vehicle types had a known distance between the wheel axles. In the case of a vehicle based on a very generic car body, the camera, which took a picture of the license plate number, could be used to make the final assessment. The camera was expensive to use and often gave false readings if the license plate was dirty or dented. That's why it only went off when the airbags failed the task. A complete set was called a "traffic monitoring station" and this was unfortunately rigged just north of Borlänge.

If not for one small detail, Tube and Funnel would have slipped past the traffic monitoring station unnoticed. The Volvo they were driving was a common sight on Swedish roads, and the camera had automatically captured its license plate. When the system cross-checked the number with the vehicle registry, it flagged something unusual: the car was officially listed as parked. All such discrepancies were automatically passed on to the police and in this case there was even a search for the license plate in question. A non-uniformed officer from the traffic offenses department had thus contacted Dan at Dataanalys to confirm the result. Dan had recognized the car and then, in the absence of further instructions, asked a traffic police officer in Borlänge to follow the white Volvo with two guys inside. Much to the chagrin of the traffic police, the tailing had not ended until the vehicle stopped at a campsite outside Westridge. There, without further explanation, a local police unit had taken over. The local police had been holding the fort for almost 24 hours now, questioning the purpose of the company.

"What do you want to do with the guys? Bring them in for questioning? You need to respond to the local police as soon as possible. These are things that are beyond my authority, but I had no choice."

"I'll take it up with Kvarnbring and then we'll contact the police unit at the campsite. Thank you very much Dan. I know this is not your area but you have done me a great favor. In fact, I have one more thing I could use help with. If I send a small bag with a moss-like substance directly to you, could you or someone else there analyze the substance?"

"In that case, it's the guys at organic analysis. You know, the ones who dig in the dirt."

"Then this job is perfect for them. I'd like to know what's in the bag as soon as you can."

"I'm sure we can fix that. By the way, where are you?"

"I'm in a hotel room in Gällivare and will probably stay up here for a few days. I'll talk to Kvarnbring and let you know what happens next."

They ended the call, and Edward immediately phoned Kvarnbring. There was plenty to discuss, and he hoped there might be some update on Niilla. Maybe he had simply turned up, dazed and disoriented, in another hospital room - or perhaps even in a broom closet. The thought struck Edward as oddly comical.

The conversation was brief. Kvarnbring had no news about either the missing patient or the delegation that went up in smoke. Edward told him about his discoveries and they decided that he would stay and watch the amphibious aircraft and wait for the results of the analysis. Depending on what the answer showed, he would then try to get in touch with Luoktajärvi. After all, it was most likely that Niilla had made it back home. Kvarnbring promised to *sort out the situation at the campsite*, whatever that meant.

Edward stretched out in bed and thought he would try to get a few hours of sleep. Then he would take a walk to a shopping center or mall. He needed clothes and stuff if he was going to stay here for several days. Outside the window, the snow had started to fall. It felt suggestive. A week ago, a rough snowstorm had plagued Stockholm and most of the country, but then spring arrived with sunshine and temperatures of around ten degrees. Now it was time for snow again. He'd need to buy some warm clothes - *and* Kvarnbring could foot the bill, he figured.

The pub was surprisingly cozy and the selection was *really good for a dump like this* as the receptionist at the hotel had put it. The lighting was dim and the decor was mostly heavy dark stained wooden furniture. The rest of the decor was a blissful mixture of everything between heaven and earth and which in its entirety could only satisfy a blind person - walls with wallpaper in indescribable color combinations, deep window niches with colored mosaic glass, lighting consisting of candles, steel lanterns and disco spotlights and on the ceiling above the bar hung an old rowing boat with oars, fishing nets and even some stuffed animals.

The pub did not claim to resemble either an English pub or a cozy inn but if mixed together, and with some props disregarded, the place was actually pleasant. Some bearded visitors had already arrived and were hanging out in the pub section, where there was a big screen showing some English League Cup football match. In the other half of the pub was an inner room with a number of booths and some round tables laid out on a shaggy carpet. One wall was dominated by a giant bookcase, crammed with books and assorted props. In the background, American country music played softly, adding yet another layer to the pub's schizophrenic clash of styles.

William sat in his own booth. Behind him towered a big bookshelf and somewhere in the background music from Kris Kristofferson streamed from hidden speakers. The adjacent booths were still empty.

Weekend or not, he'd decided to spend some of the dubiously acquired cash. So he ordered a drink menu, a bottle of Nebbiolo from Piemonte, a bottle of water, and *Tonight's Slow Cooker* special. The wine had fine notes of barrel, sweet licorice and violet and with a roughness that felt like sandpaper against the tongue and it turned out to fit even better with the food.

After dinner, he ordered an unusual American Brown Ale

followed by a robust Porter. The beer tasting quickly overshadowed the wine, which sat half-empty on the table like a flower vase stripped of its purpose. He wasn't in any rush - the indulgence unfolded slowly, almost ceremoniously.

By seven o'clock in the evening he was a little round underfoot but still in good drinking form. Unbeknownst to him, an older man had taken the booth next door. The man was gray-haired and relatively slim. His age was difficult to gauge - especially given the tasting that had been going on for some time - but if anyone had forced him to guess, he would have said between sixty and seventy. The man seemed deeply engrossed in a book and did not notice William.

By half past seven, more guests had trickled in and four bearded guys suddenly appeared in front of the gray-haired man's booth. He guessed they were miners coming for a beer and some food. The music volume had been raised slightly and William couldn't hear what was being said but he picked up the word *reserved*. It gestured towards the other end of the room and pointed to the small reservation signs placed on most of the tables. The message was not difficult to interpret. William quickly composed himself and invited the older man to his booth. He was sure that there had been no reservations in his own booth while most other tables seemed to be booked already when he arrived.

He felt a little sorry for the man and needed company, after all he'd barely spoken to any living creature in the last week, except Papusa. The man hesitated for a few seconds, then gathered his coat and book and walked over to William. He left behind an almost empty beer glass and the remnants of his meal for the bearded men to inherit. Once the gray-haired man had taken a seat, William extended his hand in greeting.

"William. This table is not reserved. I saw those signs when I arrived."

"Edward, the man replied. I hear you're a foreigner too."

"That's right. Resident in Westridge."

"Same area, Stockholm to be more precise. Are you on a business trip?"

"Vacation, actually. And I'm looking for an old friend who lives up here. I don't really know where she's been staying the last few years so it's a bit of a private detective mission you could say." William was satisfied with his improvised answer. It was barely even a white lie and he hoped he would not have to elaborate on the subject.

"What are *you* doing up here by the way?"

"You could say that I am also looking for a person. But I am here on business. I am a police officer."

William involuntarily tensed every muscle in his body. The blood left his face and he sat stiff as a board for a few moments, unable to stop it. The likelihood of the police knowing anything was microscopic, he knew that. Still, he'd reacted like a burglar caught with the family silver stuffed in his backpack. He could only hope no one had noticed.

"Are you chasing a criminal? William hoped his voice wasn't shaking."

"No, I'm looking for a person who went missing from a hospital a few days ago. He was injured in a traffic accident and may need help."

"Is there any particular reason for the Stockholm police to be involved?"

"He escaped from a hospital outside Stockholm and we believe he is in this area now. I'm actually part of the Security Service, so we work all over the country."

William relaxed. He knew now that the gray-haired man wasn't looking for him. He would hardly have pretended to be a policeman if he wanted to pump him for information or frame him.

"Can I buy the officer a beer or are you on duty?"

Edward replied that an inspector in the Security Service is always on duty, except when sleeping, but that he was happy to have a drink or two during working hours.

William laughed at the icebreaker and ordered two Guinness draught beers. He didn't know anything about the man's beer habits, but couldn't imagine that anyone would reject a Guinness.

They chatted about everything and as more orders were placed from the bar, they became more familiar with each other. Edward talked about his late wife, about the police profession and his plans to retire as soon as possible. William said that he had quit his job and was now looking for a woman named Merja with roots from Lapland.

After the third round, the inspector apologized and said he needed to relieve himself. He disappeared on unsteady legs into the noisy part of the pub and William saw that he was turning the wrong way in his search for the nearest toilet. What remained on their table resembled a battlefield of glasses and bottles. A puffy winter jacket was crumpled against the wall on the bench beside his drinking companion. A price tag from a spot outlet still dangled from the sleeve - clearly, the policeman had come in a rush, caught off guard by the sudden arrival of winter, William thought. Peeking out from the heap of jackets was a book - the same book he seemed to have been reading before the interruption by the bearded quartet.

"You won't be reading any more tonight," William said aloud to himself and picked it up. It wasn't so much a book as a map booklet. An old map booklet from the forties. He had seen enough of those lately. In the middle of the booklet was a hotel room key, the kind that looks like a credit card. William peered out of the booth towards the pub, but the inspector was nowhere to be seen. Filled with beer, wine and unbridled curiosity, he unfolded the map where the card was tucked. It showed a well-known area and in the top left corner, in the middle of the Swedish-Norwegian border, there was a hastily drawn circle around the name Luoktajärvi.

William looked at the paper for a while, trying to take in the significance of what he was seeing. If it had been earlier in the evening, he would probably have panicked or painted one conspiracy theory after another, but now things were different. He was numb - not just from everything he'd consumed that evening, but from the sheer weight of the week behind him. Nothing surprised him anymore. Out of the corner of his eye, he saw the policeman approaching the booth on round feet. William pushed in the plastic key and threw back the map booklet as if it had been a glowing lump of coal.

The policeman sat down in the booth with a bottle of beer in each hand. The corners of his mouth were up and his eyes were shining. William realized that the man was even more in the light than himself and perhaps he could take advantage of the situation for a good cause. They toasted for the umpteenth time and put the bottle to their mouths. The beer still tasted good but time was running out. He didn't think that his new friend would be able to finish the whole beer. William decided to take a chance.

"When you were in the bathroom, I accidentally spilled beer on the table and I was afraid it would have ruined both your book and your jacket. When I picked up the book and examined it to clean it, I couldn't help noticing that you had circled an area."

The policeman scrutinized him with his watery eyes as if to assess whether he was a spy. Then he took another sip.

"That's where he went, that runaway. That sneak."

"To Luoktajärvi?"

"Lokkajärve... Yes, exactly. That's where I think he is..."

"Do you know how to get there? Do you know the location?"

"I have no idea...no idea, my friend. It's in the middle of nowhere. Why do you ask? Are you going there?"

"The girl I'm looking for...Merja. Maybe she's there. An old woman she was staying with temporarily thought so, anyway."

"Then we can go together. Tomorrow..." The policeman was swaying considerably now and William suggested that they should call it a night and go back to their respective hotels. They could meet here again tomorrow at lunch and talk further about Luoktajärvi.

He helped the drunk man into his jacket and guided him toward the door. On the way out, he stopped at the bar to settle the entire bill in cash, leaving a generous tip. Outside, the crisp evening air quickly revived the man, and he managed to make his way back to the hotel on his own. They parted there, agreeing to meet again at the same place for lunch the next day to make a proper plan. "But a bit more orderly this time," the police officer added.

CHAPTER 11

Complications

At exactly twelve o'clock, Edward stepped through the pub door, nursing a mild hangover. All things considered, he thought the price he was paying for the previous night's excesses was fairly lenient. The man from yesterday was already there, waiting. He waved happily from the booth. It was the same place as yesterday, the one at the far end of the room. Edward heaved a sigh of relief. The man, whose name he couldn't remember, had kept his promise and showed up at the pub. Considering yesterday's private party, it was not entirely obvious. Besides, there was a significant risk that he'd fantasized the whole meeting. How likely was it that he would have ended up next to a stranger, a local, who was looking for the same mysterious place as himself?

"You came," said the man as Edward approached the booth. "I wasn't quite sure what we agreed on really."

"That makes two of us. I only remember fragments." Edward sat down opposite the man.

"I must start by thanking you for yesterday. It may have been a bit wet but it was nice to have company."

"I agree with you. I just hope I didn't embarrass us completely. I haven't consumed that much food and beer in years," said the policeman.

"No worries, we are both strangers to this place and the clientele here is not really upper class. I think we blended in well with the other guests. But I must confess that I forgot your name."

"That makes two of us! My name is Edward Johnson and I think you need to refresh my memory too."

"William. William Sleipner to be precise."

They both ordered today's lunch and a nice glass of Coca Cola. They chatted while they ate and the waitress brought them another round of soft drinks. When the meal was over and the coffee had been served, Edward felt it was time to bring up the common problem again.

"You mentioned yesterday that you were looking for a woman who lives in Luoktajärvi."

"Yes, you could say that. I don't know if she lives in Luoktajärvi anymore, but she must have grown up there."

"How do you know her?"

"We had a relationship many years ago and when she moved back up here we lost contact and now... well now I'm going to look her up again."

"How do you plan to get there? I assume you know where Luoktajärvi is."

"I have an old map that shows where the village is. Right on the border if it is correct. I was planning to get a scooter from a place outside Gällivare. They sell and rent out scooters and equipment. It's getting close to the end of the winter season up here so it should be possible to find everything we need.

"Sounds good, I also plan to go there and look for the missing patient. Perhaps we can go together?"

"That sounds just fine to me. I can arrange equipment for you too. He has a lot of stuff."

"Let's agree on that. I guess we need to have the possibility to stay overnight too in case we get stuck in the wilderness."

They continued planning and decided that they would meet

outside Edward's hotel at around nine the next morning. William would pick him up in his car. As they both had a lot of practical things to sort out on their own, they separated and went to their respective hotels.

Edward was pleased with developments so far. He wondered whether he should give Kvarnbring a call and inform him that he intended to go to Luoktajärvi but decided to wait until the evening. Then his good mood would not be ruined and he would also have an opportunity to disturb the old goat on a Friday evening.

What bothered him most was knowing he'd likely miss the Cessna pilot once the service was finished - but that was something he'd have to accept. It also gnawed at him that he'd left home in such a rush. He hadn't brought a thing with him, despite having shopped more than he used to at the local mall just yesterday.

But there was little to be done about his work laptop. It was left in the car - the whole car was left behind. He consoled himself with the fact that it was relatively hidden away and a good distance from Grangården's camp. The good news was that he had his service weapon with him, along with a handful of reports he'd been trying to work through whenever he got the chance.

Now was such an occasion, he reasoned with himself, and swung in through the entrance to get to work.

William was happy to have a traveling companion. Of course, he didn't know much about Edward, but they had a common goal in getting to Luoktajärvi. The fact that the man was a policeman by profession was certainly playing with high stakes, but compared to continuing alone, it was still preferable. Perhaps it would even prove to be an advantage to travel with an experienced professional in those rugged lands. After all, he'd decided to go with his gut and that's exactly what he did. Instead of feeling uncomfortable, it gave him an adrenaline rush. He hadn't told the whole story, of course. Some things were impossible to reveal without digging your own grave, but he'd been quite open about the purpose of his trip. That is, to find Merja.

Just outside Gällivare there was a large and well-stocked dealer of various brands of scooters. In addition to scooters, they also had quad bikes, trailers and accessories. They also sold second-hand equipment. On the pretext that he urgently needed a reliable snowmobile for a glacier research project, he got help quickly. He settled on a large Arctic Cat touring model from the second-hand store.

"It is the largest model available. It is designed for two people and can take a hell of a lot of luggage. A real pack-ass, and you ride like a king. It also has a navigator with satellite connection. You simply cannot get lost." The salesman's eyes twinkled with excitement as he went on.

"If you are going to be away in the wilderness for a longer period of time, we can mount two twenty-liter spare tanks as well. Then I would recommend that you attach a snowmobile sled. Then you can take the glacier home with you and study it."

William replied that he was happy to do so.

After a quick review of the scooter and a short test ride on the backside, he bought two complete sets of scooter clothes: pants, jackets, helmets, gloves, boots and some other stuff. He'd promised his newfound traveling companion that he would take care of all this and luckily the gray-haired man was about the same height and body shape, albeit slightly slimmer, so he just had to take a chance and buy double of everything. Just to be on the safe side, he oversized the boots.

In a side room, they kept extra rental gear. During the busy season, tourists could rent scooters, quad bikes, tents, backpacks, food supplies, and other equipment for their trips. Now, with winter drawing to a close, most of it was packed away.

William asked if he could buy a large tent, two fifty-liter backpacks, a couple of sleeping bags and two sturdy sleeping mats from the rental equipment. He didn't really trust his grandfather's old equipment. The salesman was happy to oblige as they were about to sort out last year's equipment for the coming season. He also helped to stock up on other equipment that might be needed in the mountains, including a satellite phone, shovels and dry food.

At last, William bought a trailer to haul the scooter and sled. The total came to three hundred and eighty thousand. To justify paying in cash, he came up with another lie - he claimed he had recently sold a car and hadn't gotten around to depositing the money. The seller didn't care. His day was made.

❋ ❋ ❋

Security Service archives, internal correspondence, scanned photo
Date: September 24, 1972
From: Arvid Svensson RPS/Sal
To: Carl Gerhard RPS/Sec

Hello Carl,

I have checked the information you gave me and it seems that this Peter Antonsson really comes from the village you mentioned. He is the son of their village elder who, by the way, has been featured in the occasional reconnaissance report from the fifties and sixties. In that case, Peter is not his real name. I attach a photo taken a few years earlier. There are striking similarities with the picture taken at Stockholm University. According to the information I have obtained, he has studied at SU for four years.

I might add that I showed this data to "the boss" and he ordered us to drop it. He was very firm on that point. Just so you know.

/A

***

Edward lay on his hotel bed, reflecting on the reports he'd read over the past few days. The villagers reminded him of the eccentric Gauls from the *Asterix & Obelix* comics. But how much of it was real, and how much had been exaggerated? Was it true that this colony or village, located north of the polar circle in frosty Laponia, sat in a dale where it stayed hot year-round? And what about the steam—was it actually steam, or just mist? But a more puzzling detail was the dates in the reports. The Mountain King was mentioned as far back as World War II. If he had been a very young man then, he'd be at least a hundred years old now - likely even older if he had already been the village leader at the time.

But the strangest thing of all was the photo in the scanned letter from the early seventies. The man in the photo was described as the son of the Mountain King. He once again held up the facial image on Niilla's driver's license next to the picture in the letter. The faces were almost identical. The same hair color, the same eyes, the same birthmark above the right eyebrow. Something was wrong.

He decided to call Kvarnbring.

"Hello, this is Edward. Hope I'm not interrupting."

"No, you don't. I'm still in the office."

"I have decided to look up Luoktajärvi and search for Niilla there. New opportunities have opened up. I met a person yesterday who knows the village and can drive me there. "

He avoided giving too many details. Yesterday was messy enough anyway.

"Well, maybe it's just as well now that you're up there. Have you heard anything from the analysis department?"

"No, not yet but I expect it may take another day or so. If you can get them to run the analysis over the weekend, that would of course be great."

"I'll see what I can do to speed them up."

"Have you sent anyone to the campsite?"

"Yes, I sent Metzner. "

"You sent Metzner? Why?"

"He did a good job actually, and it's related to the traffic accident that he will investigate anyway. Of course, I had to show him the video from the surveillance camera before he left. In any case, Metzner sent home the grumpy local police officer, who spent the night in the car, and then had a chat with the guys in the white Volvo."

"So, was it possible to get anything out of them?"

"One of them seemed to live more or less permanently in a caravan on the campsite. He had broken into every single caravan and stole electricity from a nearby service building. When Metzner pointed this out and added that they had been caught on camera in connection with the traffic accident outside Arlandastad, they became quite cooperative."

"What was their explanation for their actions during the traffic accident?"

"They didn't deny having been at the site, they had stopped to take a piss and discovered the vehicle in the ditch by chance. The man in the car was unconscious when they found him and that's why they called 112."

"But first, they stole a bag from a traffic victim?"

"Yes, that incident would have been a bit more difficult to explain but they stubbornly claimed that the bag was full of clothes and that they got rid of it afterwards."

"Do they seem credible?"

"Well... I wouldn't say that they are what you would refer to as credible persons. But anyway, Metzner didn't have a chance to look for bags, but he stuffed the guys in the back seat and drove them here for questioning. I went out to the campsite myself straight afterwards and searched the caravan and the car. In the trunk I found two plastic bags full of money... They contained six million."

Edward whistled in surprise.

"Wow... how did they explain the money?"

"I questioned them in person a few hours ago and they were pretty mellow when I finished with them. They explained that the money was in the bag in the car but that they had no idea of the contents when they found it. I believe them. These are just ordinary petty thieves. However, they are under the impression that it is the *pig* who framed them, that it is *he* who sent the police after them. They knew that they had been followed ever since Borlänge."

"So who is the pig?"

"They claim that they were robbed of the money. That the *pig* had taken the bag and then returned half of it to frame them."

"So the thieves were tricked by another thief?"

"That's what they claim happened, yes."

"Does this pig have a name?"

"They couldn't even agree on whether he was a pig or a horse but at least his name is William Sleipner. I don't know if they are telling the truth but I don't see why they would make up a complete lie, now that they have been caught with their fingers in the candy jar, so to speak. They even gave me his address. He is a forty-year-old man in Westridge. I guess they want revenge on him for some reason."

Edward's body went cold. The man in the pub had the same name, came from the same place and the age probably matched quite well. His future travel companion. It simply could not be anyone else.

"Did you say William Sleipner?"

"Yes, why? Is it someone you know?"

"No... no, I just thought it was an unusual name. Is it *Sleipner* like that eight-legged horse in Norse mythology?"

"Yes or pig," said Kvarnbring and chuckled into the phone. "Either way, we'll have to question him. And by the way, you have another question to ask Niilla, if you can locate the guy. Why is he traveling around with several million in a bag?"

Edwards' brain went into overdrive.

"I'll try to locate Niilla and will check out Sleipner when I get back. Probably they've just trotted out a name that they don't like now that they're screwed. Or maybe he's testified in some old trial against them."

"Yes, that is probably the case. Anyway, you called *me*, have you got the information you need or was there something more?"

"There are some weird things in the reports you gave me. Something that is not correct in terms of the dates. The Mountain King already appeared in the forties. It's either a different person or he's over a hundred years old. Then it's the same with Niilla.

According to the documents, he studied at Stockholm University as early as the beginning of the seventies - possibly already in the late sixties - but under a different name. I have his driver's license and pilot's license in front of me. It is the same face as in the photo from the seventies document, but slightly older. I saw him in the hospital too. At the time he was partially wrapped in bandages but now that I think about it he had the same birthmark over one eyebrow. According to the licenses he is around fifty. But if the old reports are correct, he is almost eighty years old! Or there are inaccuracies in the reports."

Kvarnbring was silent on the phone. Edward could hear him processing the information at the other end of the copper wire. He was probably twisting his moustache too.

"There are many stories about this village that have not reached the ears of the public. Some are supported by the reconnaissance reports but others are probably just rumors. One rumor says that the inhabitants do not age. This is something that has been circulating for many decades among the Sámi in Laponia. It is of course just an urban legend and nothing more."

"I'm just saying, a lot of this doesn't add up," he said, while privately thinking the whole thing reeked like an open can of sour cream. At its core, it was a smuggling operation involving a large sum of money, an injured man who had mysteriously disappeared, and a series of coincidences too convenient to be real—no matter how imaginative one tried to be. On top of that, his new travel companion appeared to be entangled in it all.

"What will you do with the guys from the campsite?"

"I have already released them. There's not much to go on and until this story is investigated, I will have to release them anyway for lack of evidence. They have stolen a bag of money in connection with a traffic accident, where the victim has escaped from the hospital and cannot be heard. I'm more interested in knowing how Niilla got this money than in arresting two petty thieves who probably had nothing to do with it. It would only create unwanted attention on the real operation. And besides, they will not go anywhere."

"Ok, I will find my way to Luoktajärvi and try to get hold of Niilla. He has some explaining to do."

"Yes, he certainly has some explaining to do - if you can find him, that is. But don't burn any bridges. Try to get him on your side. Use carrots and sticks if necessary."

The conversation ended. Niilla was no longer his main concern. Had he been completely played? First softened with alcohol, then skillfully drawn out for information. He recalled how Sleipner had ordered round after round of beer, casually brought up Luoktajärvi, and then picked up the tab. Had he really been that gullible? How much had he actually let slip? The man had seemed so sincere, so easy to talk to.

Surely it was just a coincidence that they'd ended up at the same table? Sleipner was already there when Edward arrived and had merely offered him a seat after Edward was displaced. They'd talked about everything and nothing, and Edward hadn't exactly been on guard. Luoktajärvi came up when the man spotted the map book lying openly on Edward's jacket. Then Edward had rambled on about the woman he'd traveled halfway across Sweden to find. It all felt so natural, so believable. But now he couldn't shake the feeling - what if the man had some connection to the bag those two thieves stumbled across? What if that bag had drawn him here, and their meeting wasn't a chance at all? And if he really was a criminal, sitting on a fortune in stolen cash... Why would he suggest teaming up with a police officer, or an official from the Security Service for that matter?

Edward decided to go ahead with the plan. They would look for Luoktajärvi together. He had no choice if he wanted to get there. But he would have to keep his traveling companion under surveillance.

William pulled up in front of the hotel entrance with a fully loaded Range Rover and a large trailer with a lashed scooter and a sled. It was early in the morning and the sun was shining through a sparse cloud cover. Despite folding down the back seat and throwing away a lot of his grandfather's old gear - and even some spontaneous luggage he'd brought from home - the pack climbed up to the backrest.

The car's tank was full, and he'd also filled two 20-liter plastic cans with diesel. While he was at it, he topped off the scooter and both of its spare tanks. Altogether, he'd pumped a hundred and sixty liters of fuel - by far the biggest refueling of his life.

The gun was stuffed in one of his backpacks and wrapped in a sweater for safety. It was unnecessary to take any risks with a policeman in the car, but at the same time he did not want to get rid of it. For the same reason, the cash had been carefully distributed in waterproof dry bags that could be sealed.

The policeman waited at the entrance. He had a small sports bag around his shoulders. It looked like he was going on a training session rather than a wilderness excursion. He looked at the sizable rig with wide eyes.

"You are well prepared, I see. Is there any room for my own luggage?"

"It fits in the glove compartment," said William. Welcome aboard the ship, sailor.

They chatted as they left Gällivare heading west. After half an hour they turned off the E45 to the northwest and drove along the road that ran parallel to Stora Lulevatten. William noticed that Edward was tense and slightly less talkative than before. He wondered if the inspector was caught up in the seriousness of the moment, or perhaps he'd gone off the booze again. He let it go and focused on the snow-covered road.

After a couple of hours they passed the ferry camp to Saltoluokta Mountain Station. During the summer season, there used to be a ferry in operation between the camp at the north end of the lake and across to the south side where the mountain station was located.

After the Suorva dam at Stora Sjöfallet, the road became smaller. By lunchtime they were approaching Ritsem. Across the gigantic Akkajaure reservoir, in a southerly direction, the Akka massif towered with its seven visible peaks. The locals call it the *Queen of Laponia* because it has the largest difference in altitude in Sweden.

William stopped at Ritsem Mountain Station, which had just opened for the season. The brown single-storey building was located on a small hill with a magnificent view of the snow-white lake with Akkafjället in the background. They cooked freeze-dried food in the warming hut, which offered the same magical panoramic view as the outside. After dinner, they made a preliminary route using a mountain map. William exchanged a few words with the cabin host about the thickness of the ice, suitable routes and where not to go. The host reminded them that snowmobiles were not allowed inside the national park. In order to not risk any conflicts upfront they promised to park the vehicle after crossing the frozen lake, a lie of course.

Then they started shunting at the snowmobile trailer: they loaded the cargo, backed off the snowmobile and the sled and connected them. They moved backpacks, tents and other things to the sled and Edward prepared the packing he got from William. After a short test drive in the large parking lot, they were ready to leave.

The first stretch was along the debris markers that ran in a wide arc across the frozen lake to the Akka cottages on the south side. William drove and the graying policeman sat on the prayer stool. The space was generous and they did not have to sit too close together. The driver was clearly inexperienced with snowmobiles and visibly concerned about the load on the sled. As a result, the journey progressed at a cautious yet uneven pace, hugging the markers closely—almost as if he feared they might vanish from the lake the moment he looked away. The ice was still meters thick, and it was probably a month before the floodwaters began to flow, and then a few more weeks before the ice-out would begin. Even so, the cabin host had been very distinct in pointing out that they had to stick to the debris markings.

"The ice can be treacherous even if it is still winter," he said before they took off. "If you go outside the markings, there may be cracks. You have to remember that the ice is floating on top of a river, not a lake."

The last sentence had etched itself into the minds of both men.

The first stretch went without incident and once across the other side they quickly found the Akka huts. These were used as accommodation for hikers in the summer, and this was the place where they had promised to leave the snowmobile. Instead they kept going. The planned route would not be near any settlements or hiking trails, especially not when the snow was still thick.

The second section was slightly shorter and consisted of a ten-kilometer-long and fairly straightforward trail that ended at Lake Kutjaure. The navigator showed that they had driven 27 kilometers in just over an hour. William stopped the scooter for a brief discussion with the passenger. If they continued across the lake and then turned northwest, they could use a summer trail that would take them halfway to Luoktajärvi, but they would have to cross rough terrain where all off-road vehicle traffic was prohibited. They agreed to continue with the original plan and reach the village from the south.

They continued across Lake Kutjaure and into a narrow bay

leading in a south-westerly direction. In the distance, snow-capped mountains towered in all directions. Everything was white and surreal. After four kilometers, the bay split and they turned straight west towards the eastern end of Lake Sallohaure. The lake was several kilometers long and probably frozen all the way, but William didn't dare drive any faster than he would be able to spot any wakes. This far from civilization there were no debris markers. They had to go by feel.

Nature this time of the year and this far up north was in a striking state of transition. Patches of snow still clung to the rugged slopes and high plateaus, glistening under a sun that now lingered longer in the sky. Meltwater trickled through cracks and crevices, feeding icy streams and creating a symphony of gurgling and dripping. The landscape was a blend of white and brown - snowfields interrupted by exposed tundra, where mosses, lichens, and hardy shrubs begin to stir back to life, especially on the sun-exposed slopes.

The western side of the lake passed into a stream and William could not continue as they had planned. He was forced to turn north towards land and hoped to find a suitable route that was not marked on the map. The terrain was hilly and led to higher altitudes but was nevertheless quite easy to negotiate. They covered two hundred meters of altitude and five kilometers in a northwesterly direction in an hour, reaching a reindeer herder's hut on the western shore of Lake Slahpejávrre. According to the snowmobile's built-in navigator, they were less than three kilometers southeast of the coordinate that had come to symbolize Luoktajärvi and two kilometers from the Norwegian border.

William and Edward looked at two mountain peaks that, according to the old maps, should be the mountains that surrounded the mountain village on the Swedish side. The peaks were both over fifteen hundred meters high. Between the peaks was a plateau that seemed to be the easiest way forward even though it would surely mean a climb of at least five hundred meters from where they were now.

They drove across the lake and started climbing the slope leading to the plateau. The slope was covered in rocks and very difficult to navigate. Perhaps the easiest way to reach the village was from the north or east - from the Norwegian side - but it was too late to bother about that. Moreover, it was almost impossible to turn around with the sledge on the uphill slope. They simply had to continue straight ahead and hope for the best.

On several occasions, they had to stop and use shovels and muscle power to continue. Either the conveyor belt had buried itself in the snow, or the sled's runners had sunk or become wedged between rocks. Edward had to walk alongside for long stretches, digging and pushing.

The climb up to the plateau took several hours and the sun was low when they reached the goal. They were physically exhausted but the view of the snowy and desolate landscape was breathtaking. It looked as if they were on an alien planet. They couldn't see anything resembling a mountain village, but according to the navigator and the maps, they should be very close.

A dense fog rolled in from the west and they decided to make camp for the night while they still had a few hours of light left. Just as the tent was pitched, the fog closed in around the plateau and visibility was limited to about ten meters even though the sun had not disappeared from the horizon. They ate supper consisting of canned food and water, unpacked their sleeping pads and sleeping bags, and then fell asleep almost immediately.

CHAPTER 12

Luoktajärvi

In the morning, the dense fog was gone. As William looked out of the tent opening, the morning sun stood high in the clear blue sky and golden rays illuminated the surrounding mountains. The air was crisp and fresh but at the same time pleasantly warm. It carried the scent of damp earth, pine, and the lingering cold. It was a moment of quiet awakening, where winter's grip had loosened but not vanished, and life was cautiously reasserting itself. All around there were birds chirping and the faint sound of rushing water could be heard in the background. The snowmobile was just a few meters away from the tent, where they had left it the night before. It reminded him of a friendly monster from a children's adventure movie.

As his eyes gradually adjusted to the light, he saw that he was on a plateau with a view for miles in all directions. The plateau was covered in snow, but here and there moss- and lichen-covered rocks peeked out and juniper, willow and mountain birch grew everywhere. In the background, round and pointed mountains could be seen in all directions. Far away on the horizon in the east, the white border of Sarek's mighty glaciers towered above the lakes, rivers and forests. A little further to the south were the elongated lakes Vastenjaure and Virihaure. In summer, their mirror-like surface would surely contrast powerfully with the surrounding mountain peaks and glaciers. Now, the snow- and ice-covered lakes gave an almost desolate impression.

Some thirty kilometers to the south, the snow-covered massif of Sulitelma could clearly be seen rising above the surroundings, and the great Norwegian glacier Blåmansisen could be seen further to the west. It was partly hidden behind a high, pointed peak that stood out from the other mountains in the immediate vicinity. Far away to the north, the pointed peaks of Kebnekaise towered on the horizon.

William was in awe of the mighty panorama he was looking at. He had to force himself to look away from the scenery so he could light the gas stove and boil water. With a cup of instant coffee in hand, he sat down on the nearest rock to continue enjoying the view. The steam from his cup curled into the chilly air, vanishing almost as quickly as it formed. The silence was near total, broken only by the soft hiss of the stove cooling and the occasional caw of a raven overhead. William took a slow sip, the bitter warmth grounding him in the moment. Up here, above the treeline, time seemed to move differently - slower, more deliberate. The landscape was both ancient and freshly waking, as if winter had just begun to loosen its grip on the high country.

In front of him, the mountainous landscape of Norway stretched out. According to the map, he was still on the Swedish side, but he couldn't be sure. He stood up on the rock, rising with his coffee in hand, hoping a higher vantage might help him orient himself. From there, the land ahead seemed to dip, a subtle fold in the mountains that gradually curved downward before lifting again into a distant wall of peaks. Curious, William walked towards the sink to try to find reference points. After a few hundred meters, the ground disappeared abruptly and without warning. Below, a bowl-shaped valley with steep slopes materialized out of thin air.

For a few seconds he just stood there, staring ahead. At first it looked like a large crater in the ground, but after a while it became clear that it was the surrounding mountains and highlands that were elevated rather than the other way around. In the middle of the void was a dense fog that seemed to rise out of a small lake like steam, as if the source of the fog came from the underground. But strangest of all, just below the rim of the surrounding plateau, the landscape transformed - bare earth and vibrant greenery spread across the slopes, while everything above remained cloaked in unbroken snow.

The bottom of the valley was green like a jungle, and the tree line seemed to run somewhere between the bottom and the surrounding mountain peaks. In the middle of the greenery ran a stream that branched off in different directions like arteries. Small waterfalls trickled down everywhere before disappearing into the foliage and conifers closer to the valley floor. Just above the densest vegetation, the slope was not as steep and there were hundreds of animals scattered in small groups. William assumed they must be reindeer, although the distance was too great to see with the naked eye.

At the centre of the valley and around the upcoming steam, it was possible to make out some kind of settlement. William took out the binoculars he'd found in the crawl space and now he could clearly see a small community of houses, people and the occasional motor vehicle. Small roads and paths were everywhere, and in some places stone bridges had been built over the branches of the rapids. At the far end of the valley, he saw plains of crops. Had it been the middle of summer, the contrast wouldn't have seemed so stark. But this was just after winter, north of the polar circle, over a thousand metres above sea level - yet he was looking at jungle vegetation and something that resembled vineyards.

The longer he looked through the binoculars, the more signs of life and movement he saw and the more fascinating the valley appeared. Four-wheelers used the roads, people worked in the fields and walked on the paths, children played on a landscaped area that might have served as a sports field or football pitch. In the wider and calmer part of the streams there were occasional small boats and, half hidden behind some trees, even a helicopter was parked.

He lowered the binoculars from his eyes and took out his cell phone from his leg pocket. He turned on the phone and opened the program with downloaded terrain maps from the National Land Survey. After just a few minutes, the GPS position appeared as a blue dot. It marked a place that looked like a canyon or valley surrounded by contour lines. Around the valley, he found the three nearest mountains and between all the points was an area that was marked on the digital map as a lake. There was no other useful information - no buildings, no roads or hiking trails. Not even the streams were marked.

William took a screenshot of the display and noted the GPS coordinates. Then he fished out the old mountain map from the fifties from his grandfather's cabin. It was not easy to compare the electronic map with the old yellowed paper map. The scales were different, the information was very different and the coordinate system did not follow the same standard. The terrain map on the phone had better elevation data and the mountains were clearly marked, but most of the paper map's information on hiking trails, snowmobile trails, windbreaks and the supposed Sámi village was missing. Eventually, he found two of the mountains and was able to pinpoint his position. With trembling fingers, he saw that he was a few hundred meters due east of Luoktajärvi.

He had assumed, so far, that Luoktajärvi would be like a normal Sámi settlement where at least one snowmobile trail or hiking trail would serve as a way into the village. This place was more like a northern version of Machu Picchu than a Laponia village, and he didn't even know how to get in. Was there an opening in the mountain or serpentine paths along the slopes?

"That's our village, right?".

William was completely surprised by the voice. He turned around and saw Edward looking out over the valley with a cigarette in his mouth. For a few moments he had completely forgotten about his traveling companion, excited as he was about the discovery.

"Isn't it amazing? I never thought it would look like this, but according to the map this is Luoktajärvi." William swept his arm over the spectacle.

"I read a classified letter about Luoktajärvi the other day. The letter was written in the sixties and recounted what a hunting soldier had told his commanding officer. In winter, such a valley-sink should reasonably be a cold spot, especially this far north. But most of the valley was green far up the mountainside. He must have been standing about where we are now."

"Did it say why the crater was green?"

"No, at least not in that letter. He had stayed a few days and watched the inhabitants of the village. They are supposed to be shy and difficult to deal with, according to some of the reports I have read."

William thought about what Gunvor had told him about the rumors about the villagers. Perhaps there was an ounce of truth behind all the rumors after all.

They walked back towards the temporary campsite. The water in the jug was still warm. They gulped down some porridge and ate a chocolate bar each.

"I suggest we leave the snowmobile, the tent and most of the luggage," said William.

"I was thinking the same thing. I mean, how the hell would we get everything down the slopes?"

"We could pack a backpack each with the essentials and then try to find a way down the slopes."

"Do you have any idea *where* to get down? I looked for a natural trail or blasted serpentine road but all I saw were steep rock walls except for the pass on the west side, but that's a long way and the terrain is rugged."

"No, not a clue. But maybe that will change when we start searching. I'm more worried about what we'll say when we meet the first person."

"Leave it to me. They can't argue with a police officer."

In the same breath, Edward thought of the report that described how the inhabitants had sunk a German company in a lake and humiliated and sent home a Swedish fighter platoon.

They finished the chocolate cake and prepared the backpacks. The tent was left behind along with the snowmobile, sled and most of the equipment. Then they set off on foot towards the village. Now the tricky part of the operation began.

✳ ✳ ✳

Security Service Archive, registered email

Date: August 11, 2012

From: Kenneth Ringbom, Security Service, Operations North

To: Sven-Erik Dahlman, Head of Security Service

Sven-Erik,

I am sending you a short summary of the observations made over the last three years.

- *Sporadic border surveillance has been observed from the Norwegian side*

- *Movements within and outside the area bounded by the valley floor have increased significantly*

- *Two Swedish-registered seaplanes, one Norwegian-registered helicopter, a number of scooters and quad bikes have turned up in the valley*

- *A number of new buildings have been constructed*

- *The infrastructure (if you can call it that) has been improved. Examples include the internal road network (read: paths), bridges over river sections, lighting, a supposed telecommunications mast on one of the mountains, and tunneling work*

- *It seems that some kind of underground source is the explanation for the warm microclimate. In the winter months (October-March) they use some kind of artificial sunlight to extend the days. We have compared new satellite images with old ones from the archive and the valley seems to have become significantly greener in the last fifteen years alone.*

In conclusion, there are no indications of illegal activities. On the other hand, it is rather unbelievable that there is no official documentation about this village. Not least the unique microclimate and the incomprehensible border problem should have reached the ears of the public, or at least the occasional journalist or researcher.

I have looked through some old classified reports and my personal assessment is that the inhabitants have managed to take advantage of both the border issue and the geographical location, the village is extremely inaccessible and surrounded by protected national parks, most of the infrastructure and sign of life are obscured by the steam that comes up from the small lake (which resembles clouds from above) but also the fact that they are protected by the Sámi Reindeer Husbandry Act - although they seem to have no contact at all with other Sámi.

Best regards /Kenneth

They stood at the edge of the valley, looking for a place to descend. No way seemed better than any other and the snow made the descent even more treacherous as it effectively smoothed over any obstacles. They decided to continue straight ahead and hope for the best. If they could only make it down a couple of hundred meters into the valley, they would reach bare ground and then there would be no apparent problem.

William led the small group down the mountainside, being careful where he put his feet and using a walking stick to point out any hidden rocks or other obstacles in front of him. In some places the snow was extra loose and deep and he sank down to his knees. Edward formed a rearguard and tried to put his feet in the already trampled tracks, which had the advantage that the snow was more easily forced but the disadvantage that it did not cushion so much against the rocky surface. It was very slow going and after an hour they had only reached halfway.

As they descended, they noticed that the snow grew thinner the closer they got to the bare ground. At first, this seemed like a sign of relief—but it quickly became clear that the hardest part still lay ahead. From the plateau, it hadn't been visible, but now he could see the steep slope below, littered with sharp rocks hidden beneath a thin layer of snow. Every step was a precision job and there was no visible detour that would make the descent easier.

When they were only fifty meters away from some kind of green field, Edward lost his balance. He flailed his arms for a second before falling forward and dragging his traveling companion down with him. He spun around half a turn in the air and landed backwards in the snow. The slope was steep and he continued to rotate, touching several snow-covered rocks on his way down the slope but mostly remained on top of the snow-layer like a rampant snow sled. Despite the violent descent he felt no real pain until he ran foot-first into one of the last rocks sticking up through the snow cover. He felt his ankle break and the pain only came when he had stopped completely. By then he was on bare ground just above the treeline.

The pain from his ankle was immense, but he also felt pain from his temple, collarbone and one wrist. He barely caught a glimpse of his traveling companion's motionless body before he passed out.

The first thing he noticed was the visible wooden beams. They were rough like birch trunks and uneven in shape. About ten beams together spanned an arched wooden ceiling. He was lying on his back in an oblong room. The bed - or bunk - was covered with straw, mostly hidden under a thick blanket. The head end was against the sloping ceiling, while the foot end was crowned by two sturdy pillars that apparently helped to support the ceiling.

The last thing he remembered was climbing down the mountainside with Edward. He had gone first. They were on the final stretch, where the snow gave way to green moss and low shrubs. Then, suddenly, everything went black.

A woman dressed as a nurse suddenly appeared out of nowhere. She stopped a few meters from the foot of the bed and held a tray table in her hands.

"You've slept all day and must be hungry." She put the tray down on the bed across William's stomach.

"You got off lightly compared to your friend; no broken bones and no open wounds. Just a big bang over the elbow and probably a slight concussion, says the doctor. You have a deep cut on your forehead. Your friend is in the room next door. We use it as a hospital."

She left him without waiting for a response and after a few seconds she was engulfed by the building. William tried to stand up using his left elbow and pain flashed through his body. His elbow was tightly wrapped and when he tried to move his arm it hurt like hell and the pain radiated out in the whole body. There was a plaster in the middle of his forehead. He gently touched and moved the other parts of his body to see if anything else was damaged, but fortunately the pain seemed to be limited to the wrapped elbow and the head.

He looked down at himself. Someone had apparently removed his clothes—only a dark-grey night-suit of some kind covered his body. It resembled a japanese kimono. Propping himself up on one elbow, he grabbed a large pillow and wedged it behind his back. On the tray beside him was a hearty, English-style breakfast, complete and generous—nothing seemed to be missing.

Once he had finished his breakfast, or whatever time it was in the day, William sat up in bed and looked around the room. He seemed to be alone. The room seemed inspired by Vikings or the Middle Ages. The walls were decorated with animal skins and reindeer horns. There was a kerosene lamp hanging between each bunk, but only the one next to William was lit. Something made the light in the room brighter than should be possible with just one lamp on. Light seemed to seep in here and there through windows in the ceiling.

He stood up on unsteady legs and saw his backpack and clothes lying on the bed next to him. On top of the small pile of clothes were the glasses. It was a relief to see them even if he wasn't completely depending on them, only while driving. Suddenly he remembered the gun and went to the backpack and started looking. Everything seemed to be there except the gun. His hosts had obviously found it. What first impression would they now have of the two visitors?

William put his feet in a pair of slippers and limped slowly across the floor on shaky legs. On the other end was a door. He opened it cautiously and the summery air hit his nostrils. The evening sun was coming over the snow-covered ridge and the sky all around was red and slightly hazy. On the outside there was not a trace of snow on the ground, instead everything was covered in a magnificent green. One of those indefinable mountain greens that were so clear and contrasting in the summers, but were conspicuous by their absence in the winters.

In the distance he heard the sound of running water. He descended a small flight of steps outside the building and continued towards the sound across a hilly lawn. Out in the open, he saw that slowly flowing water surrounded him on both sides. The small house stood on an island in the middle of a lake or a wide stream of water. All over the island and on the other side of the rapids, various plants flourished, not only the plants one would expect so far north, but also more exotic elements. A short distance away, where the rapids were slightly narrower, there was a long footbridge leading to the other side. In the middle of the bridge stood a person with a fishing rod. When William looked in his direction, he looked away and continued fishing.

He walked back up to the house and from outside it looked nothing like a viking house, more like something derived from a fantasy movie. As he approached the house he saw a second door on the side. There was no sign of anyone. He entered the house and found himself standing in a small sickroom. Edward was lying in a hospital bed with a large plaster cast on one ankle. His wrist was wrapped, as was his shoulder and head. At the far end of the room, a couple more patients were sleeping.

He walked up to Edward who seemed to be awake, if a little dizzy.

"I'm glad you're alive," William said happily.

"Same to you. I feel pretty clear-headed after all. But the right ankle is fucked. Broken in two places. The shoulder has dislocated but it's not the first time you know. A shitty shoulder is what it is. The wrist and head are just scraped up they say. Looks worse than it is."

"It is good that you take it that way. You look like you've had a difficult seven years. What really happened?"

"I put my foot in a pit and lost my balance. The snow is treacherous, it levels the ground. Dragged us both down in the fall. Then I probably hit some rock and lost consciousness and woke up here while they were working on my ankle. Then I must have passed out again from all the painkillers they put in me. By the way, do you know where we are? Have you talked to anyone?"

William nodded thoughtfully and looked over at the other patients. They were still asleep.

"A nurse left some food but she disappeared before I could open my mouth. I woke up in a room next door and just caught a glimpse of the outside. It seems that we are on a small island in the middle of a river. When we saw the valley floor from above, there was an oblong lake surrounded by a light mist and with a number of branches partially hidden by the greenery. I think we are at one of these branches or at a narrower part of the lake."

"Then we are prisoners on the island. That's why it's so deserted. There is no need to watch us."

"I saw a footbridge leading over to the other side. There was a person fishing in the middle of the bridge but I got the feeling he was watching me."

Edward looked worried and glanced around the room.

"Maybe we are lucky that we made such a dramatic entrance. Otherwise they would perhaps have thrown us out immediately."

"The thought has crossed my mind. Anyway, I guess we'll have to answer some questions now that we're awake." William gently touched the wrapped elbow. It was sore but nothing seemed broken.

"I have an idea," said Edward in a subdued voice. "We've made it through the first part of our journey. When we left Ritsem yesterday on the snowmobile, I didn't think we would get this far - maybe I've read too many reports about this place. But all reports come from the outside and now we are on the inside and we have to make the best of it. I don't think they would have put in so much work on us just to throw us out in the snow with broken legs and everything," Edward continued.

"But as soon as we can walk out of here - or maybe it's enough that we can be transported out of here - we will probably be sent away very quickly."

William wasn't sure where the policeman was going and he was afraid they didn't have much time to come up with a plan now that one of them was on his feet. He looked around the ward but so far only the snores of the two sleeping patients could be heard.

"My mission is sensitive. I have no idea how they will react and maybe the person I am looking for is not even here. But your case is quite innocent and you are looking for a woman you already know. I suggest I go back to sleep and you try to get a foot inside the door in the village. You are on your feet and the last time someone was here I was probably sleeping. I can continue to do that when someone comes here."

William had no time to answer before he heard footsteps on the stairs outside the entrance. He gave the policeman a quick nod as he pretended to fall into sleep. A man wearing a wrinkled white coat entered the hospital room and walked up to the duo with determined steps. He was in his late fifties, with dark hair and a blank face that didn't reveal anything.

"Good evening. My name is Matti and I'm in charge of this small infirmary here. How is your friend, has he woken up? The man spoke in a broad melodic dialect that he'd never heard before."

"No, he is sleeping. Is he seriously injured?"

"He'll recover. And you are already on your feet."

"A blow to the elbow and one to the head so I guess I was lucky?" William looked at Matti to get confirmation on his condition.

"Those are some tough slopes you tried to climb. Especially this time of year. Did you get lost? That's usually the case when someone comes to us, although it almost never happens these days."

"If this is Luoktajärvi, we're in the right place."

The doctor stiffened a little and looked alternately at the two men with inscrutable eyes.

"Have those men got it wrong too?" William added, pointing to the two sleeping patients in the corner.

"No... no, it's two young guys from the village who drove too fast with four-wheelers. What a mess those vehicles are. Couldn't they do it with scooters? They don't tip over as easily. Well, what are you doing in Luoktajärvi?"

"I am looking for a person who is from here, a close friend. It is a person I got to know in Stockholm several years ago and I need to get in touch with her."

"Does the person have a name?"

"Her name is Merja. The surname is unfamiliar to me. She used a different surname when I got to know her. She is a few years younger than me, quite tall and has big dark brown hair."

He was content with that description for the time being. Had he given the same brief and general description in Stockholm, or in any other city for that matter, he would have been declared an idiot. But it seemed to have made an impression on the doctor. Without saying anything, he picked up a phone and walked off in the direction of the entrance to talk in private. After a few minutes he came back.

"Your sleeping friend, is he here for the same reason as you?"

"No, he's here for completely different reasons. We met just a few days ago and decided to go together - this is an inaccessible place. He also wants to meet a certain person, but he has to explain himself when he wakes up.

"Well, if you're in good enough shape, you'll come with me. I'll take you to a person who can answer your questions."

"I feel bruised, that's all."

Doctor Matti nodded and signaled for him to follow. William cast a quick glance at the policeman who made a discreet nodding motion with his head. He took it that Edward had understood everything and gave his approval. He followed the doctor out through the entrance. The sun was slowly disappearing behind the mountains but still lit up the sky with a red glow. They crossed the island and continued down towards the water, but not in the direction of the bridge, to William's surprise. Instead, they followed a beaten path that led down to a jetty, where there was a boat. On the dock was a kerosene lamp that cast an eerie glow over the place. The reddish indirect sunlight and dense jungle-like vegetation helped to create a surreal setting by casting long shadows across the river.

"The fastest way to get to the person you will meet is by boat. It only takes a few minutes."

William obediently sat down at the back of the five-meter-long steering console.

"Here, use this on. There may be mosquitoes on the way." Matti handed over a thin coat and a mosquito hat with a net covering the face.

William put on the clothes when he saw that the doctor did the same. His escort then started the outboard, which was powered by electricity and made hardly any noise at all. In eerie silence, the craft glided across the river with the two men on board. Soon they came to a wider section where there was less current. The boat continued across to the other side. It was hot and humid in the evening air. Occasionally there were mosquitoes when they passed close to vegetation but the coat and the hat kept them away.

A light mist rose from the water mirror. William felt his fingers in the water and it was even warmer than in the air, perhaps as much as thirty degrees.

"How can it be so hot in early April? On the mountain ridge this morning it was thick with snow and only a few plus degrees in the sun."

"All your questions will be answered soon. Enjoy the journey."

William asked no more questions during the boat trip. The doctor wasn't grumpy, but he seemed to be a little bit clenched and not in a chatty mood. When he thought about it, it was a strange doctor and a strange hospital. Everything was strange. In the distance there were occasional points of light along the river and further up the hill. They were faint because it was not quite dark yet.

The boat passed the wide section and turned into another bay where the vegetation was even thicker and trees hung out over the water. Were it not for the snow-capped mountains in the background, and the occasional patches of the typical mountain flora and fauna, one might have been led to believe that they were on the Amazon River. William sat spellbound, watching what increasingly seemed like a dream world.

After a few minutes, the cove ended at the foot of a mountain slope and another pier became visible. It was lit by a light hanging on a post on the jetty.

The doctor parked the boat at the dock and motioned for William to follow. They left their coats and hats and walked as a group across the jetty and up a path that led into a crack in the rock where a steep stone staircase began. The steps were long and winding and William estimated that they had been walking up the mountain for at least ten minutes when suddenly they came to a plateau and a large house came into view. It was a brown and white duplex mountain house with a huge balcony and a dizzying view of the river, the greenery and the surrounding mountains now lit up by a bright full moon.

They walked across a grass lawn and then went up a wooden staircase that led to the first floor and a large terrace. The doctor asked him to wait on the terrace and then disappeared through a door. After a while, he came out with a man who looked very much like his traveling companion, at least in terms of his injuries: his head was wrapped in gauze, one wrist was in a cast, and he was hobbling on crutches with one foot dragging behind. William wondered for a moment how the hell this man had made it up the stone steps.

❋ ❋ ❋

Edward opened his eyes as soon as the two men had left the infirmary. He felt frustrated that he had to stay in bed. Carefully, he got up into a semi-sitting position with the help of his working shoulder and looked around the room. To his surprise, his backpack and clothes were lying on a chair next to the hospital bed. He reached out as far as he could and grabbed the back of the chair. Slowly he pulled the chair closer and soon he had both the backpack and clothes within reach.

He searched his backpack and clothes methodically. Every motion was a battle - slow, painful - but it didn't take long to confirm that everything was there, except the service weapon. That was a problem. He wouldn't need it while lying helpless in a hospital bed, but being disarmed could seriously damage his standing with the villagers.

He picked up his phone and was once again surprised to see that he'd received both the call and the message - and the coverage was excellent even though the operator was unknown. It came from Kvarnbring and was recorded during the morning. He read the message:

Tried to reach you but without success. The lab has examined the contents. They think it's some kind of moss. The odor is most likely animal feces. No sign of any illegal substances. Are you sure this is the contraband you've been chasing around half of Sweden?

He read the message once more. Animal droppings and moss. It was good news, but also completely absurd. Would they go to all that trouble to smuggle moss undisturbed, and if so, who was paying for it? He wondered if anyone else had read the message but it was highly doubtful given that the code lock was on. The policeman sank back into bed and wondered how his traveling companion was doing. He had to rely on him now.

✻ ✻ ✻

The doctor nodded briefly towards them and then walked across the grassy plateau towards the stone steps and was soon engulfed by the crack in the rock. William realized that he'd now been left alone with this bandaged creature, whose wounded body looked ominous in the moonlight. He felt uneasy, left out and lost in the most unlikely place he could think of. Perhaps the man sensed this because he held out his hand and said in a friendly tone:

"Welcome to Luoktajärvi. My name is Niilla."

"William." He held out his hand and looked at the man curiously but could think of nothing more to say.

"I must apologize for my appearance. It was a traffic accident, a self-inflicted one. I drove off the road in the middle of a storm. It's not quite as bad as it looks. My ankle's the worst, but I can get around on crutches. But you've been through a lot yourself," he said, pointing to the patch on his forehead.

"I fell on the way down here. Couldn't find a better way in."

Niilla nodded without commenting on the slightly sarcastic statement and then made a gesture with his hand.

"Let's go into the house and talk about your business. We rarely get visitors so I hope you will be able to stay a while and let me show

235

you our hospitality."

"My calendar is empty and my traveling companion won't be going anywhere for a few days so I'm happy to stay."

"Excellent, let's go up to the big balcony. He turned and limped with some problems through the open door with his crutches. William followed. There was not much else to do. He didn't really know where he was, and darkness had fallen. But the worst of the unease had subsided somewhat and curiosity took over. It struck him that this was the man Edward was talking about. The person who had escaped from the hospital. But he didn't know much more. The policeman had been reticent about details. Even when he was drunk.

The house resembled an Alpine house even on the inside. Thick stained logs on the ceiling, a giant curved staircase and large heavy wooden furniture formed the focal point of an oblong room that ran across the house on the first floor. His host led them up the stairs to a large entrance hall, probably on the main floor. The entrance hall had a ceiling height of at least six meters and was enclosed by an open upper floor with a protective railing. In the middle of the opening hung a gigantic chandelier made of reindeer horn.

They went up another flight of stairs and came to a large sitting room. In the center of the room was a magnificent pool table lit by an oblong brass lamp. In one corner was a chesterfield set on a thick and colorful rug. At one end of the room was a bar, and on the wall hung a dartboard next to a Winchester rifle and a number of evocative oil paintings. The room was decorated like an English gentlemen's club, William thought. Whether it was tasteful or tacky was up to the viewer to judge.

Through the room ran an invisible corridor parallel to the landing, with a number of doors on either side. William gasped when he saw a painting of Merja's face. It hung on one of the walls in the sitting room among the other paintings. It was a picture where she was younger but her face was unmistakable. The beautiful features were hers and no one else's. But what was she doing here? How had she ended up on the wall of this house? Before he could ponder this further, Niilla beckoned him to come along.

At the back of the room was a long sliding section framed by heavy curtains. They fluttered lightly in the breeze, revealing that somewhere it was opened up. Niilla parted the curtains and a gentle evening breeze seeped into the room. They stepped out onto a huge balcony with pleasantly dim lighting. Half the balcony was roof covered but the rest was open under the sky and the view was magical. William gazed in wonder at the grassy plateau he'd just crossed. Just beyond the plateau, he saw the small cleft in the rock that led down to the private harbour. From the balcony's elevated position, he could see down to the bay that connected the harbor to the lake beyond. In the background, the snow-capped mountains rested under the moonlight. Here and there, points of light could be seen in the valley and on the mountainsides. The air was humid and mild.

"Please use that armchair. Niilla pointed to a gigantic rattan armchair that could easily have swallowed two people."

"Are you hungry? If so, I'll make sure to get some food sent up."

"No, thank you. I was served food on the bed when I woke up. But preferably something to drink."

His host disappeared into the bar and returned with a bottle of wine, some water and a tray of cold cuts. He sat down in the armchair opposite William and poured them each a glass of wine. William smelled and tasted the delicious red wine as he looked out over the valley.

"We are very proud of our wine. The grapes grow along the southern and western slopes, not far from where you tried to climb down. Red wine does very well up here, but we haven't had success with white grapes yet. We're still trying to find the right type of vine, but their roots are particularly sensitive to the soil and the special climate."

"It really is an excellent wine. But how is it possible to grow grapes this far north? How can you have such a mild climate?"

"Yes, you've noticed that we have a slightly warmer winter climate up here?" Niilla smiled broadly as he watched his guest's reaction to the rhetorical question.

"Never seen anything like it. Saw smoke rising from the lake when we left the infirmary. Is there something underground heating up the valley?"

"Yes, you could say that. There is a so-called hot spring right under Luoktajärvi, which provides a mild climate all year round."

"Like the bottom of a volcano?"

"In a manner of speaking. It's called a thermal spring and is actually found all over the world. Mainly in the United States - you've heard of Yellowstone, right? - but also in Iceland and Japan. In our case, fifty-degree water seeps up directly under the lake instead of in a small cavity in the rock. Therefore, we never notice any geyser-like eruptions; there's always a bit of a sizzle under the deepest part of the lake, and because the lake is constantly fed with fresh and cold meltwater from the surrounding mountains, hot and cold water are constantly mixed. The result is that the lake has crystal clear water at a comfortable temperature all year round. Even the surrounding soil is warmed by our magical spring. This is one of the reasons why we can grow wine all year round. The valley-sink works as a big reservoir of heat and this is what makes it unique. Perhaps you and your friend noticed that it is snow-free well up the mountain sides?

"Yes, we noticed it, but we never got that far down the valley-sink before we tripped." William took a sip of wine and looked in the direction of the lake. It was so dark that it was no longer possible to discern any fog.

"But how do you get everything to grow this far north? The center of the valley looks like a jungle, and vines need a lot of sunlight too, don't they?"

"You are of course right. But it is now well into spring, otherwise you would have noticed that the valley is illuminated by a faint glow during the winter months."

"A faint glow? I don't understand."

"Between October and March, we extend the days with artificial sunlight. It's really nothing more than an advanced system of UV-lighting that is spread throughout the valley. Much like around a soccer field but not as intense and with light of the right wavelength."

"I haven't seen any light poles," replied William.

"Most of the lights are hidden around the mountain sides but also in the center of the valley. If it weren't for the fog, you would see that the whole green area in the middle is perforated by a large light system, at least during the winter months. The fog makes any light poles disappear but at the same time it lets the light through."

"So that's why you have like a jungle in the middle?"

"Well that combined with the heat and humidity and some other unique conditions. But if you had come just a month earlier, during late winter, you would find lights everywhere. On rooftops, in the trees, on high poles above the vineyard and even on the hillside. But even the light beams themselves are not that visible to the naked eye, they are a different wavelength. And, of course, artificial lighting consumes a huge amount of energy, but we have that in abundance, as you might have guessed."

William did not answer, but looked as if he were searching for something in the distance. The stars of the night sky seemed to shine only over the valley. The mountain ridges cut off the sky in all directions.

"By the way, how is your friend?" Niilla asked. I was informed that he is doing well but needs to heal for a few weeks.

"I'm sure that's true. He was unconscious when I saw him an hour ago but he seemed to have been well looked after."

"Good. Excellent, excellent." His host sipped his wine contentedly and then became more composed. As if gathering himself for an uncomfortable question.

"Matti, the good doctor who brought you here, told me that you have come to Luoktajärvi to see Merja."

"Yes, that's right. Do you know her?" William's heart skipped a beat as he thought of the painting hanging inside the balcony door.

"Yes, I know her, but first I would like to ask you something about your friend. What is his business here in Luoktsajärvi?"

He felt that the conversation was reaching its breaking point. Niilla knew who Merja was and that was encouraging, but now he'd asked sensitive questions about the police officer. What could he answer? After all, he knew nothing about his case. Except that he was most likely looking for the man sitting opposite him. He decided to tell the little he knew.

"I met my travel companion a couple of days ago in Gällivare by chance. We decided to join forces when it turned out that we both wanted to go to Luoktajärvi. He is looking for a person - a patient - who has disappeared from a hospital. A person who has been in a traffic accident. I think he's looking for you."

"That may well be true. I recognize his face. He came to see me just after the accident a few days ago. A gray-haired policeman in his sixties."

Niilla's sincerity made him shake the glass so that a few drops of the precious wine spilled on his clothes. It reminded him that he was still wearing slippers and a kimono of some kind. Despite this, he felt quite comfortable. Perhaps it was because his host also looked like a hospital patient. Equal children play best.

"As I mentioned earlier, visitors to our remote village are rare - especially those who are armed, including at least one who is a policeman." He fell silent, watching William with a scrutinizing gaze. Perhaps he was waiting for a reaction that did not come.

"We did, of course, go through your clothing and packing, once we got you into the infirmary. We have been following you since you camped last night."

"It's... what I said is absolutely true. We met a couple of days ago. The reason why I am armed is a long story, but at the same time it has nothing to do with me being here, and I guess my travel companion has a weapon in the service. Our intentions are purely good."

"Well, you are not here for questioning but because *you* wanted to ask a question. The rest I will have to take up with the police officer."

William thought for a while while he took a decent sip of the wine.

"I suddenly have a thousand questions but I am happy if I can get answers to three of them."

"Sure, go ahead." Niilla leaned back in the rattan armchair with the glass in his hand.

"First, I would like to know why I am here. Who are you? Are you the chief of this village?"

"Sáhkár Kuoljok is our chief," if you can call him that.

"But then who are you?"

"I am the one who holds everything together. Sáhkár is my father. He is our chief, our all-father, the spiritual leader of the village. But of course he's not very spiritual. No one is in Luoktajärvi. The old man is getting old and leaves the operational side to me. Now, let's hear your second question."

"Merja... is she here? You said you know her."

"I spoke to her just before you arrived, after Matti called. She's not in the village at the moment but she was keen for you to be here when she gets back. You must have made a good impression on her at some point."

William felt the blood pumping throughout his body and was unable to respond. He had embarked on the adventure of a lifetime, with little hope of finding even a sign of life. Now he'd found her in the strangest place and under the most unlikely circumstances he could think of. And she wanted to meet him.

He wanted to ask about the painting in the parlor, but instead he said: "When is she coming here?"

"It may take a few days. She usually works for a few weeks at a time and then goes back to the village to attend to her commitments. I suggest you stay here as long as you are my guest. There are plenty of rooms and I think it will coincide well with your companion's recovery."

"I am very grateful for the hospitality and I am happy to stay here until Merja comes back."

"Excellent! Now, you have a third question, right?"

"Yes... I have more questions than you would have time to answer but I would love to know how you got the pool table all the way up here."

Niila laughed heartily and long before answering.

"It is a legitimate question. If I remember correctly, it weighs between eight and nine hundred kilograms, so it couldn't be transported by our little helicopter. But... there are other ways in, even if you don't see them. The pool table was transported on a sled behind a scooter."

William was satisfied with the answer, although he wanted to know where these "other ways" are. He didn't want to test his host's patience too much now that he would be here for a few days.

"As for the snowmobile, we still have our camp with clothes and supplies up on the mountain plateau…"

"I'll send someone tomorrow to bring it all down here. The weapons will be returned to you when you leave Luoktajärvi. It's not that we don't trust you, but only a select few are allowed to carry weapons here and they have special duties."

William nodded and took another sip of the wine. The red fluid ran slowly down the throat and warmed his whole chest. The two men sat on the balcony until well after midnight, chatting their way through another bottle of the native drink. The rattan chair was soft, the wine was delicious, the air warm and pleasant and, for some reason he could not understand, there was no other place he would rather have been than this very balcony.

CHAPTER 13

Reindeer's Gold

Sunlight streamed through the few windows in the infirmary through gaps in the drawn blinds, and he guessed that it was between ten and eleven in the morning. During the night he'd slept on and off and at some point a nurse had checked on him and the other two patients. They still seemed to be snoozing as deeply and peacefully as hibernating bears.

He felt restless where he was lying and William had been gone ever since that doctor came to get him the previous evening. It made him feel even more uncomfortable. He swept his eyes across the room for the umpteenth time and this time he saw a pair of crutches. They were leaning against one of the empty beds. Perhaps they belonged to a patient who no longer needed them? He decided to make an attempt to get up. If only to kill some time.

It was slow going at first and the stiff sore body told him off but soon he was sitting on the edge of the bed and once the blood had left his head it didn't feel so bad under the circumstances. After all, the night had done wonders for his body. He carefully stood up on the floor and immediately felt that he could support his cast foot. At least as long as he did not put too much strain on it. He felt somewhat numb and guessed that the painkillers were still working. Both the injured ankle and shoulder felt numb. He moved slowly towards the crutches, leaning on the headboards. Soon he had wedged them under each armpit and after that it was somewhat easier, although the arm under the injured shoulder did not really respond to his commands.

He took his cell phone and limped down the hallway, each step echoing faintly behind him. Outside, the morning air wrapped around him, fresh and invigorating. Birds chirped from the canopy above, and somewhere nearby, the gentle sound of running water beckoned. He followed it, the gravel crunching beneath his shoes as he moved toward the place William had described the night before. Soon, he reached a broad, weathered rock that overlooked a stream and a narrow footbridge. Easing himself down onto the stone, he let out a quiet breath.

He decided to try to call Kvarnbring now that he was alone and in contact with the telephone network. It was just after ten in the morning and his colleague answered on the second tone.

"Good morning, Johnson. How have things been going for you? Where are you now? Did you get my message?" His voice was thick and raspy, as if he was still in bed.

"I am in Luoktajärvi now and have read your message. Had a little mishap on the way here. Broke an ankle and dislocated my shoulder but the Luoktajärvi people have taken good care of us."

"About us? Is it the travel company you told me about?"

"Yes, he also fell on the way down the slope to the village. But he did better than me. Nothing broken."

"Are you bedridden? That sounds serious."

"I'm ok. My foot is in a cast so there is nothing I can do about it. It's my shoulder and wrist that slow me down. It hurts when I jump on crutches."

"Have you found Niilla?"

"No, not yet, but of course he is here somewhere. As soon as I get on my feet, I will find him. Maybe sooner than that. But what do I say to him?"

There was silence on the phone for quite a while before

Kvarnbring's raspy voice returned.

"We have nothing to go on. No case, no carrot and no stick. I say we call it off. "

Edward couldn't believe what he was hearing. It took several seconds for the words to sink in. He had chased this person across half of Sweden, worn himself down to the bone - only to come this close to the end, and then stop? The thought was almost too absurd to grasp.

"Are you serious?"

"I am serious about this. We'll try to get you home somehow. Or will you make your own way home?"

"A few days ago it was a matter of national interest and now all of a sudden you want me to stop and go home. Aren't you even curious about what the man has to say? Don't you want to know what business they have up here? What makes the village go round?"

"It is not illegal to grow moss and escaping from a hospital is not a serious crime. Besides, I don't think you'll have much success in persuading the savages to work for our cause. I think you'd better round off nicely and retire as soon as your body allows you to."

"I haven't met any savages yet! Edward started to get upset and felt a headache coming on. He looked around but there was no one else around. The rock at the rapids was partly hidden behind some bushes so he wouldn't be spotted immediately as long as he didn't make too much noise."

"What about the bag?" he tried. "Don't you want to know where the money comes from?"

There was silence at the other end, almost a faint roar. Then he heard the sleepy voice of Kvarnbring again:

"Try to dig into the matter as discreetly as possible. Ask Niilla what he knows about the bag. If he doesn't have a good explanation for the money, don't press him. Then return his belongings - driver's license, phone - and then abort the mission and head home as soon as you can."

"We've been shut down, haven't we? So you don't want any more reports?"

"Edward, believe me when I say that I am doing you a favor. We are both up to our ears in this mess and I am trying to back out the door as neatly and discreetly as possible. You can report back when you get back. Metzner has already given his report. The investigation into the traffic accident is in the register. And there's one more thing... I'll be retiring soon. I've already been granted a retirement. I won't be working many more days."

"Did... did you just think of that?

"No, I've been thinking about that for a long time. Just like you. But I decided this morning. It's about time... we're not getting any younger Edward..."

"That doesn't sound like you. Just checking out like that. Has something happened? I mean, except being shut down."

Another long pause. Edward did not recognize his colleague at all. Neither in his voice nor in his actions. Something was not right.

"The smoking... It's the smoking Edward. I knew that bastard would catch up with me eventually."

"What do you mean?"

"Same as Beatrice. Same shit. Same ending."

"Cancer... Do you have cancer?"

"Lung cancer. The worst kind. I have six months left, the doctors say. If I'm lucky."

Edward was shocked. All the repressed memories washed over him again.

"I'm sorry... really. How long have you known about it?"

"They did some tests a few weeks ago. I had coughing fits and chest pains. I knew it was bad but you always hope for the best. Then I got the test results yesterday. I was completely shocked."

"You don't sound well. Have you slept?"

"I have been awake all night. But apart from that, I feel quite relaxed in the body. The doctor has given me enough morphine for a whole company. It takes the edge off the anxiety, coughing and shortness of breath. Knocks everything out. He thinks I can use it as much as I want to, the cancer will get me long before I become an addict, he said."

"So, this is it? We'll close the case and say goodbye?"

"Edward, if you think about it you will understand that this is the best way. The best way for both you and me."

The words puzzled him, but it was not the right time to delve deeper into the meaning right now. They chatted for a while and then ended the conversation and Edward sat on the stone with his head leaning against the healthy shoulder and deep in thought. He thought about Kvarnbring and the fate that awaited him. Edward, of all people, knew what it meant to be broken down piece by piece until all that was left was a body that no longer served any purpose. He thought of all the memories he shared with Kvarnbring. Memories from a whole working life. Both good and bad, of course, but nothing of that mattered anymore. They seemed petty in the context. Insignificant and petty. And Beatrice - it all came back. Unconsciously he had repressed everything - not only the last difficult time but most everything else as well. It was probably a protective mechanism that had kicked in. By repressing everything that could be associated with a particular event, there was no risk of anything unpleasant bubbling up to the surface again and making itself felt.

He didn't know how long he'd been sitting on the stone but when he looked up he saw a person standing on the bridge. He was quite sure that there had been no one on the bridge when he sat on the stone. There was no doubt that he was being watched, but his guard made no attempt to approach him, looking indifferently out over the stream. A few minutes passed without the bridge guard taking the slightest notice of him. Edward relaxed and allowed himself to enjoy the sun a little. There was nothing else he could do and in the light of the conversation that had just taken place, everything else seemed rather harmless.

He reflected on Kvarnbring's words: *if you think about it you will understand that this is the best way.* What could he have meant by this? Why would it be easier or better to cancel an unsolved case than to for example hand it over to someone else? The last time he had spoken to him was three days earlier and he'd just sent the two bag thieves home but there was not a hint that the case would be closed, quite the opposite. What's more, the two thieves had named his travel companion - *the pig* - as an accomplice. He felt powerless and lost, sitting on a rock in the middle of an island at the bottom of a crater, wrapped in gauze and plaster.

❋ ❋ ❋

William sat on the recessed balcony of the guest room, enjoying the view while sipping a cup of coffee. In the morning light, the lush valley seemed even more exotic than it had the previous evening. The greenery was more tangible, the streams and the mists rising from the lake were more visible, the mountains seemed to be even more magnificent, and more details were revealed the longer he looked at it. A waterfall stood out against the western mountainside, and here and there along the mountain sides reindeer roamed the dark moss just below the snowline. A flock of birds, probably black grouse, took advantage of the thermals in the center of the pot and circled slowly upward in a spiral motion, seemingly without moving their wings. Domestic cattle grazed peacefully in fenced pastures below. Barn buildings, crop fields and greenhouses were scattered across the bare areas, linked by small paths. The roofs and chimneys of small farmhouses poked up through the greenery. The occasional voice or shout echoed through the valley. A saw went off and muffled hammer blows clattered in the background. It was the sound of people working. The forgotten valley, which existed only in the form of three mountain peaks and a lake on the map, was bursting with life and movement.

He'd slept soundly in the spacious guest room, and in the morning, breakfast was delivered to his door by the host himself. With a brief apology, the man explained he had to step out for a few hours but would return in time for lunch. William was more than content with the arrangement. He enjoyed his breakfast out on the balcony, surrounded by the stillness and quiet rhythm of life beyond the railing. As he leaned back in his chair, a thought crossed his mind - had he ever experienced anything quite like this before?

It's always easy to be seduced by beautiful settings or exotic cultures when on vacation. A moment of freedom and unbridled pleasure. In contrast to the gray everyday life at home, the exaggerations tend to assume large proportions. A tour of the ruins of ancient Rome, a day-hike between mountain villages in the Alps, a skiing trip in the Scandinavian mountains, a swim in the ocean, a visit to the Great Wall of China or just a simple cup of java in a cozy café in a big city - everything seems magnified in the rush of temporary happiness. You promise yourself dearly that you must visit this place again, that you must experience the same feeling once more.

But things rarely turn out as planned. Memories fade and everyday life gets in the way. When it's time to go on an adventure again, you tell yourself *it would be great to go back there again* and soon after *but there are so many other places to experience*. And in the same moment, you realize that the romantic image has been replaced by a fleeting memory among many others.

But this time he knew it was different. This wasn't a vacation (the destination didn't even exist) and nothing was predetermined. This was the adventure of a lifetime and if all went well, he would soon meet the person he most wanted to meet right now. But perhaps most importantly, this time there was no gray everyday life waiting for him at home. Whatever happened in the next few days, even if he was thrown out of Luoktajärvi head first, the gray everyday life would be gone forever. Either the adventure would continue in the same style as it had begun or everything would go straight to hell, but it would not be gray. Possibly pitch black but never gray.

Around noon there was a knock on the door. It was Niilla who had returned.

"I have some good news about your friend. He is apparently up and about and has been seen hopping around on crutches this morning. I have suggested that he should be moved here instead of lying alone in the dreary infirmary. Perhaps he has already arrived with the doctor. If so, he could join us for lunch."

They moved to the same place as the night before and sure enough, the policeman was waiting for them. Edward and Niilla had immediately recognized each other from the brief meeting at the hospital in Uppsala and when the pleasantries had been said, the doctor left as discreetly as last time. Their host was relaxed and made small talk the whole time. He told them that the snowmobile and trailer had been brought down to the village and the rest of the equipment had been transported to the house during the morning. Edward, who first felt a little tense, began to relax. William couldn't help but smile a little secretly at the disheveled trio. All of them had bruises, scratches and bandages to varying degrees. Both Edward and Niilla each had a splendid plaster cast and a pair of crutches standing next to the seating area on the balcony.

"I guess you're the person I'm looking for, said Edward."

"That's probably true."

"I hope that you will be able to clarify some of the questions."

"All your questions will be answered. But first, I'd like you to meet Sáhkár - our village elder and chief. He is expecting us later today and can help clarify the concepts."

"I... we... are very grateful for you taking care of us and for the hospitality you have shown", said Edward.

"We don't get many visitors here, or rather we rarely let any visitors in, so it's exciting when it does happen. And right now I have plenty of time because of my current condition"

William and Edward looked at each other quickly, both wanting to ask the obvious question. Edward turned to Niilla again.

"Is there any particular reason why we were admitted and treated so well?"

"Well... not all visitors are... so to speak... so keen to meet us that they come rolling down the eastern slope." Niilla fired off his wide smile again to break the ice and show that he was joking with them.

"Jokes aside. Yes, there are several reasons why we are sitting here having lunch together. First, of course, there are your respective cases. That is, the reasons why *you* chose to come and see us." Niilla paused and looked at the lunch guests before continuing with a more serious expression.

"Secondly, the village needs your help. You don't realize it yet but you are actually very timely. There are big things going on. But I'd like to come back to that when we meet with Sáhkár."

He let the expectations hang in the air and continued chatting about other things for a while. Then Edward was shown to a room that was next door to Williams. His luggage had already been moved there. It was decided that they would meet at the entrance in half an hour and then go to the meeting with the village chief. For the second time in a couple of days, Edward reluctantly had to admit that he was mighty impressed with the professionalism in the whole arrangement.

The vehicle resembled a heavily modified golf cart. It ran on electricity and had both front and rear seats and heavy-duty tires. William had been trusted to drive. The other two were not in driving condition. Niilla sat next to them in the front seat and led the way while Edward sat in the back and enjoyed the ride as much as possible - as soon as the vehicle lurched because of some bump in the road, his limbs ached. The village chief lived on the opposite side of the valley and so the party got a good sightseeing tour. William got the feeling that they were not taking the shortest route and soon their guide confirmed his suspicions.

"I want you to observe as much as possible. As you can see, we have built gravel roads in many places. Someone calculated that we have over ten kilometers of road in the valley."

"How do you get in and out? I mean with vehicles like quad bikes and scooters." William gave a fleeting thought to their own scooter which was now somewhere in the village. At least according to their tour guide.

"Originally there were only small paths along the mountain slopes. Towards the Norwegian side it is not as steep and that's where the reindeer are led out for winter grazing."

He pointed to the western slopes.

"It is also possible to drive snowmobiles there. But nowadays we have blasted a tunnel through the mountain on both the east and west sides. It's not wide enough for larger vehicles, but a quad bike or snowmobile can easily get through."

They ran parallel to a rapid and in some places simple bridges had been built to cross to the other side.

"We only have electric vehicles in Luoktajärvi," said Niilla. "Some scooters are of course gasoline-powered, but they are only used for transportation in and out of the village. But here in the community, everything runs on electricity."

"How do you get electricity then?" Edward blurted out. "I don't see any power lines and I find it hard to believe that you've run a cable under the mountain."

Niilla laughed heartily.

"We have been self-sufficient in electricity for many years. Most of the electricity is generated by underground heat. If you drill deep enough, there's no limit to the amount of energy you can get. But we have also been experimenting with other natural sources to find alternatives."

He pointed to the west side again and told us about how they extract energy from the waterfall and the flowing rapids below.

"We have also installed solar panels on as many rooftops as we can—at least on the communal buildings. The villagers aren't too excited about it, though. Especially the older folks—they're skeptical. They think the shiny panels might somehow make the houses catch fire. But anyway, speaking of houses—we're rolling through the village now!"

A motley collection of buildings along a wide dirt road apparently formed the center of the village. Almost all the buildings were single-story wooden houses but there were also some stone houses. There were small cross streets and additional houses along them but essentially the center was a two hundred meter long dirt road and two rows of buildings. A short distance away on the left, water ran parallel to the village street and on the right there was a small football pitch on one of the few flat areas. With the exception of a few kids playing football on the pitch, the village itself seemed to be empty. Compared to the rest of the valley, this place was far from idyllic. Rather, it gave the impression of having been built for purely practical purposes.

"How many people live here?" William asked.

"Here along the village street there are not that many. Most of the houses are community buildings. But in the whole of Luoktajärvi we have around two hundred inhabitants. About half of them are scattered in the valley and the other half we count as villagers, although they actually live elsewhere - both in Sweden and Norway. They work, study and live like any other people. Some go to school and bring their knowledge here, like our doctor, whom you have already met. Some stay and some come back. Like Merja," he said, turning to William.

Edward curiously leaned forward in the carriage to participate in the discussion.

"So how come no one has heard of this place? I mean, surely at some point all these people who have left have been asked where they come from or had to give an address while waiting for their first home."

"A legitimate question." Niilla fell silent and let the answer hang in the air for a while, as if wondering how to continue.

"Because we don't want to draw attention to ourselves, there is a tacit agreement among all the Luoktajärvi people - an agreement never to talk about the village. But if someone gets into a situation where they have to explain themselves, they usually say that they come from one of the three Sámi villages located a few kilometers outside the valley. These places are run and used by various families who live here - these families are by the way real Sámi. Almost no one lives there anymore, but they are often used for winter grazing or fall hunting, and all three are marked on the map. So these places really exist, unlike Luoktajärvi."

The party passed a broad gravel square that stretched from the village street up to a stone building and next to it a wooden house that looked newly built. It was the only structure of its kind in the village, its most striking feature a grand, oversized balcony. All around it - on the steps, the square, and the balcony - villagers bustled about, clearly preparing for something. Niilla offered a brief explanation: the town hall was being readied for an upcoming celebration. That was all he said, and the group moved on without further comment.

They turned off at one of the last cross streets and headed away from the rapids up the northern mountainside. The road was winding but the vehicle's powerful electric motor took them quickly up the serpentine road. In some places, the road had been cut into the mountainside and reinforced with stone, concrete or oil gravel. In some places, meltwater had been channelled under the road using stone grooves.

They drove past the vineyards and came to what looked like a large farm. All the feed barns, stables, machine sheds and other buildings were equipped with solar panels. Cattle were in pastures and people were working on the sloping fields. Somewhere there was the rumbling sound of a diesel engine. Niilla apologetically explained that not everything could be replaced by electricity or hand power.

On the edge of the farm was a huge greenhouse. It was at least a hundred meters long and thirty meters wide. On the roofs of all the buildings were grass, but also something that William assumed was part of the lighting system. Now that he knew what to look for, he saw more and more large lights. Many were cleverly hidden among trees, integrated into buildings and other things that made them blend in with their surroundings. The buildings themselves blended seamlessly into the valley's greenery, and would be almost impossible to discover from the air.

As he made new discoveries, Niilla gave a vivid description of everything that was grown there: tomatoes, cucumbers, eggplants, melons, peppers and lemons.

"We grow everything that is not suitable for outdoor cultivation in the greenhouse. We are virtually self-sufficient. From the cows we get milk, butter, cream and cheese. From the reindeer and cattle we get meat and skins. We have planted fish in the lake and the rapids and potatoes and root vegetables grow in the soil. The vines and apple trees produce fruit, must and wine. Mushrooms grow in the old quarry. The fields produce bread, grain and animal feed. The rest we grow in the greenhouse or transport here by air."

Niilla turned to his guests but got no response. They were both dumbfounded, like children in a giant toy store, where every room, corner and nook offered a new surprise. The journey continued through a varied mountain landscape, and everywhere there was something to look at and be mesmerized by. As they approached the western part of the valley, Niilla told them that they had just crossed the official border with Norway, at least according to official maps.

Soon after, they came to a small, mirror-like mountain tarn on a plateau at the western wall of the mountain. At the far end of the tarn stood a solitary Sámi hut. William realized that they had now arrived.

William and Edward were each sitting on a reindeer skin that covered a crescent-shaped wooden bench around the fireplace in the Sámi hut. Niilla was stirring the logs with a stick. Sáhkár stood across the fireplace, smoking a pipe. His appearance was more reminiscent of Zeb Macahan than the typical Sámi chief they had imagined. The ancient man stood tall and wore a sun-bleached and worn leather suit. On his head he wore a fur garment that looked like a bird's nest. It was pleasantly cozy near the crackling fire, and both visitors were pleased that the weathered mountain king was as far away as the small tent offered.

Niilla dropped the stick and walked over to a wooden cabinet at the back of the hut and returned with a bottle and four small glasses. He poured a considerable amount of a clear liquid into each glass and handed them out. Then he raised the glass, uttered a few incomprehensible words and swallowed the contents. The others did the same. William's throat burned and he could not help but grimace. He looked at Edward and saw that he had the same problem.

"We distill our own potato spirit. It's a bit stronger than the stuff you're used to." Niilla gave a big smile and sat down on a sheepskin between the guests and the village chief.

The Mountain King looked up from his pipe for the first time and noticed the visitors. Then he turned to Niilla and said something in an incomprehensible dialect.

"Sáhkár asks if you would like to smoke a pipe with him."

They both nodded, and soon all four were sitting with a stuffed log each, puffing in silence. William, who was not used to tobacco, coughed a few times. The tobacco had a sweet animal smell that was not entirely unpleasant.

After a while, the old man looked up from his pipe again and spoke to Niilla, who then turned to the visitors.

"Sáhkár wants to know what the Swedish Security Service is doing here."

Edward slowly blew the smoke out of his mouth as he steeled himself. This was it. They had reached the point where he would either get answers to his questions or be sent out head first. Just a few hours ago, this had been the whole purpose of the trip. To come here and get answers to questions. He was representing the Security Service in an extremely sensitive case, where unfortunate events had occurred on Swedish soil and under questionable circumstances. But this morning's conversation with Kvarnbring changed everything. He no longer had a mandate or clear guidelines. At the same time, he couldn't just claim he was here to pick mushrooms. But given the surprisingly good reception and the great goodwill Niila had shown, he decided to proceed cautiously with the original plan.

"I have a number of questions concerning your activities in Stockholm. First, I would like to know what Reindeer's Gold is?"

Niilla flinched where he sat on the chair. Whatever it was, he'd obviously not expected this particular question. He glanced at the chieftain who was still puffing on his pipe. He made a friendly gesture with his hand towards the two visitors and said something inaudible to Niilla. Their host nodded and spoke.

"Have you heard of Yarchagumba?"

"Jajagumba? No, I can't recall that I have ever heard that word," said Edward.

"Yarchagumba. It is a mushroom that grows in Nepal. The name means "summer grass" or "winter worm" and is a type of mushroom that is said to increase sex drive. At least that's what they say in China. The goodies are formed when a parasitic fungus attacks the caterpillars of a particular butterfly living in the soil. The fungus turns the caterpillar's organs into a cobweb-like mass and then shoots out a sprout through the dead insect's head. In China, the mummified caterpillars are mixed with food, ground into powder and given as a gift or used as a bribe."

"Who could possibly want to taste a dead caterpillar?" William got unappealing images in his head and grimaced.

"It's just like rhino horn or snake gall bladders. They are supposed to increase potency or improve the immune system, but really it's all about impressing people. The secret is in the exclusivity and the grotesque price. A kilo can sell for up to a million."

"So, it doesn't matter if it's ineffective or tastes like a dead caterpillar?"

"Not in the least. Then there are probably some who really imagine that the witchcraft mixture has an effect."

"So what are you trying to tell us? I don't think I have understood the context. Do you grow jajagumba up here?" Edward waved his palms up in an uncomprehending gesture.

"No, it only grows in Nepal. We have found something similar but much better. Something that works. But keep your mind on the parasitic fungus for a while longer and I'll explain." Niilla's eyes sparkled as he spoke. You could tell this was his business. His baby.

"Yarchagumba grows only in Nepal and at an altitude of five thousand meters. The caterpillars are collected by hand by villagers or farmers who are taxed by the Nepalese government before selling the goods on to traders in Tibet. Chinese middlemen buy the goods in Tibet and then sell them to markets in central China, where retailers resell the mushrooms to Beijing and elsewhere. Finally, the goodies end up in the hands of the end customer. That is, wealthy Chinese. These are mainly younger, newly rich businessmen, but also older, wealthy men who cannot resist buying when everyone else does.

"So the price rises many times before it reaches its final destination?"

"Exactly. Then imagine that we are the farmers who provide the raw material - which, of course, only grows in an exotic inaccessible place in the Laponia World Heritage Site. Then remove the tax and most of the middlemen. Do you see where I'm going with this?"

"I kind of understand," said William. "But what is it that you have actually found? A northern mushroom that makes Asians horny?"

"Haha, yes you might say that. But our mushroom has nothing to do with caterpillars and it does not contribute to increasing potency. If you are precise, it's not even a mushroom but a rare variety of moss. It's called *Blue Grimmia* and grows freely on our hills and the only special nutrition they need comes from our horned friends."

"You mean the reindeer?"

"This is exactly what I mean. You could say that manure is the main nutrient for moss. And sun and water, of course. We call the moss "Reindeer's Gold."

"You mean this moss thrives in reindeer manure?"

"Yes, it seems so. The moss is extremely rare and only grows in a few places. In Sweden, it officially grows only at Kvikkjokk. But what almost no one knows is that it grows particularly well in our small mountain village. The special fertilizer makes it unique."

"Who buys such eccentric products?"

"More than you might think. Most of our customers come from China, Japan and Korea. They believe that the sponge prolongs life."

"What makes them think so? Do you believe it yourself?"

"Here in Luoktajärvi we have used moss for centuries. We don't mix it with food, of course, but the elderly people dry the moss and put it in their pipes along with tobacco." He pointed to his father, who was quietly puffing on his pipe.

William had tried to locate the animal scent since they stepped into the hut and now that he knew he regretted his curiosity.

"You seem to have been successful in cultivating the myth of the magic moss," Edward insisted, looking at the old man and the bandaged man with a mixture of skepticism and admiration.

"It is not a myth. We don't know exactly why, but the moss does seem to have an effect. The Reindeer's Gold, combined with our lifestyle, might add. For example, we eat a lot of fish from the river and the water is crystal clear and full of minerals. Then there's the environment, of course. We believe that the mountains and the underground spring - and the mist it creates - have a calming effect on the inhabitants. Here there are no stressed souls and no influence from the outside world. Wars, natural disasters, environmental pollution, financial crises, career hustle and ordinary everyday stress do not affect us. We don't process our food and we don't dump our waste into Luoktajärvi's only watercourse. Cancer and stroke are virtually unknown phenomena among the elderly. Here people die from accidents or old age.

He paused and looked at the two visitors with amusement. William met his gaze. Although everything Niilla had told him made sense, it was hard to believe that the moss would have any contributing effect. Not to mention the reindeer shit.

"I see that you have doubts. By the way, I forgot to tell you that the water and the mist are good for the skin, they smooth out the wrinkles. Well, I'll let you guess how old I am. If you guess the correct age, I promise to run naked through the village singing any song you like." He then picked up a timeworn photograph and held it in his hand, upside down.

Edward looked uncomfortable. "One of the reasons for coming here was to hand back your cell phone, driver's license, and pilot's license."

Niilla nodded. "We already found them while you were asleep. I thank you for bringing them back".

"Well, then I know your age and do not have to participate in the guessing game."

"Those are Swedish and Norwegian licenses. I need them to be able to travel outside of this village. The birth date is not correct".

"Ok, fine," said William. I don't know what you are talking about but I would say that you are a few years older than me. Let's say 45 years."

"And I remember from the licenses that you are around 50", said Edward.

Niilla looked amused as he held up the yellowish photo in front of William and Edward. It was a picture of him from the Winter Games in Calgary 1988. The photo was taken on Niilla together with a couple of famous Swedish gold medalists from the cross country ski competition. The olympic rings could be seen in the background.

It was undoubtedly the same person, thought Edward, with the characteristic birthmark above the right eyebrow, albeit a slightly younger version of himself.

"I was born in 1948 and was 40 during the winter games in Calgary."

"Then you should be approaching 80 today," said Edward, shaking his head for himself.

"I don't believe you," said William.

Edward looked at his friend, then at Sáhkár and turned his head back to Niilla again.

"I would agree with William but there are actually some reconnaissance reports that support your claim. According to one report, you studied at Stockholm University over forty years ago under a false name. Is that correct?"

"Yes, that is correct."

"Why did you use a false name?"

"We didn't want to draw attention to Luoktajärvi and a false name was the easiest solution. Nowadays, when so many people live and work in places other than Luoktajärvi, they always give their real names, but use the nearby Sámi villages as their place of birth when necessary."

"So you want to tell us that you are almost eighty years old... is that the reason for using a fake birth date?" Edward glanced at William as if seeking support for his doubts.

"Yes, as you now have proved yourselves, it wouldn't have been a good idea to use the correct birth date on the driver's- and pilot licence. And I wouldn't know the real date anyway. I am probably 77 or 78, he replied, shining like the sun again. The numbers are not that important in Luoktajärvi. Sáhkár, my father, is about 110 years old."

They both looked at the old man, whose face was partially obscured by tobacco smoke. He certainly didn't look young, but neither of them would have guessed such a respectable age.

"Ok, let's drop it for now. Why did you disappear from the hospital?"

"I would have had to answer a lot of uncomfortable questions that I couldn't possibly answer without giving away our entire existence. After your visit, I knew I had to get out of there as soon as possible."

"Did you get help from here?"

"Yes they came for me. It was apparently just to roll me out and roll someone else in. The guard was sleeping like a baby."

Edward grunted and buried his hands in his face while he thought about how to continue. The brandy and tobacco had dulled the pain somewhat, but instead another nagging feeling emerged - a craving. The urge to smoke came over him and for a moment he almost asked if he could light a cigarette, but immediately dismissed the idea for fear of ingesting another pipe of reindeer shit. He decided to take a chance again since Niilla had proved to be more than cooperative.

"We know that Reindeer's Gold is dried and mixed with tobacco before being flown down to Stockholm to be packed in small containers resembling snuff boxes. The snuff boxes are sold by a company in the harbour, the packing is done in a boathouse north of Stockholm, and the goods are delivered by amphibious aircraft out at sea. I myself have flown in the Cessna that is parked at your pier. Edward paused and for a moment he thought Niilla looked worried but he quickly washed that look away."

"Legally, it is about smuggling. That's why I'm here in the first place, not because you escaped from a hospital."

"But... there are no illegal substances in the boxes," Niilla tried tentatively.

"No, but it is still a black market. Why do you go to such trouble to keep everything secret?"

Niilla took a deep puff from his pipe and poured another glass of potato-spirit, which he swigged. Then he passed the bottle to the visitors. Both Edward and William joined him.

"The trade is done on international waters, not in Sweden. And where would we report the trade anyway? Who would be registered with the company? Where would the tax be paid? Should we apply for an export license? We do not even exist on the map."

"What about the customers? Are they also incognito?"

"Yes, we have a handful of Asian customers. They have contact persons on site and pay in cash in connection with the handover. So what happens now? Will there be a raid on the boathouse?"

"No... I can't imagine that. If you had smuggled heroin, it would of course have been a different matter, but now it is a fairly harmless activity. But why haven't you worked to become part of Sweden or Norway? Wouldn't that have been easier?"

"There is nothing there that we need. Look around and tell us what we are missing."

Edward thought about the journey through the valley and everything they had seen. The mountains, the greenery, the waterfalls, the rapids, the vineyards, the farms and the pleasant temperature.

"Ok, but then I don't understand why you let us in at all. It would have been a simple matter to just patch us up and drive us away on some snowmobile sled. If I remember correctly, that's how you would prefer to do it. Why this hospitality and openness? Why do you tell all these secrets to us outsiders?" Edward wondered.

"Because we need your help. As I told you earlier, big things will happen in a few days. All the secrecy will soon be a thing of the past."

William and Edward looked at each other and then at Niilla and finally at the puffing old man who still hadn't moved a muscle.

"What big things are going to happen?" William asked.

"You are our humble and grateful witnesses to what will soon become known to the entire world. You are the hikers who lost their way, fell, and were badly injured—only to be rescued by the kind people of Luoktajärvi, who tended your wounds and welcomed you with open arms."

"So you have used us?" Edward gave Niilla a sharp look.

"No, I don't think so. You found your way here yourselves and decided to climb down the steep eastern mountain wall in deep snow. We have taken care of you as we would have done with any injured person. And you have certainly proved to be unusually interesting guests afterwards. You happened to be a police officer, a representative of the state who has secretly chased me through half of Sweden. And William here has apparently had an affair with my daughter. No, we haven't planned anything or set any traps, but I must admit that you are very timely."

William flinched as he realized the obviousness of the words that had just been spoken, *my daughter*. The pieces of the puzzle fell into place. Niilla was Merja's father. It matched the age Niilla had given, and when he looked at the man's face he immediately saw similarities. Similarities that had been in front of him all along but which, because of all the other impressions, had passed unnoticed. It also explained why he had seen Merja's photo on the wall of the mountain house. Somehow it made him feel relieved that he now had an explanation. A logical, simple and reasonable explanation. He looked around the cabin at the other three men, but no one seemed to have taken any notice of his reaction.

"But what will happen in Luoktajärvi? Why do *you* need *us*?" Edward flung his arms out in a theatrical gesture.

"You will witness something that has never happened before. In three days, Luoktajärvi will declare itself an independent state. We will declare ourselves free from both Norway and Sweden. And as for you two, we ask a favor: as the first official foreign visitors, tell us how well you have been treated and all the beautiful things you have seen here. We want to convey the image of a civilized society that has managed to survive without outside help - despite the pressures of a century. In return, we will offer you the chance to stay and become the first immigrants in our new state."

The little party sat in silence for a long time. Niilla refilled their glasses and neither William nor Edward protested when he filled their pipes with reindeer dung-scented tobacco and moss for the second time.

Budapest, January 17, 1945

The frozen winter air hung heavy over Budapest, laced with the acrid scent of war. The city was crumbling under Soviet artillery, and Raoul Wallenberg knew his time was running out. Though he had saved thousands of Jews from Nazi extermination, he had become a hunted man - by both the retreating Germans and the advancing Soviets.

Word had reached him: Soviet officers were searching for him. In the chaos of occupied Hungary, his diplomatic immunity meant little. But Wallenberg had one final hope - an old Hungarian resistance contact had arranged for a secret escape. A German aircraft, returning from Narvik with troops to reinforce the Eastern Front, was scheduled to depart from a remote airstrip west of the city.

Under cover of darkness, Wallenberg left the Swedish Legation under the pretense of a meeting with Soviet command. Instead, he slipped into a waiting vehicle driven by a trusted resistance fighter.

The journey was perilous - Soviet patrols roamed the roads, and German snipers haunted the ruins - but just before dawn, they reached the snow-covered airstrip. A small courier aircraft waited, its propellers already spinning. Wallenberg climbed aboard, disguised as a Gestapo officer with forged papers and a fabricated mission. The pilot and his wingman didn't question him. Their orders were to transport personnel back, not ask questions.

The flight through the frigid night was long and dangerous, crossing enemy lines and war-torn landscapes. But hours later, as the jagged Norwegian coastline came into view beneath the pale light of morning, Wallenberg finally exhaled. He had survived the first part.

The plane touched down on a frozen runway just outside Narvik. A biting wind swept across the airfield as Wallenberg stepped out, his Gestapo disguise flapping loosely around him. The illusion had served its purpose, but now it was a liability. Norwegian resistance contacts were supposed to meet him, but the airstrip was nearly deserted - just a few German mechanics busy refueling another plane and a lone officer scanning paperwork in a small outpost. Wallenberg kept his head down, moving quickly toward the edge of the field where a nondescript black truck idled in the snow.

A man emerged from the driver's side, tall and gaunt, his breath clouding in the cold.

"Wallenberg, is it you?" he asked quietly in Swedish. At Wallenberg's nod, he gestured to the truck. "We have little time. There's already word that the Soviets are asking questions - here, in Norway."

As they pulled away from the airfield, the man handed Wallenberg a bundle of clothes.

"Get out of that uniform before someone sees you. We're taking you north - there's a fishing vessel in Tromsø that can get you to Sweden. But it won't be easy. The Germans still control most of the coast, and the Soviets have agents everywhere."

Wallenberg changed quickly in the back of the truck, the disguise discarded like a second skin. Exhaustion clawed at him, but his mind remained sharp. If he reached Stockholm, if he lived to tell the story - maybe then the world would understand what had happened in Budapest.

CHAPTER 14

Independence Day

Two days before the announced declaration of independence, people began to arrive in Luoktajärvi. They came on quad bikes, on snowmobiles and on foot. People came via the east and west tunnels, but some walked across the slopes, just as they had always done. Some had heavy packs in tow, but most came more or less empty-handed, carrying a small rucksack or other light luggage. All along the surrounding mountainside, the snow cover had eased significantly.

When the day of the big event arrived, the population had doubled. The whole valley was now bustling with life. Niilla explained that it was all the returnees who wanted to take part in the celebrations. A number of selected guests had also been invited in secret. They were mainly journalists, but also a number of representatives of the United Nations. These were officials normally tasked with monitoring the electoral process in troubled parts of the world. The election observers would also serve as guarantors in case either of the two mother countries started to oppose.

William and Edward had chosen to stay to participate in the process. For William, it was mainly about getting a chance to meet Merja who would arrive in connection with Independence Day. For Edward, staying had been mostly a matter of having nothing better to do - though it also gave him time to let his body recover. They remained at Niilla's alpine house, where they were treated like honored guests and wanted for nothing. During the days they explored the valley in all corners and in the evenings they enjoyed the local food and wine. The small electric car had been at their disposal and Edward in particular was grateful for this favor, even though the plaster bandage around his right ankle was now the only visible trace of the mountain climb a few days earlier.

In the days that followed, the unlikely pair had not only forged a strong friendship, but had also - perhaps without realizing it - grown deeply fond of Luoktajärvi. The village had a quiet pull, and it was impossible to resist the steady stream of impressions it offered: the warmth of its people, the rhythm of its days, the haunting beauty of its isolation. Niilla's words had not been forgotten either: *In return, we will offer you to stay and become the first immigrants in our new state.* It was an offer that grew more and more attractive with each passing hour. At one point, Niilla had taken them to the hot spring that made Luoktajärvi the unique place it was. They had floated around like retirees at a spa in almost body-temperature water. The boiling mineral-rich water rose from the invisible coal seam of the underground and mixed with the cooler surface water of the lake, which was constantly fed with fresh and ice-cold mountain water from inflowing rapids. Water vapor rose from the lake and settled like a light mist in the middle of the bowl-shaped valley.

Edward had put a plastic bag over the cast and that was that. They had bathed for hours, just enjoying the warmth and the view in the background. On a few occasions, villagers had made their way down to the site for a ritual washing. Everyone seemed to have their own favorite spots.

Now the hour for the Declaration of Independence had struck and the two men were sitting in the borrowed electric car and were on their way down to the gravel square at the town hall, where the event was to be held. The sun was shining brightly without a single cloud in the sky, but Edward was deep in thought. He had not heard anything from Kvarnbring since he'd been asked by phone to drop the case. He was still dismayed by the cancer news. It wasn't just because they'd spent a quarter of their lives together in the service - it also stirred memories of what he and Beatrice had been through just a few years earlier.

It felt unreal, but at the same time it was not entirely unexpected. His colleague had been smoking like a chimney for far too many years and now his body had given up. It was simply time to take stock and Kvarnbring had made the only right decision - to push himself out of the job as soon as possible and make the most of the time left.

Over the past few days, he'd been pondering his colleague's strange explanation for why he wanted to close the case. *Edward, if you think about it, I think you will understand that this is the best way. The best way for both you and me.* Now the words seemed obvious.

Firstly, the operation was obviously closed-down by someone other than Kvarnbring. Again. When he recalled the various reports from the past hundred years, they had always ended in an abrupt shut down. Someone else pulled the strings, possibly a small group of people or an organization with high influence, that effectively seemed to have killed all attempts to unravel the truth about the shady mountain village for more than a century.

Secondly, there was probably no one other than the two colleagues who were familiar with the details of the case. Kvarnbring had probably only reported the information he considered appropriate to pass on, and he guessed that the money and the details of the smuggling did not belong there. Metzner certainly knew some of it but had no overall picture, only fragments of a traffic investigation.

Kvarnbring's personal incentive to keep the lid on was probably that no one else knew about the money, at least no one who could do anything about it. So the big question would obviously be: if you find out that you have six months to live and at the same time stumble upon six million that no one knows about, what do you do? At least he himself knew what he would have done.

At that moment, only one thing occupied his mind: the man sitting beside him in the electric vehicle. What was his connection to the two young men who had stolen the bag from Niilla's car? And why had they accused William of cheating them out of money? There was only one way to get answers - he would have to ask.

* * *

William noticed the policeman slouched beside him, lost in some deep, silent thought. His eyes were fixed straight ahead, vacant and unblinking. He hadn't said a word since they left the chalet. It was unlike him - over the past few days, the gray-haired man had seemed lighter, almost ten years younger, moving with surprising ease despite his injuries. But now, that vitality was gone, replaced by a heavy stillness William couldn't ignore. It was as if the environment had a magical effect on both of them, and William felt that they had become familiar with each other and talked effortlessly. Now the policeman seemed gloomy and melancholic. Suddenly he turned to William and said:

"There is one thing I have to ask you. I want you to answer honestly."

William was so taken aback that he jerked the steering wheel and hit the brakes at the same time. He recovered and resumed driving while wondering what had gotten into the older man.

"Ask away and I will do my best. What are you thinking about?"

"Police took two men in for questioning last weekend. They were arrested at a camping site in Westridge and are suspected of robbery.

275

A couple of plastic bags containing several millions were found in the trunk of their car."

William got a lump in his throat. Two men. A camping site outside Westridge. Two plastic bags of money. Could they be the same people? What did the police want from him? His thoughts were racing and he had difficulty concentrating on driving.

"Both men are former juvenile offenders and we believe they acted alone. But they claim that there is another person involved. Someone who conned them out of money and set them up to get away with it. The person they've named is you. They've given your name."

The policeman stared blankly past him, straight out into the dense green vegetation, as if trying to fix his gaze on something else.

William thought long and hard before answering. In any case, these were the same people he'd given six million to and who had now been caught and subsequently turned him in. Probably out of frustration. But if it really had been a premeditated robbery, then they had lied to him - deceived him into believing they'd stumbled upon the money by chance, and he had fallen for it completely. Whatever it mattered. He was very much an accomplice. Maybe more than that? He had manipulated and lied and been aware of every step he'd taken. There was no turning back. He decided to tell everything as it was. He stopped the car at a small meeting point, just wide enough for two four-wheelers to meet. William buried his face in his hands and started to tell the story. He left out a few details like the exact amount, the location of the cabin, the weapons in the crawl space, and the car swap at his uncle's place. When he was done, he looked at Edward and asked:

"Are you going to arrest me now?"

The policeman looked at him for a while but finally burst out laughing.

"Are you going to share?"

William was so surprised that he almost fell out of his chair. At the same time, a great weight was released from his chest. A burden that he'd been carrying for almost a week now. A story that had to be told to someone. He turned to Edward and said:

"I would be happy to do so! But... who did they steal the money from?"

"The man we are on our way to listen to. Niilla drove off the road during the snowstorm and ended up in hospital. That's why his face looks like mine. During that accident his money was stolen by the two guys that tried to turn you in"

Edward glanced at him with a puzzled look.

"How is it possible...? What is the probability of that?"

"It's not that surprising if you think about it. All evidence points this way."

"The bag... it came from here."

"The bag?" Edward rubbed his forehead.

"Yes, the bag where the money was originally. It read *Luoktajärvi* engraved on the inside of the lid."

"Then it's Niilla's bag you found," replied Edward.

"And above all, Niilla's money."

"You must tell him everything."

"Yes, of course... but it won't be easy to explain that six million are missing and that I've come here empty-handed and haven't mentioned anything during this time."

"It can't be helped."

William nodded and then sat in silence for a long time. Then he asked:

"Have you thought about staying here?"

"I've been thinking about it ever since Niilla asked. I guess I was going to wait until this whole thing was over and then see what happens. What if all these people decide to stay?"

"Have thought about the same thing. But I think most people will leave again. They have built their lives elsewhere and invested too much to just give it up. It's not like you and me, standing here like two blank pieces of paper."

"What about you? Do you want to stay here?" Edward looked at William.

"It depends entirely on Merja. If she wants me to stay, I'll stay. Otherwise I'll probably have to leave Luoktajärvi."

"Where do you go then?"

"I do not know. Maybe I will go abroad for a while."

The wind shifted, carrying with it the sound of people shouting and cheering. It was coming from the direction of the village center, which was only a few hundred meters away. It was almost six o'clock in the evening and the live broadcasts were about to start. William stepped on the gas and turned back onto the road.

❋ ❋ ❋

The village square was filled to the brim with excited people. There was cheering and laughter and some joined in song. It was about times gone by, about setbacks and victories - and about Luoktajärvi. Many were dressed in colorful folk costume-inspired clothes while others looked like people on vacation. William guessed that most of the village's two hundred inhabitants were there plus some specially invited guests. At the front, a number of journalists were looking expectantly towards the balcony.

The newly built town hall looked magnificent. The facade and the balcony had been decorated with flowers, colorful fabrics and flags, and the result was impressive. A large screen was set up next to the gravel area, showing the full width of the balcony and part of the sea of people. To a TV viewer, it must all look pretty impressive.

They were almost at the back of the gravel square but had a good view of the big screen. William discreetly scanned the sea of people in the hope of catching a glimpse of Merja. Her father had told him she was coming to the Declaration of Independence but it was unlikely he would be able to find her among all the other people.

* * *

The large clock on the façade struck six and the noise level dropped until only a scattered murmur remained. Eyes turned to the balcony and journalists stood ready with their cameras and notebooks. Three large flags swayed gently in the wind - the Swedish, Norwegian and Sámi flags. They were each hoisted on a long flagpole attached to the roof of the building.

Suddenly a figure appeared on the balcony and then another. William glanced at the big screen, where the image had now been replaced by a live broadcast from the Swedish National Television, and saw Niilla step up to the makeshift microphone. His face bandage was completely removed and there was no trace of what he'd been through. In the background, a tall, hulking figure that looked like Sáhkár could be seen. Two standard-bearers and two soldiers stood neatly lined up behind the protagonist. A little to the side, five men in blue berets stood in a group, looking both lost and out of place. Niilla looked out over the sea of people and then grabbed the microphone. It crackled and added to the drama. Everyone's eyes were now fixed on the person at the microphone.

"Dear friends, citizens and children of Luoktajärvi, honored guests and TV viewers, welcome to this unique event. Welcome to the Declaration of Independence of the Principality of Luoktajärvi!"

A big cheer broke out and flags waved in people's hands. He was forced to pause briefly before continuing in flawless English:

"A special welcome to our invited guests - journalists from all over the world and representatives of the United Nations, who are here to make sure everything goes smoothly."

For a moment, the TV cameras were focused on the hooded men who, in the camera's close-up, seemed to be cast in the same mold.

"For almost one hundred and thirty years, we have been in a no man's land. Everywhere we have been driven away. We are not part of Sweden, not part of Norway and not part of the Sámi community. According to the reindeer grazing convention, we have not been able to move across the border, and no one can even agree on where the border is. We have thus, in practice, been foreigners for over a hundred years and in a place that does not even exist. We have finally concluded that, with the help of the international community and in front of the world's cameras, it is time to make a number of demands. Our hope is that the free states of the United Nations - including our closest neighbors and brothers - will accept these demands."

Niilla paused as applause and cheers filled the village. The image on the big screen panned across the sea of people, which appeared much larger than it actually was. The sound faded slightly and the camera panned back to the balcony where Niilla spoke again.

"For all these years, we have managed on our own, without help from the outside world. We are self-sufficient and self-governing, applying our own laws and rules. We have never needed any help, nor do we expect any."

He looked into the cameras with a serious look. Then he picked up a piece of paper and read from it:

"As the elected representative of Luoktajärvi, I wish to express the unanimous demands of our inhabitants. Before the international community and its honorable representatives, before our closest neighbors Sweden and Norway, and before our Sámi brothers and sisters, I hereby declare the independence of Luoktajärvi. Its borders will consist of the area bounded by the mountains Virijåkko, Sadjhelanta and Karelieppe and the contiguous reindeer grazing land belonging to the three neighboring Sámi communities in the north, south and west, which have belonged to our families for generations. From today's date, this area will belong to the Principality of Luoktajärvi."

Niilla raised his arms in the air in a dramatic gesture and a huge cheer erupted. The three flags were lowered and replaced by a single giant light blue flag adorned with a white symbol. When the flag had been hoisted all the way and stretched by the wind, the silhouette of a mountain could be clearly seen against the blue background. William immediately recognized the figure on the coat bag. It symbolized one of Luoktajärvi's three surrounding mountains - the pyramid-shaped mountain to the west. It had been there all along, but only now did he realize that the embroidered symbol on the bag was the same silhouette he'd seen every evening and every morning from the balcony of the alpine house.

Church bells began to chime with full force. The sound waves bounced off the rock walls and created a faint echo. William couldn't recall seeing a single church during their guided tours, but the effect was powerful and added to the impression of a civilization that already had it all and was best left to its own devices. The pre-recorded sound of church bells died away and was replaced by a firework display emanating from the roof of the building.

When the fireworks subsided, the live broadcast on the big screen was replaced by a couple of pre-recorded interviews with William and Edward. The recording had been made the day before by Swedish Television and neither William nor Edward were mentioned by name. They were two anonymous mountain hikers who got lost and injured in the rugged terrain. Thanks to first-class medical care and great hospitality, the two hikers had now fully recovered and were offered to stay and settle in Luoktajärvi. They spoke highly of their experience: the medical care, the food and wine, the self-sufficiency, the climate and beautiful surroundings, and last but not least, the friendly people.

William and Edward looked at each other. They felt a little uneasy when they realized that the interview was being broadcast around the world. It had been done in English to the best of their ability and to add to the drama, the lights were dimmed and both interviewees had been provided with extra plasters and gauze on their faces. This allowed them to remain anonymous but possibly appear somewhat ridiculous. This was followed by an interview with the UN observers, which then turned into a live studio debate on the subject of

Luoktajärvi.

The balcony emptied and some of the elderly people started to leave the gravel field but most of them stayed to join in the celebrations which were expected to last well into the night. A group of local musicians had taken their place on the balcony and soon folk music was blasting from the speakers. Beer and wine were served directly from barrels pulled there on a hay wagon behind a tractor. Makeshift tents were erected, barbecue barrels were filled with charcoal, long tables were brought out and set up. A roasted pig was rotating over an open fire. Lamps and torches were lit as the sun began to disappear behind the mountain ridge. William and Edward stayed to join in the festivities, walking around and talking to the villagers. They had more or less become local celebrities in just a few days.

It was towards evening, when the sun had long since disappeared behind the pyramid-shaped mountain peak to the west but still cast a faint backlight across the sky, that William saw her. She was too far away for him to see her face, but it was her silhouette that ultimately revealed her presence.

She appeared to be helping serve at the long tables and was talking to some other people. She was a head taller than those in front of her and her hair was clearly visible. Then, as she moved towards one of the makeshift tents with an empty tray in her hand, he was completely convinced; the swaying elegant gait, like a desert ship, and the long legs. For a while he didn't know what to do. Should he wait or should he go forward? So far, the adventure had been the thing, and the thought of seeing her again had been the icing on the cake, but it had only been there in theory. It had never been real. Not until now. Everything so far had turned out to be an amazing experience, far beyond what he could imagine. But now it was all in danger of falling apart like a house of cards in a few short moments. Either he would become very happy or he would become very disappointed. But he couldn't turn back now that he'd come this far and everything had turned out for the best as long as he'd just followed his gut.

He looked around and realized that Edward was not around. That was a good thing. He didn't want to be interrupted now that he was gathering himself. He gritted his teeth, took a few deep breaths and started walking towards the tent.

CHAPTER 15

The Principality

News of the Principality of Luoktajärvi spread around the world. For several days, it was front-page news in most of Europe, and in Sweden and Norway it was top news for several weeks. At first, no one knew how to tackle the problem. The governments of each country were asked for a statement, but not a single person had heard of Luoktajärvi. The questions were passed around and eventually ended up with the Security Service, where pieces of the century-old story began to unravel. Classified reports were published and journalists did their own investigations. Soon, everyone knew about the village and the evergreen crater that was the heart of the Principality. But not a word was said about the Reindeer's Gold. The secret had remained with the inhabitants, but it was understood that it was only a matter of time before Luoktajärvi's biggest, and so far only, source of income became known to the public now that the village's existence was no longer a secret.

When the stories of the secret investigations, the border dispute and many other inconvenient things became public knowledge, there was no turning back. Both Sweden and Norway were forced, after some customary wrangling over the actual demarcation of the border, to accept the new breakaway state. After a few months, the Principality's request for independence was formally taken up at the UN, where it was passed by an overwhelming majority. No country voted against, but a few abstained - including Russia and China, which feared that similar ideas would take hold in the various vassal states. They wanted to avoid a new disintegration.

When Luoktajärvi's sovereignty was no longer in doubt, the infrastructure was expanded; there was plenty of investment money. The tunnel on the west side was expanded to allow larger loads to pass, and a small asphalt road connected the E6 highway on the Norwegian side with Luoktajärvi. However, all gasoline vehicles had to stop on the Norwegian side of the tunnel. On the Swedish side, it was trickier to get good access because of all the prohibitions in Padjelanta National Park. In the end, a completely new tunnel was built in a northerly direction and a small gravel road, running north along the Norwegian-Swedish border, connected Luoktajärvi with Rietsem. Small vehicles such as quad bikes and scooters were allowed on the new road, but no cars or trucks.

The road network inside Luoktajärvi - if one could call it a road network in the true sense of the word - was expanded and strengthened, electricity networks and street lighting were installed, and a proper water and sewage system was built. A new mobile phone mast was erected and the whole village center got a big boost; several community buildings were renovated, the municipal building was repainted and a small village pub opened its doors. Another seaplane was acquired and a small terminal building was added to the seaport.

But even though there was activity everywhere for a while, in the end the inhabitants could recognize themselves. It was still the same old village, albeit slightly more modern. Many expatriates chose to return with their families. The population grew in just a few years to three hundred permanent residents.

Curiosity about the mythical mountain village grew and many

people wanted to come as tourists. They wondered how best to handle the situation; the place was really too small to accommodate so many visitors. Eventually, they were forced to impose visa requirements, and only relatives or people with a special reason were given access to a visa. One such special reason was, for example, guest workers hired to build the infrastructure.

Given the pace at which the mountain village was modernizing, uncomfortable questions were soon asked about how to finance the whole shebang. Soon the media got wind of the miracle drug *Reindeer's Gold*, which was exported to Asia and brought in fantastic sums of money. Exports, which were already underway, had by then multiplied as a result of the enormous attention generated by Luoktajärvi. Public awareness of the Reindeer's Gold increased demand even more, and soon the demand could not be met. The effect was to drive up the price to unbelievably high levels, and money poured into the small village.

After Luoktajärvi became a real nation, running the village as a family affair was no longer enough. The population grew, the village expanded, and soon goods were flowing in and out. Hired labor needed wages, and with growth came complexity. Laws, regulations, and a functioning structure were no longer optional—a proper society had to be built from the ground up. Imported goods required customs clearance, sales had to be tracked, infrastructure maintained, and public order enforced. People began demanding grocery stores and other basic amenities - services that had never before existed within the village's borders. A team of bureaucrats was set up to deal with all this. Some had experience of the outside world, while others found it a little harder to take in everything that was happening around them.

As Luoktajärvi became a sovereign state, and everything that followed by being a real nation, more and more figures and statistics became available to the outside world. These were unofficial figures on the country's GDP, life expectancy, population and the like. At first, the figures were received as a joke, but as more official figures and explanations were unveiled, the laughter turned to skepticism and finally to admiration. GDP was well above the neighbouring countries, principalities or microstates that came closest behind and life expectancy was reported to be an improbable ninety-three years. The explanation for the high life expectancy was given as climate, diet and lack of stress. Not a word was mentioned about Reindeer's Gold, although its existence was by now widely known, the alleged miracle effect was widely regarded as hocus pocus.

For most of the inhabitants of Luoktajärvi, life went on as usual and they were usually unaffected by everything around them. Every now and then, some of the older villagers would vent their innermost feelings about the state of things, but they were usually about some local remodeling that affected the accessibility of the village, and not about the principality's newly acquired place in the universe.

Secret Service Officer Edward Johnson decided to stay and make a life in the village on the very day it declared independence—though it would be some time before he could fully admit it, even to himself. Once his injuries had healed, he returned to Stockholm aboard one of the air transports to take care of the practicalities of retirement.

Kvarnbring was not there and no one knew where he'd gone. According to his closest colleagues, he had *gone on a long vacation* to *try out his wings as a newly retired man.* Edward suspected that no one knew anything about the advanced cancer that was methodically and relentlessly breaking down his skin-dry body. He never saw Kvarnbring again, but a few months later he received a short handwritten letter, forwarded to his new address in Luoktajärvi.

Dear friend, I hope that everything is well with you and that you are in good health. I took the liberty of doing some private research and found out that you, like myself a few months ago, had retired and are now living in Luoktajärvi. What a coincidence! I have followed developments in the newspapers with great interest. You could say that the assignment finally worked out, even if it wasn't quite what I had in mind.

I myself have found my place on earth. White beaches, warm climate, good food and nice people. I have had two fantastic months. In the last week, my body has started to give up a little. I'm more tired than usual and feel that the disease is starting to make itself felt. The doctors here want to stuff me full of medication but I only pour it out when the quacks have left the room. But for now, the old man is still alive. I'll go as long as I can and when I can't take it anymore, I will disappear nicely and discreetly.

Now I'm going back to Hemingway and my umbrella drink. Hope you get peace of mind and can disconnect from the past. Live well and long!

Your friend K

Dear friend, that's a surprise, thought Edward. He was even a little moved. The letter bore Cuban stamps and postmarks - clear signs it had traveled far. It wouldn't be impossible to trace where it had been sent from, at least down to the city. For a time, Edward had even considered going to Cuba to find him. But the thought of arriving only to meet an old, broken man who no longer wanted visitors held him back. In the end, this letter was all he received.

Edward put down roots in Luoktajärvi and helped to build up the village police force. There wasn't really much of a police force, two older villagers in all, and there wasn't much crime to fight. The two recruits also had a fairly flexible approach to law and order - there had never been any crime to fight or any law to enforce, but as the permanent population and the number of visitors increased, they needed to stay visible and available.

For a hobby smoker with poor self-discipline, it was almost impossible not to fall into the local pipe smoking. Instead of a cigarette or two a day, it was now a couple of big pipes stuffed with tobacco and dried moss. He quickly got used to the animal scent and the inhabitants didn't seem to take harm anyway. On the contrary, it seemed that people remained healthy well into old age. Perhaps one could buy himself a few years and at the same time get a pleasant nicotine rush at regular intervals.

Funnel and Tube never saw the money again. At first, during the next few days after the police interrogation and the strange incident at the campsite, they were anxious and expected to be arrested. There was no point in running away now that they were caught, and they had in fact been caught with their hands in the cookie jar. And they had also confessed how they got the money. Given their backgrounds, they would surely get a long and severe sentence.

But the arrest was never carried out and instead of worrying about legal action, the mood turned to confusion and then frustration. Frustration should have turned to relief, relief at having escaped the long arm of the law, but that feeling would not come. Instead, they felt cheated again. For which time in the order they could not agree on, but they were cheated in any case. Who was this chain-smoking policeman really and why did he not come back with questions about the Pig? Were they in cahoots or were all living creatures simply complete idiots?

However, they decided not to challenge fate and seek out their antagonist once again, now that they seemed to have very unexpectedly fallen off the hook. They did not want to end up behind bars again. Especially not when summer was coming.

It was Funnel who finally hatched the idea that they should start a haulage business. He had a truck driver's license and knew how to get hold of a cheap Eastern European truck and use it legally in Sweden. They started driving around doing small jobs in the area. Mostly small jobs that did not bring in any large sums of money. In its simplest form, it could be a load of filler to be transported from point A to point B. Funnel handled the driving and Tube picked up assignments. On one occasion, they came into contact with a person who needed to transport goods from Laponia to Stockholm. It turned out to be the start of a very lucrative business.

Funnel collected the goods from a parking lot at Stora Sjöfallet, outside the mountain station in Ritsem, at a warehouse in Porjus or at various places outside Gällivare. The pick-up location varied for some reason that Funnel could not understand, but the drop-off was always at one and the same place; it was at an old house located near the water between Märsta and Sigtuna. The customer paid cash and the only counterclaim was fast delivery and no questions asked. That suited Funnel and Tube just fine.

At some point, Funnel couldn't resist peering into the packing crates to find out what it was that they were hauling all over the country. To his great surprise, the entire truck seemed to be filled with some moss-like substance that was spreading a light manure aroma in the cargo area.

After a while, the customer's procedures were changed and

tightened. Goods were delivered from a place called Luoktajärvi to Porjus and cleared through some kind of checkpoint. Each shipment now involved some paperwork. The money was not paid out in plastic bags, but the amount had to be invoiced. Funnel and Tube were forced to form a real company and invest in a new truck. It was a tough adjustment, but after a few months things settled down and the orders continued to flow in. Before long, they owned two trucks and had hired a full-time driver. His name was Pedda - a guy they'd gotten to know during their time in prison. Pedda had a shaved head, arms like tree trunks, tattoos snaking across his body, and a perpetual trickle of snuff under his upper lip. They knew he wasn't the most presentable or reliable creature who walked on two legs, but he was an excellent truck driver and with a little bit of equipment and a hefty advance payment, he fell into line.

Tube took care of the bookkeeping and finances, and Funnel and Pedda worked in the field. The business grew and prospered and Tube arranged for new office space. The caravan, whose rightful owner never showed up at the campsite, was demoted to a sleeping place. As usual, he dragged the caravan with him and parked it outside the office. It was a solution that seemed to please all parties, not least the manager of the campsite and most of its guests.

A few weeks after William slipped down the mountainside and literally stumbled into a new world, he was summoned to the new head of state. On the same balcony where they had first met, Niilla and Papusa were waiting. Papusa had crossed the same ridge that he and Edward had passed earlier. Once on the other side, she had tried to reach someone—anyone—who could confirm whether William was in the village. Eventually, she managed to get in touch with the new head of state, and together, they now had an incredible story to tell.

After she'd left William in Gällivare, she went on to Kiruna and then across the border to Narvik and further out along the coast to Tranoy Lighthouse. There she'd broken into the lighthouse tower itself and found the window marked with a cross on the postcard. After hours of searching, she finally found a loose stone and behind the stone was a wrapped letter. The letter was dated the end of March 1945 and addressed to Papusa's great-grandmother's sister in Hungary. This time the letter was addressed *To my Schatzi* and signed by *Your Raoul*. The letter contained a brief description of how Raoul had tried to escape from a German unit outside Narvik and then sought shelter at the lighthouse with a couple of Norwegians. Their plan was to try to steal a German transport plane together and cross the border into Sweden.

Niilla said that a German plane had crashed outside the village around the end of the war, that a German unit found the wreckage shortly afterwards but that Sáhkár had blown the whole company through the ice. One person survived, wearing a German uniform but speaking Swedish and wanted to be called *Raol*. He was badly injured and died just a few days later. He was buried just outside the village, according to Niilla. It was only now, after meeting Papusa, that he realized that the anonymous *Raol* was none other than the famous Raoul Wallenberg. Instead of being tortured and dying in a Russian prison, he had instead ended his days on a mountainside under reindeer dung and moss.

Once the circle was closed, Papusa was able to settle down. She stayed in the village and got a job in the new city apparatus that was being built. During the first few months, she thought about writing a book about what really happened to Raoul Wallenberg, her great grandfather, but finally decided against it. In any case, her distant relative had been dead for a long time and it was possible that he'd fallen victim to his own countrymen rather than the Germans. What actually happened on the day the Mountain King blew up the plane was unclear and Sáhkár himself had nothing more to say about it. Perhaps he no longer remembered anything about the incident. Papusa let the matter rest.

It soon became clear that William had worried for no reason that night in the square. In a way, it was as if the time and distance between them had never existed. It seemed like yesterday when they met again. Effortless and uncomplicated. They both agreed to give it another try but at the same time there was an unspoken but mutual condition. It was a tacit agreement that two middle-aged singles with no experience of long-term relationships and an unusually high need for freedom should not be kept too tightly chained. Undemanding and gradual were the key words.

Merja quit her temporary job in Kiruna and moved back to the village. William, with Niilla's permission, had been allowed to build a log house for them both on one of the mountain slopes. Fortunately, Niilla's goodwill remained intact despite William's somewhat convoluted - yet sincere - explanation of how he had come by the money. On the contrary, he had shown remarkable patience, almost an ocean's worth.

He might have raised an eyebrow at the moment when his future son-in-law explained how, in just a few days, he'd returned a small fortune to the criminals who had seized the bag the first time. After William's confession, Niilla suggested that the new couple keep the money. They could use it to build themselves a proper house. But he really wanted the leather bag back.

William took on the task with great enthusiasm. He had logs and other materials shipped in from both Sweden and Norway. The construction workers he brought from the forests of eastern Finland. They were rough, bearded men who knew how to cross-lay logs. With their help, he built a large house in the best Alpine style on the western slope. Inspired by the first evening on Niilla's balcony, the house was built with both a large terrace and a large balcony. The location was chosen to give a fantastic view of the valley and was right next to a meltwater stream. On the advice of the Finns, a sauna and hot tub were also built next to the rapids.

The site of the timber construction was adjacent to Sáhkár's private vineyard. He'd been forced to promise the old man dearly that he would take care of the wine-project, which had fallen into involuntary disuse in recent years. Although the crops had been neglected, the soil was well-drained, the vines old and the roots deep. William assured Sáhkár that the vineyard was in safe hands and that there was hope for the future.

The new head of state, the son of the Mountain King and William's benefactor, had tried several times to persuade him to take a seat on the Governing Council. It was a chance to be part of the action and make a difference at the same time. Starting up a new state had proved more difficult than anticipated, and William had *long experience of being a good citizen in a functioning society* as Niilla expressed it. At least if theft and exile was removed from his record.

William, who was bored with politics in general and administration in particular, found a very good reason to refuse by referring to the management of the vineyard and the sacred promise to the Sáhkár. Such a promise could not be broken just like that. Merja was also more interested in tilling the soil and taking care of the home than in political bickering. Thus, the offer could be humbly rejected.

Together, they got the farm and vineyard in order and by the fall they were able to harvest their first grapes. Sam, the eldest son of Luoktajärvi's only farmer, was delighted at finally meeting like-minded people - people who were passionate about the art and not just interested in the consumption of the final product. William reciprocated the kindness as best he could by injecting money to invest in Sam's own farm. After a year or so of barrel aging, the wine was absolutely world class and even Sam was surprised. William and Merja participated in international wine competitions and won several awards. The wine, which was a blend of red grapes from both Sam's and their own farm, was named *Reindeer's Gold.*

They proudly claimed that it was a combination of the old vines, the well-balanced blend of grapes, the unique climate of Luoktajärvi and many years of experience and hard work that had contributed to the success. William thought the wine had a hint of manure in the aroma but did not want to research the cause further. Wine connoisseurs described the smell as *animalic*, which in wine language is something positive. Despite this, William and Sam each put up a hunter's fence around the vineyards to avoid the soil being too animalic.

After the awards, they decided to join forces with Sam. They used the entire harvest to produce ten thousand bottles of Reindeer's Gold for delivery to selected distributors abroad. The limited production helped to drive up the price. Three thousand bottles stayed in Luoktajärvi for the residents and a hundred bottles were kept for their own use. William suggested that they should deliver a few boxes of Reindeer's Gold to Sáhkár as a thank you for using his vineyard. Merja explained that they might as well pour the wine out at once, since her grandfather mixed it with brandy anyway. The last time she'd visited him in the cabin, she'd even tried to hide the brandy bottles. Then the old man got angry and drove her to the door.

Over the next few years, production expanded slightly as less experimentation was needed and manufacturing was optimized and automated. It was enough to make a living and enough to avoid drowning in work. This suited William and Merja perfectly.

Edward often came to visit. They liked to sit on the balcony with a glass of wine in front of them, looking out over the valley and puffing on a pipe. Maybe it would prolong life, maybe not. But when the rest of the village was sitting with their pipe, it was easy to follow along. And as long as one disregarded the animalic contribution, it was actually not so bad. Both soothing and sociable.

They often talked about how they met in Gällivare, the trip to Luoktajärvi and what happened next. Sometimes they talked about the time before. It felt both close and distant at the same time. These were memories and nostalgia from a world that no longer existed and that followed a different count of time. The seasons did not have the same meaning. A week did not have the same length and the concept of a *working day* had no meaning.

At such times, William often thought of the snowstorm and the Night Owl. He wondered if the roadside inn was still open and what had become of the two young men. He wished them no harm. They were lost souls, like himself. He thought of the willow tree just before the dark stretch of road, and with that image came a quiet certainty - he'd made his choice. And he felt no regret.